VALERIE S. MALMONT AND
**THE TORI MIRACLE
MYSTERY SERIES**

"Malmont has introduced a likable heroine
whose adventures are worth reading."
—*Albuquerque Journal*

"Tori Miracle is a fresh and appealing new amateur
sleuth who charms you, then pulls through the dark
caves and sinister secrets of Lickin Creek. Delighted
with her company, you willingly follow along."
—Sister Carol Anne O'Marie,
author of *Murder in Ordinary Time*

"Malmont does a fine job of creating atmosphere . . .
and Tori makes a resourceful heroine."
—*Roanoke Times and World-News*

"Tori is an engaging, believable character, and her
adventures in Lickin Creek are highly entertaining."
—*I Love a Mystery*

"Likable, eccentric characters, frothy hullabaloo,
and humorous situations."
—*Library Journal*

DELL BOOKS by Valerie S. Malmont

Death, Snow, and Mistletoe

Death, Guns, and Sticky Buns

Death, Lies, and Apple Pies

Death Pays the Rose Rent

A Tori Miracle Mystery

DEATH, SNOW,
AND
MISTLETOE

VALERIE S. MALMONT

A Dell Book

Published by
Dell Publishing
a division of
Random House, Inc.
1540 Broadway
New York, New York 10036

Dell® is a registered trademark of Random House, Inc., and the colophon is a registered trademark of Random House, Inc.

ISBN: 0-440-23601-0

Printed in the United States of America

Published simultaneously in Canada

November 2000

10 9 8 7 6 5 4 3 2 1

OPM

For Stephanie and Paige

ACKNOWLEDGMENTS

Once again, I want to thank the members of my critique group, Françoise Harrison, Helen O. Platt, and M. Joan H. Juttner, M.D., for their help and support, not only with this book but all four in the series.

I am grateful to Silver RavenWolf for answering my many questions about Wicca and helping me write a more authentic description of a winter solstice ceremony than the one I first made up. However, there are mistakes, and they are all mine. I highly recommend her book *To Ride a Silver Broomstick*, for anyone who wants to learn more about the Craft.

Thanks go to Luci Zahray, who has provided much information about poisons.

I also want to thank Maggie Crawford, Danielle Perez, and George Nicholson for believing in me.

And last, my heartfelt gratitude goes to the mystery book dealers who have supported me since the beginning. I love you guys!

CHAPTER 1

O come all ye faithful

THE STONE SPIRES OF TRINITY EVANGELICAL Church hovered like gray ghosts in the star-studded darkness above Lickin Creek. Brilliant splashes of colored light streamed from the church's authentic Tiffany windows and lay on the snow-covered brick sidewalk like gleaming jewels spilled from a pirate's treasure chest. The air was warmer now than earlier this afternoon when the first snow of the season had fallen on this small, pre–Civil War town.

Garnet had left his huge blue monster-truck with me to use while he was in Costa Rica, but I still had trouble manipulating it in tight places, so I parked on the street rather than trying to squeeze into one of the narrow spaces in the church parking lot.

I was scheduled to photograph the cast of the Lickin Creek Community Theatre rehearsing the annual Christmas pageant, and as usual I was running late—but only by half an hour tonight, a definite improvement. Was it my fault that three churches in the borough had *trinity* in their names? I'd been unfortunate enough to visit the other two first.

I grabbed my canvas fanny pack, my notebook, and the *Chronicle*'s antique camera, and ran toward the neo-Gothic building. After trying the front doors and finding them locked, I finally entered the church through a side entrance, which was an anachronism of glass and aluminum decorated with a wreath of plastic greenery and ribbons. I found myself in a long beige hallway, facing a row of closed doors on either side.

After disturbing the choir at practice and barging into an Alcoholics Anonymous group meeting in the nursery, I followed a trail of noise down a flight of concrete steps and through a set of double doors into a basement room that ran the length of the church. To my left was a small kitchen, separated from the larger room by a waist-high counter on which stood several stainless-steel coffee urns and many heaping platters of cookies.

The main part of the hall, on my right, was packed with people, mostly women. I recognized several members of the Lickin Creek borough council as well as several county commissioners, and I guessed this was the politically correct basement to be in this cold winter evening. Some people wrestled with an enormous pile of evergreens in one corner, while others sat on metal folding chairs in small groups, chatting and drinking from Styrofoam cups. The rows of flickering fluorescent lights overhead cast an odd lavender glow on everyone there.

Six women stood on the stage at the far end of the room, silently studying their scripts. I relaxed when I realized that the rehearsal had not yet begun. I'd be able to get my pictures and be on my way home to feed my cats in a few minutes. The thought of a cozy evening at home with Fred and Noel, watching a good sci-fi film on TV, was almost too pleasurable to bear.

A middle-aged woman filling sugar containers at the kitchen counter waved at me. "Hey, Tori. Nice to see you again. We've got some great goodies—if you like chocolate." The congenial speaker was Ginnie Welburn. I'd met her a few times at various functions, and although she was ten or twelve years older than I, we were drawn to each other by virtue of both being relative newcomers to Lickin Creek.

I grinned at Ginnie and patted my fanny pack. "Do I like chocolate? Where do you think these hips came from?"

"Good, that Lori Miracle's here from the paper." The voice came from a woman on the stage who was swaddled in a politically incorrect but drop-dead-gorgeous mink coat. I recognized her as Bernice Roadcap, who, along with her husband, was a well-known local real estate developer.

"Come up here, Lori," she ordered. "We'uns is ready to have our picture taken."

Before I could say "It's Tori," a full-bodied matron stepped forward and protested, "We are *not* ready, Bernice. Weezie's not here yet."

As I walked toward the stage, Bernice turned to the woman who had just spoken. In my limited experience, nobody had ever crossed Bernice Roadcap and I expected a battle, but she surprised me by saying in a meek voice, "Sorry, Oretta. I hadn't noticed."

The woman Bernice had addressed as Oretta stepped to stage front, planted her hands on her hips, and balanced herself on wide-apart feet. She wore an enormous pale-blue polyester pantsuit and a blouse covered with pink and purple hibiscus blossoms. Around her throat was a choker of silver and amber beads, so tight I wondered how she swallowed. Looking at her, I promised myself I most definitely would restart my diet tomorrow. I know how it happens; one night you go to bed a size ten and you wake up the next morning an eighteen.

Not a hair dared to move in her bright gold bouffant

as she glared down at me. "You're the new *Chronicle* editor?" It was more an accusation than a question.

I couldn't keep from staring at her gravity-defying bosom. I had no idea anyone still manufactured corsets like that. Maybe a special order? I fought back a giggle and said, "I'd like to take the picture now. I have other stops to make."

"We always have our picture taken during the final, dramatic ending of the pageant rehearsal. You'd know that if you weren't new to town."

"I really don't have time to wait," I said. "I'll just snap a picture or two and—"

Oretta tapped her foot. She was staring at me as though I'd lost my mind. "You'll wait until the end. It's the way we've always done it!" she announced.

In the short time I'd lived in Lickin Creek, I'd become very familiar with that phrase and its evil twin, "We've never done it that way." Hit me with a two-by-four half a dozen times and I get the idea. There was no use in arguing; I might as well find a comfortable place to park myself for the next hour.

Oretta turned to face her cast. "No point in waiting for Weezie any longer. She doesn't have any lines near the beginning, anyway. Places, everybody. Bernice, stand over there—stage right—next to the palm tree. Have you all highlighted your parts? It would be nice to hear you reading the right lines tonight." She glared at one of the hapless women, who seemed to shrink several inches. Another rummaged through her purse, extracted a bright yellow marking pen, and began to diligently mark her script.

Silently cursing myself for being such a wimp, I shrugged off my jacket and took a seat on a metal folding chair in the front row. Ginnie Welburn appeared next to me bearing a cup of steaming coffee and a couple of cookies wrapped in a red paper napkin. "Thought you might like some nourishment," she said with a grin.

"How did this happen to me?" I whispered, accepting the gift. Little Santa faces smiled at me from the napkin.

"Whatever Oretta Clopper wants, Oretta Clopper gets," Ginnie said. "She's one of those natural forces you just can't fight."

"Who is she? The name's familiar. Isn't the new borough manager named Jackson Clopper? Are they married?"

Ginnie snickered. "Don't let her hear you ask that. Oretta's the ultimate snob, and in her opinion, Jackson crawled out of the lower depths when he was hired to be borough manager and should be made to return there as soon as possible. I believe her husband, Matavious— who's almost a doctor—and Jackson are some sort of fifth cousins once removed, or whatever they call it around here."

"What do you mean by 'almost a doctor'?" I asked, curious about her strange choice of words.

"Chiropractor." I could practically see the sneer in her voice. Apparently, Oretta was not the only snob in the room.

Ginnie continued. "The Clopper men don't speak. It's one of those Blue and Gray family squabbles."

"You mean a family feud going back to the Civil War?" I remarked. "Now that's what I call holding a grudge!"

"A lot of people are still actively fighting that war here in Lickin Creek."

"Quiet down front!" Oretta snapped. "Ladies, let the play begin."

Ginnie groaned, winked at me, and moved back to the kitchen. I tried, but failed, to find a comfortable position on the cold metal chair and nibbled on a heavenly chocolate-macadamia-nut cookie.

Before any of the actresses spoke, a tiny woman fluttered down the center aisle and shrugged off her red ski jacket to reveal a most un-Christmasy yellow cotton housedress covered with tiny blue flowers. "I'm so sorry," she twitted. "You'uns know how my husband is. He don't like me to go out at night, so I thought it best to wait till he fell asleep."

Oretta nodded sympathetically. "We do indeed know how he is. Let's get started, or we'll be here all night."

I silently breathed an amen to that.

She stepped to the edge of the stage and peered down at me. "Just wanted to make sure you're still here, young lady."

I sniffed at the "young lady." After all, I am a tiny bit past thirty, and Oretta, despite her imposing size, was probably in her forties.

Without moving back, she announced to the audience, "*The Nutcracker*, an adaptation by Oretta Clopper. Music, please, Matavious." She stared down at the man sitting next to me. He pushed a button on the portable cassette player on his lap, and the Overture to *The Nutcracker* reverberated through the hall.

"Too loud, Matavious."

"Sorry, dearest." He lowered the volume.

I studied him for a moment. Physically, he was the exact opposite of Oretta, small and thin, with thinning sandy-colored hair that was beginning to turn gray, and rimless glasses. Thanks to Ginnie's crack about him, I'd probably never be able to think of him as anything but "almost a doctor."

Oretta shared stage center with Bernice Roadcap and the late-arriving Weezie. They alternately referred to themselves as sugar plum fairies, angels, and goddesses.

Although Oretta had announced the pageant was an adaptation of *The Nutcracker,* I recognized nothing from that lovely ballet except the background music. Thankfully, the middle-aged angels/goddesses/sugar plum fairies didn't dance.

The blank verse the three women spouted had far more to do with Greco-Roman mythology and New Age mysticism than it did with Christianity's most sacred season. The other four cast members had little to do but hold up scenery and chorus back the ends of some bad verses.

The three lead actresses spent most of the next half hour perched on kitchen stools, reading from their scripts in stentorian tones. I padded the seat of my hard chair with my jacket and concentrated on making my final cookie last.

I guessed the ending was blessedly near when the goddesses jumped from their stools and danced around a pedestal on top of which sat a Styrofoam cup, while Dr. Clopper's tape player boomed out "Ode to Joy." I recalled with amusement the wonderful "Ode to a Grecian Urn" in Meredith Willson's *The Music Man.* All these middle-aged goddesses needed were flowing togas, which led me to wonder what exactly they *would* wear for the pageant.

Bernice waved her fur-covered arms in the air and wailed, "What does this mean, my lady?"

Little Weezie paused in her dance to read, "The King doth wake tonight. He is to the manor born."

I clapped my hand over my mouth so I wouldn't laugh out loud.

Oretta, only a little out of breath, sang out, "By the tolling of the bell, someone wonderful has come to dwell." She raised the white cup above her head with both hands and cried, "What light from yonder manger breaks? It is the star from the east and the mother is the sun. Hail to the great mother." She paused, then glared at the woman in the chorus who had only just finished highlighting her script with her yellow pen. "Janet . . ."

"Sorry, Oretta. Hail to the great mother." She looked embarrassed. I didn't blame her.

"Hail to the wyccan."

"Hail to the wyccan." What the heck was a wyccan?

"Hail to the Goddess."

Goddesses I know about. I winced as Janet hailed this one with slight enthusiasm. A little artsy feminism goes a long way with me.

"And now we drink from the Goblet of Life." Oretta brought the cup to her lips and drained it. "Hold your places, ladies. Dorrie, you may take your pictures now."

"It's Tori," I protested, even though nobody paid any attention to me. I got to my feet stiffly, suffering the effects of sitting on that torture chair for over an hour.

I snapped half a dozen pictures of the cast at different exposures and shutter speeds, hoping at least one of them would develop into a photo good enough for the paper. Photography is not my strong suit.

As I wrote the names of the ladies in my notebook, Oretta barked, "Good work, ladies. Take ten and we'll run through it again. Without scripts this time. Somebody refill the goblet. Make it spiced apple cider this time. That coffee was cold."

"Now look here, Oretta . . ." Bernice waved her script in Oretta Clopper's face. "You'uns got it all wrong."

"Really, Bernice! I did write it, you know."

I left the stage and nearly bumped into Ginnie. Her face was all crinkly from laughing. We walked to the kitchen together, where she filled a cup with coffee and handed it to me.

"I'm surprised the minister hasn't run them out of here on a rail," I said as I doctored my cup with fake cream and artificial sugar.

Ginnie's lips twitched. "Oretta has everybody snowed. She almost had a play produced Off-off-off Broadway once. Now, she's executive director of the LCLCT. That's the Lickin Creek Little Community Theatre, spelled *t-h-e-a-t-r-e*," she explained, answering my unspoken question. "The town's convinced she's the next Eugene O'Neill."

"She certainly doesn't mind whom she steals from, does she? The only line from Shakespeare she didn't rewrite was 'Double, double, toil and trouble.' "

"Perhaps she should have," Ginnie said with a smile. "They did rather resemble the three witches, didn't they?"

"That reminds me," I said, "doesn't the word *wyccan* refer to a modern-day witch?"

"Haven't the foggiest. But then I'm a little behind on my feminist readings."

"I haven't seen the little goddess in the yellow housedress before," I said. "The one with the unfortunate name."

"In my opinion, they all have unfortunate names," Ginnie replied with a grin. "But I assume you mean Weezie Clopper."

That name again. "Another Clopper? Is this one married to the borough manager?"

Ginnie nodded. "Unfortunately for her, yes. I understand Jackson is a real tyrant. Word about town is he doesn't want her to associate with Oretta—partly because of the family feud, and partly because he and Matavious are fighting over some family property. That's why she had to sneak out to be in the pageant. If—I mean, when Jackson finds out, she'll pay dearly. I've seen her with some nasty bruises."

"That surprises me," I said. "As borough manager, he's in a very public position."

Ginnie snorted with indignation. "You know damn well abuse happens anywhere."

"Some life for a goddess!" I commented. "If there's such a grand feud going on between the two branches of the Clopper family, why doesn't Matavious insist that Oretta stay away from Weezie?"

Ginnie exhaled something between a laugh and a whinny. "Can you imagine Matavious making Oretta do anything?"

I couldn't, and we both chuckled at the preposterous idea.

At that moment Oretta bore down upon us. "Corey, I hear you're an animal lover."

"It's Tori, Mrs. Clopper," I said firmly, "and I do have two cats—"

"As you must know, I'm president of the Lickin Creek Animal Rescue League," she interrupted. "Sometimes I need a temporary home. Can you help me out?"

I guessed that it was animals that needed temporary homes and not Oretta. "I don't think I can . . . You see, I'm just house-sitting . . ."

"That's grand," she said. "You'll be hearing from me, Victoria." She swept away, leaving me spluttering unheard protests.

"I know how you feel about your name," Ginnie said with a sympathetic smile. "She calls me Virginia all the time. Wrong name or not, you should feel flattered that she's approved you to be a temporary care provider. Not everyone is so honored."

I groaned. One more animal was all I needed. "Maybe nothing will come of it," I said hopefully.

"Not a chance," Ginnie's look told me.

"How about us two outsiders getting together some time soon?" Ginnie suggested. "We need to stand united against the closed circle of Lickin Creek's high society."

I thought a minute before answering. Ginnie's sense of humor was caustic, her snobbery was appalling, and her dedication to gossip was shameful, but I had to admit I found her amusing, perhaps because she was so different from most of the people I'd met in Lickin Creek. She reminded me of Alice Roosevelt, who also loved gossip and said, "If you can't say anything good about someone, sit next to me."

I'd already come to the conclusion that I needed to reinvent myself—be more sociable, not so much a loner. For most of my life, I'd moved about with my foreign service family, and friendship always meant saying good-bye. It had been easier to be aloof than to continually suffer the heartbreak of separation. In recent years, I'd worked at opening my heart to others, like my neighbor and good friend in New York, Murray. And then there was my budding relationship with Garnet Gochenauer— one of the two reasons I'd moved to Lickin Creek.

The other reason, of course, was Alice-Ann, who'd been my best friend since college. It was because of her I'd first visited Lickin Creek, and she was a major factor in my decision to stay in town for six months as temporary editor of the *Chronicle*.

Ironically, after I committed myself to moving closer to the two people I most loved, Garnet accepted a position with the foreign service, leaving me alone in Lickin Creek for at least six months.

And I was truly alone, because something had come between Alice-Ann and me. She unreasonably blamed me for the loss of her fiancé last fall, and we'd gone from sharing our deepest feelings to barely nodding when we passed on the street.

I missed her dreadfully, and that's the real reason I decided to pursue a friendship with Ginnie. It would be nice to have a someone, once more, to do things with.

"Sounds like fun," I finally answered. "Want to do lunch someday this week?"

"You sound like a typical New Yorker, Tori. I'd love to 'do lunch,' as you put it, but I'm on the high-school substitute-teacher list and can't make any plans ahead of time. Say, I've got an idea—since I moved here I've become quite fond of playing bingo. How about going to a game with me one night?"

Bingo. It would be a new experience. "Sounds like fun. Uh-oh, the rehearsal's starting up again. I think I'll sneak out while I can." At last I could get home to my cats and the evening I'd planned.

The kitchen stools were at center stage once more. Oretta perched one hip on hers and tapped her foot impatiently while the others took their places.

Ginnie reached for my coffee cup. "I'll call you."

I went up front to collect my coat and camera.

The ladies were on stage and Oretta began to speak. "This day is called the feast of Christ, he's born this day and comes safe home."

Bernice continued. "We'll stand a-tiptoe when this day is named, and rouse him at the name of Christ."

Weezie said, "I will be brief, the noble son is . . ." Her voice trailed off as the double doors at the back of the hall burst open. All heads turned toward the dark, menacing giant filling the door frame, and who resembled the monster in the movie *Frankenstein*—the good, classic version starring Boris Karloff.

The creature stepped inside, peeled off a heavy quilted

blue down jacket, and became Luscious Miller, the town's only full-time policeman, and now, in Garnet's absence, acting police chief. His tall, scrawny frame had been enlarged to enormous proportions by the ill-fitting jacket. He was breathing hard and opened and closed his mouth several times as though struggling for air. I figured he was probably exhausted from doing his rounds on that new bicycle the borough council had decided he should ride to save the town money.

When he finally managed to catch his breath, he squawked, "Emergency! Folks, we got a real big emergency on our hands!"

After the squeals of surprise and exclamations of astonishment died down, Marvin Bumbaugh, who was the president of the borough council, moved forward and guided the gawky policeman to a chair. Luscious pulled off his knit cap and replaced three long strands of blond hair over his bald spot with shaking hands. We gathered around him in a semicircle.

"What's up, Luscious?" the council president asked.

"Missing kid, Marv. Playing with his cousins in the woods above Stinking Spring. Wandered away from them a couple of hours ago. When they came back alone, they said they thought he'd come home by himself. His mom called me 'bout ten minutes ago. Said she'd been all over the hills looking for him."

Oretta uttered a gasp and clutched at my arm. "My God! How dreadful! Who is it?"

"Name's Kevin Poffenberger. He's only five years old."

Oretta's fingernails dug into my skin, but I hardly noticed the pain. My thoughts were with the five-year-old boy, alone and terrified in the snowy woods. He was the same age my brother Billy had been when he'd wandered away from me during that minute when I was inattentive—so much can happen in a minute. Would the child's cousins suffer guilt for the rest of their lives as I did?

Murmurs from the crowd pulled me back to the present. Marvin looked from one face to another. "Anybody know him?"

There was some discussion. Finally, one man said, "I do maintenance out to the Iron Ore Mansions Trailer Park near Stinking Spring. There's three or four trailers full of Poffenbergers out there. They got lots of kids 'tween them."

"What've you done?" Marvin asked Luscious. "Did you call the state police?"

"Of course I did, Marv. They said for me to go ahead and get search parties started. Captain of the fire department's mobilizing his men right now."

I could tell by his shaking hands and nervous stammer that Luscious was already in over his head.

Marvin's brow creased, and I assumed he knew even better than I how poorly prepared Luscious was to manage a tragedy.

I opened my notebook and wrote down the commands as Marvin gave them.

"Call for fire companies from Gettysburg and Mc-Connellsburg to come over. And see if we can borrow up that people-sniffing dog from Hagerstown." Marvin turned to face the crowd. "We'll set up a command post at Corny's Feed Store, out at the junction of Iron Ore and Bright's Church roads. Who wants to be in charge of getting out the volunteers for a search party?"

A gray-haired man raised his hand.

"That's J. B. Morgan," Ginnie whispered in my ear, "president of the Lickin Creek National Bank."

Marvin acknowledged him. "Good, J.B., go door-to-door if you have to. I want three, four hundred people up there within the hour. Get moving."

J.B. was already jamming his arms into his parka.

"I'll be in charge of serving refreshments to the volunteers," a woman offered. "At least until the fire company's ladies' auxiliary can take over."

"That's Primrose Flack, wife of Trinity's minister," Ginnie told me.

"I know who she is," I said, beginning to feel slightly annoyed with Ginnie. "She's on the borough council." I wrote Primrose Flack's name in my notebook.

"The token woman," Ginnie said.

"I'll help you, Primrose," Oretta offered. "Come on, Weezie, grab the cookies and coffeepots and let's go. My God, that poor little boy . . . it's so cold, and so dark out there."

"I'd like to help, too. May I ride with you?" Ginnie asked Oretta. She shook her head despairingly. "What kind of animals those cousins must be . . . deserting a little kid like that."

Oretta sighed. "They are probably very young and didn't know better. Let's go. We can stop at Dunkin' Donuts on the way out of town. Matavious, you're still here! You *are* going with the men, aren't you? They might need a doctor."

"Of course, dearest. I only wanted to make sure you were taken care of first." He scurried out the door without even bothering to put on his coat.

"You coming, Tori?" Ginnie asked.

I shook my head. My job was to put on my reporter's hat and interview the lost boy's parents. I dreaded turning back into one of those insensitive media pests who intrude into other people's grief. It was a role I'd never felt comfortable with.

There was a noisy rush for the coatrack, and then the

hall was quiet. Only some tipped-over chairs, a few white cups that hadn't quite made it into the trash cans, and the scattered evergreen branches on the floor indicated that a few minutes ago we'd been involved in preparations for a gala Christmas pageant.

CHAPTER 2

On a cold winter's night

THE STREETS IN THE DOWNTOWN HISTORIC district were dark as I drove past the fountain in the square. In Lickin Creek, even the fast-food restaurants closed early. As my truck rattled over the brick-paved streets, I mentally rehearsed some questions I could ask the Poffenbergers about their missing child. Questions that I hoped would satisfy readers of the *Chronicle*, but wouldn't add to the family's anguish.

I was near the *Chronicle* building, and a light shining from the front window caught my attention. The paper couldn't afford a large electric bill; I'd have to stop and "out the lights," as a true Lickin Creek native would say. This wasn't a delaying tactic, I assured myself, but simply a necessary detour.

Somehow, I maneuvered the truck down the dark alley without adding any more scrapes to either the truck or the buildings on either side and pulled into the slot marked EDITOR. That was a new enough experience to still give me a thrill.

I paused for a second in the doorway of the narrow brick building to admire the shiny brass sign that said 1846. Polishing off a century of tarnish had been my first official duty as editor. As I reached for the door handle, I noticed something on the sill. Apparently, our janitorial service had forgotten a broom. I carried it inside.

Cassie Kriner, the paper's only other full-time employee, was at her desk, nearly hidden behind stacks of yellowed paper and piles of bound newspapers. She glanced up over the top of her half-moon reading glasses, noticed the broom, and said, "Coming in to redd up the place?"

"Found it on the stoop. Cleaning people must have dropped it." I stood the broom in the corner.

Sinking into the red imitation-leather sofa with chrome arms, a relic from the thirties, I said, "I saw the light in the window and thought I'd forgotten to turn it off."

"I came in as soon as I heard about the missing boy on my scanner," Cassie said. She jumped to her feet and nearly stumbled over a large box on the floor next to her desk. "How about a cup of coffee?"

I nodded. "Thanks. What's in the box?"

Cassie's cheeks flushed, and it seemed to me she avoided my eyes as she filled two mugs from the freshly-made pot of coffee. "Something I ordered from the Home Shopping Network." She fixed mine the way I like it—with a lot of artificial cream and sweetener—and brought it to me.

"Better move it out of the way," I suggested as I accepted the steaming mug. "Last thing we need is someone tripping over it and suing us."

"I will." She changed the subject abruptly. "I've found some information about the Poffenbergers in our morgue. Thought you might need it for your article."

Although she spoke calmly, I could tell by the way she'd dressed how upset she was. Instead of one of her usual elegant cashmere suits with matching shoes and handbag, Cassie had thrown on paint-splattered slacks and a Lickin Creek centennial sweatshirt, and her silver-gray hair was drawn into a ponytail rather than the usual Grace Kelly–like French twist. She wore no makeup—a sure sign of distress. Despite all this, Cassie still looked like a million bucks, which actually was a lot less than what her late husband had left her.

"Bless you. What've you got?"

"There's a lot of Iron Ore Road Poffenbergers on the police blotter. It's a large family—and apparently they're all related. Nothing unusual: in the past year a few were picked up for DWI, one for making terrorist threats at the Crossroads Tavern, two for issuing bad checks, and one for discharging firearms within borough limits . . . and—oh my!" She began to laugh. "Did I really say nothing unusual? Here's one who was charged with . . ." She blushed. "It had to do with a goose. Shall I go on?"

"I get the idea. Charming family."

"Salt of the earth."

"Thanks, Cassie. I don't know what I'd do without you." I meant it, too. Once, when I'd goofed up the front page half an hour before it was due at the printers, I'd half-seriously threatened to throw myself off the Main Street Bridge. Cassie had made me laugh by reminding me that the creek under the bridge was only eighteen inches deep. Then, together, we'd repaired the damage.

Almost daily, she single-handedly saved the *Chronicle* from disaster. P.J., the editor, once told me Cassie had come to work for the paper shortly after her husband had suffocated in a silo. I guess she wanted something worthwhile to do, since she surely didn't need the meager salary we paid her. With me at the editorial helm, her forty-hour work week had expanded to nearly eighty. She worked day and night without protest, except for one night a week, which was saved for her club meetings.

I gulped down the last of my coffee. "I'm off," I announced. "God, I hope by the time I get out to the Poffenbergers' house the little boy will have come home."

"Better to hope the temperature doesn't drop."

⌒

The borough of Lickin Creek sits in a basin, surrounded by mountains of the Appalachian chain. The surrounding dark, hulking hills have been silent witnesses to the valley's history: the bloody turf battles between the Delawares and Iroquois; the arrival of the early settlers, who carved their farms out of the wilderness; the tragic battles with the Indians; the French and Indian War; the Revolutionary War; and the event that seemed freshest in the minds of most residents—the Civil War.

In the daylight, covered with a soft lavender haze, the mountains were a landscape artist's dream. But at night, they looked menacing to me, especially when I had to drive into them. I could imagine how they might seem to five-year-old Kevin Poffenberger tonight.

Stinking Spring was high in the mountain range to the south of town. Garnet's truck seemed to grow wider by the minute as I slowly inched it up the very narrow mountain road, which had been wrenched from the dense forest. I drove slowly, not only because I was nervous about the icy road and the steep drop-off—which I was—but because I was part of a long procession of cars, sport-utility vehicles, fire engines, ambulances, and trucks winding its way toward the place where Kevin Poffenberger had last been seen. It seemed as if everyone in Lickin Creek was headed up the mountain tonight.

Despite the lack of a sign at the crossroads, I knew I was in the right place. Vehicles, more abandoned than parked, littered the fields on either side of the road. A sign over the weathered wooden building on the north-east corner announced that CORNY'S IS YOUR FRIENDLY FEED STORE. I was glad of that—who'd want to shop in an unfriendly feed store?

A traffic director, somewhere on the leeward side of eighty, wearing a fluorescent orange vest, directed me with his flashlight beam to a parking place. The trucks, mine included, made a circle around a field, and in the center, like besieged travelers of a wagon train, were the support units for the rescue teams.

In the light from a dozen campfires, volunteers were erecting tents where searchers could rest between shifts. Long tables bowed under the weight of the huge urns of coffee and trays of doughnuts, cookies, and sandwiches. Several steel watering troughs, with the name Corny's Feed Store on the sides, held ice and canned sodas.

Hundreds of people milled about, shouting orders, calling out names, asking for directions. They all were so bundled up in heavy clothing as to be unrecognizable. It warmed my heart to see the community's overwhelming response to an emergency.

I stopped a navy-blue parka and asked if it had seen Luscious. The silver-fox fur on the hood bounced vigor-ously as it nodded and pointed toward the largest of the tents on the edge of the encampment.

"Hey, Luscious," I said as I lifted the canvas flap and peeked inside. "Any news?"

The acting police chief looked up from where he sat at a folding card table on which were three cellular phones, piles of yellow legal pads, a stack of topographical maps, and a flickering kerosene lamp. His pale face was drawn, his eyes red. "Hi, Tori. I'm glad you're here. Come in and sit down."

I sat across from him on a metal chair, the coldness of

which seeped through the double layers of my wool slacks and thermal underwear.

"I've tried to think of everything, but I'm scared to death I forgot something." His usually bland face was creased with worry. "Look this over and tell me what you think."

He handed me a yellow lined pad on which he had printed a checklist in childlike block letters. He gnawed on the eraser of his pencil while I read through it.

Garnet had not only been Luscious's boss, but also his father figure. The young policeman had depended on him for guidance, professionally and in his personal affairs. When Garnet had left Luscious in charge of the public safety of Lickin Creek, he'd shown, in my opinion, a surprisingly large amount of faith and an equal amount of poor judgment. Gradually, over the past month, Luscious had taken to dropping in at my office several times a day with questions on police procedure. It took me a little while before I realized Luscious had chosen me as his mentor by virtue of my relationship with Garnet.

"Looks fine to me, Luscious," I assured him. "Garnet couldn't have done better." I wondered how much of the plan had been suggested by Marvin Bumbaugh, the council president, but that wasn't of any real importance. What was important was that the search had been well organized.

His sallow face reddened at my praise. "There's more than five hundred people out there hunting him right now. And more coming from Adams and Fulton counties."

"You might want to lay off the brandy till he's found," I suggested. The faint odor of alcohol told me that his facial redness wasn't entirely from embarrassment.

His color heightened.

"Perhaps I'm overly sensitive, Luscious, but I grew up with that smell. Are the boy's parents here? I need to interview them for the paper."

"The mother wanted to help with the search, but I told her it's better she stay home, in case he comes back on his own. They're on up the mountain 'bout half a mile on the Iron Ore Road. Just past the junkyard. You can't miss it."

I thanked him, then an idea suddenly came to me. "Have you questioned the cousins yet? The ones who were with the boy when he got lost?"

" 'Course I did, Tori. See this map of the mountain? The X is where they seen him last. That's the center of our search—we'll spread out from there."

Apparently, Luscious didn't really need my help, only my assurance, so I left him studying his maps. Outside the tent, I paused for a moment to get my bearings and take in the surreal scene before me. In the flickering light from the bonfires, the volunteers appeared almost inhuman—strange, unidentifiable creatures from another world.

Suddenly, Ginnie Welburn's familiar voice called my name. The outerspace creatures were, once again, ordinary people.

I walked to a table piled high with doughnuts, where she and Oretta Clopper stamped their feet and blew on their fingertips in a futile attempt to stay warm.

"I saw you coming out of Luscious's tent. Any word?" Ginnie asked hopefully.

"Not yet, but Luscious is doing a fine job."

"I suppose there's a first time for everything," Oretta sniffed.

"Give him a chance," Ginnie said. "Doughnut?"

I absentmindedly accepted one.

"I guess we have to put up with him, now that Garnet's gone." Oretta stared pointedly at me, as though it were my fault he'd left. Great! Now the town had something besides last summer's burning down of the historical society to blame on me. One would think accidents didn't happen to anyone but me. I took a bite of the doughnut and ended up with white splotches of powdered sugar all over the front of my jacket.

"We could use another pair of hands. Especially unfrozen ones," Ginnie said with a smile.

"I'm sorry, but I have to talk to the boy's parents."

"Better talk to his cousins, too," Oretta said. "I'll bet they know more than they're saying."

Exactly what I'd been thinking, but I wondered why she thought so. "Why do you say that?" I asked. I stuffed the rest of the doughnut into my mouth and ineffectually tried to brush the sugar off my bosom.

"I don't trust children. Mark my words, there's more to this than meets the eye." Oretta's chins bounced with indignation.

"You seem to know a lot about children. How many do you have?" I asked.

"Matavious and I were not blessed with a family," Oretta said. "But as a playwright, I am somewhat of an expert on human behavior."

"You don't really believe that those kids would have deliberately hurt their cousin, do you?" Beside me, Ginnie's usually cheerful face registered horror.

"Things like that have been known to happen," Oretta said. "In fact, I recently finished a play on that theme—it's much better than *The Bad Seed*. Maybe you'uns would like to read it."

"I would," Ginnie said. "How about you, Tori?"

I'd heard a sample of Oretta's playwriting skills earlier

that evening, so I fibbed, "Love to. Soon as I find the time."

"I'll print out a copy and bring it by your house," Oretta said to Ginnie.

The two women were talking as I left to continue my ride up the side of the mountain, only now I traveled alone on the narrow road. The moon in the cloudless sky was only a few days short of being full, and it brightly lit the twisted way before me.

As I completed a corkscrew turn, I nearly drove into an acre of heaped bedsprings, old recliners, and cracked toilet bowls . . . the junkyard Luscious had mentioned. A little past this charming landmark stood a crooked sign, punctured with bullet holes, telling me the unpaved, deeply-rutted drive to my left was the entrance to the Iron Ore Mansions Trailer Park.

Inside were rows of trailers, with only inches of space between them. Many of them looked as if they had been salvaged from the neighboring junk heap. Light streamed from every window, and although I saw no one, I heard children's voices.

As I turned in, the undercarriage of Garnet's truck scraped on something, and the screech made my teeth tingle. Almost at once, the door of the nearest trailer flew open. The man who stepped out onto the porch wore only jeans—no shirt or shoes—and his shotgun was pointed right at me. I mouthed the prayer I'd often said as a child, "Dear God, if you get me out of this mess, I'll be a good girl . . . and I mean it this time . . . a really good girl."

First, I glanced at the lock buttons on the door to make sure they were all depressed, then I rolled the window down about an inch. "I'm a reporter from the *Chronicle*," I yelled, "looking for the Poffenbergers."

He lowered the gun. *Thanks for listening, God.* "The

ones what got a lost kid? Fifth house on the right. Can't miss it—it's the one with the tires."

I didn't have long to wonder what he meant about the tires. They were stacked, six high, all around the trailer, making an odd-looking but effective fence. In the small yard there was a lone tree with a truck-tire swing dangling on a rope from a bare branch. Car tires, standing upright, bordered both sides of a cement walk. Others, lying on the brown grass, were filled with dirt and held withered plants.

Reluctantly, I left the safety of my truck and entered the yard. The stench of rubber turned my stomach, and I wondered how anybody could live with it. For that matter, how could anybody live in a place as depressing as the inappropriately-named Iron Ore Mansions? Next to this place, my apartment building in Hell's Kitchen looked like Club Med.

The woman who opened the door in response to my knock was small and shriveled, with a swollen red nose and bloodshot eyes. I explained I was a reporter and needed to ask a few questions about Kevin.

"Come in," she said, and I saw she was missing several teeth. She clutched at the front of her overly large gray-green sweater with one hand and held a wad of pink Kleenex in the other.

"Karl," she called over her shoulder. "It's a reporter. You want a beer?"

It took me a second to realize she was offering a drink to me and not her husband. "No, thanks. I won't take much of your time. I know how upset you must be." I sat on the orange-and-brown plaid sofa, which smelled almost as bad as the front yard but in a different way, and groped in my bag for my notebook.

A man who I assumed was Karl swaggered into the living room carrying an odoriferous infant wrapped in a spotted yellow blanket. "Kara's dirty," he said, handing the child to her mother.

"Sorry. Be right back." She scuttled sideways out of the room.

"Beer?" He picked up a bottle from the coffee table, drained it, and carried the empty bottle into the kitchen area. He brought back two and put one in front of me. His fingernails couldn't have gotten that black in one lifetime . . . no way would I touch that beer.

The front door burst open, and the room was suddenly full of children, some barely toddling, all with silvery-blond hair. "My kids: Kirsten, Kathy, Ken, Kim, Karol, Klark, Klaire. All with a *K*—makes 'em easy to remember. Them other two is my brother's brats. You'uns sit down and shut up," he shouted—at them, not me. "This cute little gal's from the TV, and she's gonna put us on the news."

I stopped writing down the names of all the little Poffenbergers "with a *K*" and explained to them I had nothing to do with TV. Their small round faces showed obvious disappointment. There would be no TV stars discovered in the Poffenberger mansion tonight.

After Mrs. Poffenberger came back without the baby, I asked my questions—beginning with the usual human-interest ones about the boy: age? did he go to kindergarten? what games did he like to play? As I wrote down the answers given to me by the child's mother, I realized how little the average child of five has to show for his years on earth; it is the loss of everything that is still to come that makes the death of a child so tragic.

I had to keep raising my voice because the little Ks and their cousins were arguing over a TV show. Karl Poffenberger, nearly prone in a blue velour recliner, had downed his beer, my beer, and another fetched by his wife, and was taking offense to just about everything she said to me.

"Has he wandered off like this before?" I asked the mother, thinking it was time to be on my way.

"Never," began Mrs. Poffenberger.

Mr. Poffenberger belched softly. "That's enough yakking, woman," he said to his wife. "You ain't yet said what you're paying." This was directed to me.

"Mr. Poffenberger, newspaper reporters don't pay for interviews."

"Then get the hell outta here. You'uns got some nerve barging in when we'uns is all upset about Ken's being lost." His eyes drooped shut, and a soft snore erupted from his nose.

"Sorry," Mrs. Poffenberger whispered to me at the door. "He's real upset."

"I can tell. So upset, he forgot his son's name is Kevin."

"He's waiting for someone to call back 'bout a made-for-TV movie. You know, like the one they did about that little girl in Texas what fell in the well. We sure could use the money."

"I understand."

"I can't watch the little ones all the time, not with nine of 'em underfoot, you know."

I nodded. I felt real pity for the woman. Neither she nor those nine kids had much of a life, nor much chance of it getting any better.

"It's time to get to bed," she said to the waist-high towheads crowded around us. "Pearl and Peter, you'uns go home now. Good night, miss." She closed the door, leaving me on the stoop with the two children, who followed me to my car.

"Were you guys with Kevin when he got lost?" I asked them.

They shuffled their feet in the dirt, shared sideways glances, and poked each other with their shabby elbows.

"Can't either of you speak?"

The girl stepped forward. From her height, I assumed she was the oldest. "I guess so," she said.

"You guess? Don't you know? What's your name? How old are you?"

"Pearl Poffenberger." Her green eyes glinted with something I hadn't seen much of at the Poffenberger home this evening—a hint of intelligence. "I'm near twelve."

"I know you weren't alone. Who else was with you?"

Reluctantly, it seemed, she said, "My brother, Peter."

The other child stepped forward. "I'm eleven," he said.

"Anybody else with you?"

The shiny heads shook their denial.

"Aren't you two a little old to be playing with a five-year-old?"

"He always tags along," Peter said.

"What happened up there?"

Pearl, who seemed to be the leader, answered. "Kevin got tired of playing. Said he wanted to go home."

"We wasn't ready," Peter said. "He was blubbering, so we told him to go home by hisself."

"We didn't know he was lost till we got home 'bout an hour later," Pearl put in.

I had to express my incredulity. "You mean, you just let a five-year-old boy go off by himself in the woods?"

"Sure, why not? He done it all the time. Didn't he, Pearl?"

She nodded vigorously. "All the time."

"If you guys think of anything you haven't told the police, call me at the paper. You won't get into any trouble." I handed Pearl a *Chronicle* business card with my name handwritten on the back. Peter extended his hand, and I gave him one, too.

I decided to get creative. "There's a reward," I told them. Maybe that'd get one of them talking.

For a brief moment, it seemed that Peter wanted to tell me something. But then he turned to Pearl, and his eyes seemed to search her face. She placed her hand on his upper arm and squeezed until he grimaced. Whatever he'd been about to say, he thought better of it.

"Okay," Pearl said. "But I can tell you right now, there ain't nothing we didn't already tell the cops."

They were keeping something back, I was sure of it. I've interviewed enough people in my life to know when someone is lying or telling a half-truth.

"Kevin's lost out there," I said. "He's very small, and he's cold and frightened. Do me a favor. When you get into your warm beds tonight, think about that."

Their sullen faces showed no emotion. I left them and drove back to Lickin Creek as rapidly as the slippery road allowed. All I wanted to do was get into a hot shower and steam away my distasteful encounter with the Poffenbergers.

CHAPTER 3

What child is this?

MOON LAKE MARKS THE SOUTHERN BORDER of the Borough of Lickin Creek. Where once a sandy beach stretched along the shore of the crescent-shaped lake, there is now a thorny forest extending to the water's edge. Where once ladies in long white dresses and men in natty suits and straw hats strolled along well-tended paths, there is now only desolation. Where excited children once rode the carousel, there is now only the vine-covered ruin of a pavilion. A decaying dock is a nostalgic reminder of times when renting a rowboat on a dreamy summer day was the stuff memories were made of.

Great mansions, built before the turn of the century as the vacation cottages of the very rich from D.C. and Baltimore, have crumbled for years beneath the ancient trees. In the summer, the area is heavy with the fragrance of wild honeysuckle and old rosebushes. Only in the winter, when the bare branches admit the sun and the snow hides imperfections, can one imagine the original grandeur of the old summer colony.

World War I, the stock market crash, and the development of rapid transportation brought the glory days of Moon Lake to an end. But in the past few years the development had once again sprung to life, and many of the huge homes were now occupied by young professionals, some of whom commuted daily to the cities of D.C. and Baltimore. They arrived in their minivans and BMWs with grand and often unrealistic plans for remodeling the enormous white elephants and filling them with large families.

I entered the colony through the rusted iron gates, turned off the main road circling the lake, and drove down the narrow dirt lane that approached the largest, grandest, and gloomiest of the lakefront mansions: my temporary home-sweet-home. It was the perfect setting for one of the gothic novels I'd loved to read in junior high, even rumored to be haunted by the ghost of a woman who died during childbirth in one of its fairy-tale turrets. I've often thought it would be fun to don a long white nightgown and flit about the yard like a heroine on the cover of a gothic but have decided to wait until the weather gets warmer.

The reason I was living in such unusual splendor was that I was house-sitting for a college professor on sabbatical in England to study the use of contractions in medieval writings. It was a mutually beneficial arrangement. I had a free (except for utilities) place to live for the six months I'd committed to editing the *Chronicle*, and all I had to do for Dr. Ethelind Gallant was make sure the house she'd inherited from her grandparents didn't collapse while she was gone.

It was fun having all that space to spread out in, but the utilities turned out to be a huge expense. I really hadn't considered what it would cost to heat a thirty-room house in the winter. That's why I was angry with myself tonight, for I could see a sliver of light shining through the chink where the velvet drapes didn't quite meet in one of the front-parlor windows. I couldn't afford to be so careless with electricity.

I left Garnet's macho-man pickup truck in the roundabout in front of the mansion and shuffled through the light dusting of snow to the kitchen entrance in back. Some of the new owners had successfully renovated their homes, but Ethelind was not one of them.

Right before she flew off to merry olde England, she'd casually mentioned that the front porch roof was on the verge of collapse. "Don't go slamming the front door," she'd cautioned me. I hoped the warning note I'd tacked on a pillar near the steps was sufficient to protect unwary visitors.

I hung my coat on the oak hall tree on the enclosed back porch, slipped off my boots, and opened the door into the kitchen. Funny—I thought for sure I'd locked it. I was getting to be more like the natives every day.

Before I could turn on the lights, my nose began to twitch. My nose is unusually sensitive, and I recognized the sweet, spicy scent drifting in the air; it was the aroma of carnations, mingled with the smoky smell of burning firewood.

Good grief! Ethelind had said not to use the fireplaces because she hadn't had the chimneys checked for safety. I hadn't lit any fires. Who had?

As I groped for the light switch next to the door, I realized something was dreadfully wrong. There were no warm, furry cats rubbing against my legs, begging for food and affection.

"Fred . . . Noel . . . ?" I called in a soft voice. No answer.

I sniffed the air and identified the scent. Only one person I knew wore Bellodgia, a distinctive and expensive perfume from Paris, and that person was Praxythea Evangelista!

Praxythea was the best-known psychic in America, thanks to the many TV talk-show hosts who desperately needed guests. She was always a welcome addition to their shows because of her glamour, intelligence, and her well-publicized talent for helping police departments solve hopeless crimes. Now, she reclined on an antique chaise longue in my front parlor. On her lap lay Fred, curled into a round orange ball and grinning like a big dope. The more sophisticated Noel rested her chin on one of Praxythea's shapely ankles and appeared to be enjoying the unexpected luxury of the fire blazing in the marble-faced fireplace.

On the index finger of the hand that held a crystal goblet half full of amber liquid, an emerald of immense proportions, surrounded by diamonds, glimmered in the firelight. Praxythea's hair, hanging loose around her shoulders, was the color of the flames that threatened to burn the house down. She looked at me through those amazing catlike eyes, which matched her emerald, and smiled. "So glad you have Glenfiddich. Double malts cause psychic confusion—too many clashing vibrations."

I collapsed into an armchair and stared at her in amazement. Praxythea was not someone I knew well. We'd only met last summer when Alice-Ann's husband was murdered and Praxythea supposedly had been in town to find the long-lost diamond known as Sylvia's Star. Since then we'd "done lunch" a couple of times in New York, but still, she was the last person I'd expect to find camped out in my living room.

"Not that it isn't nice to see you," I said, "but what are you doing here?"

"I had a vision of a little boy, lost in the woods, and knew I had to help the police find him."

"Could that vision possibly have been on the evening news in New York?" I asked.

She grinned. "My sources are private."

"How'd you get here so fast?"

"A friend put his plane and pilot at my disposal."

I should have thought of that. Don't we all have friends with planes and pilots?

"That delightful man with the taxi, Uriah's Heap, met me at the airport. He told me you were staying here, and I was sure you wouldn't mind a houseguest."

When I didn't say anything, she said, "You can't expect me to stay at a Days Inn. By the way, you really should pick a better place to hide your key, Tori. Those phony rocks from a catalog are too, too obvious. You might as well leave the door unlocked with a note on it saying 'Help yourself.' "

While she spoke, her long, elegant fingers drifted through Fred's soft orange fur. He writhed in ecstasy.

I heard myself repeating what I'd heard so often from local people. "This isn't New York, you know. We don't worry about things like that here."

It isn't that I don't like Praxythea; it's just that I feel totally inadequate every time I'm near her. She's beautiful while I'm ordinary, tall while I'm height disadvantaged, and has a perfect figure while my weight would be okay if I were eight or nine inches taller. On top of all that she's rich, and her first book, *Adrift on a Psychic Sea*, which had just come out, was already on the *New York Times* best-seller list. Unlike mine, which was due to be remaindered any second now.

"You don't mind my staying here, do you?"

"No, of course not." Praxythea hadn't become famous only because she was beautiful. She was also intelligent and witty. As a houseguest, she would be better company than those traitorous animals of mine.

"Would you get me another drink please, Tori? I don't

want to disturb these darling cats." Fred squirmed with pleasure and adjusted his tail.

I glared at him as I carried Praxythea's glass to the bar, where I poured an inch of Scotch into it. I didn't want to cloud those psychic vibrations she'd mentioned. Then I poured about three inches in another glass for myself. I had no vibrations to worry about, and as late as it was, I'd welcome a cloud—all I wanted to do was take a hot shower and get to bed. Tomorrow would be a busy day: I still had to write up my interview with the Poffenbergers and, of course, I'd want to keep up with the progress of the search parties.

I handed her the glass. "I'd better extinguish that fire," I said. "The chimneys haven't been cleaned in years."

"It's safe, Tori. I checked it out."

"Physically or psychically?"

"Don't worry about it."

I slumped into the armchair and hoped Ethelind had a good homeowner's policy. Still, I did have to admit it was nice to have a fire going. For the first time since I'd moved in, I was warm. The firelight cast a cozy glow upon the room, camouflaging the dust and the shabby upholstery, and making it easy to imagine how grand it must have been ninety years ago.

We sipped our drinks, and Praxythea filled me in on her most recent psychic adventures. Lulled by the warmth, her melodic voice, and the Scotch, I was nearly asleep when the sound of a car approaching on the gravel driveway startled me awake.

"What time is it?" I'd been meaning to get my Timex repaired for months.

"Only a little past one. That should be Luscious Miller."

"Luscious! Why?"

"I called him a few minutes before you got home. I've offered to help him with his search for the boy."

A moment later, there was a loud pounding at the back door.

"I'll get it." Did I have any choice?

Luscious stood on the back porch, stripping off layers of clothing. I asked, "Any luck?"

He shook his head, so upset he didn't even bother to rearrange his hair over his bald spot. "Praxythea Evangelista called me—said she's come all the way from New York to help us," he said. "She found a missing murder victim for us back a few years ago. We're real lucky to have her."

"Indeed we are." I tried not to sound skeptical. After all, it couldn't hurt to have her here, despite what I thought about her psychic abilities. "Luscious, if I were you, I'd ask those kids more questions. The ones that were with Kevin before he got lost. There was something peculiar about the way they acted—I don't trust them."

"Thanks, Tori. I'll do that. First thing in the morning."

Praxythea was standing when we entered the parlor. Now I saw she wore a creamy raw-silk pantsuit with a purple scarf artfully draped around her neck. Purple, I recalled, represented spiritualism. I couldn't help feeling shorter, heavier, and more poorly dressed than I had a few minutes ago.

She held her arms out, and Luscious, with a goofy smile on his face, stepped right into her embrace.

"So good to see you again," she whispered huskily into his right ear. His bald spot glowed like a fuchsia in full bloom.

"Let's start at once, shall we?" Praxythea said. Looking at me, she said, "We'll need a small table and some straight-backed chairs."

"Wait a minute," I protested. "You're not going to hold a séance, are you?"

"I prefer to call them *readings*." She spotted a carved Chinese table, rosewood inlaid with mother-of-pearl, in a dark corner. "That table will do nicely. Chairs, Tori?"

Luscious and I carried in three oak chairs from the kitchen and set them around the table Praxythea had selected.

"Very nice. I need one more thing. Something convex with a reflective surface to concentrate on."

"You mean a crystal ball, don't you?" I said. "I'm surprised you didn't bring one with you."

"Mine is far too heavy to carry with me and is really not necessary. I'm sure you can find something suitable."

"Would you like some background music, Praxythea? I have an Enya tape."

Her cool stare told me my attempt at humor was not appreciated. A few minutes later, the three of us sat in a circle around the rosewood table, holding hands and staring at an upside-down one-and-a-half-quart Pyrex baking dish. As Praxythea had ordered, all the lamps were turned off and the only light in the room came from the burning logs in the hearth.

"Concentrate on the reflection," she told us. "Let your eyes relax until you feel you are falling into it."

"Just like looking at a 3-D computer picture," I commented, crossing my eyes.

"Whatever it takes for you, Tori. Relax. Empty your mind. Be receptive to what comes." Her eyes narrowed to nearly closed slits. I was afraid if I did as instructed I'd fall asleep, so I concentrated on a baked-on gravy stain on the side of the bowl.

We sat that way for a long time, while the fire died down to embers and the room turned cold. Once or twice I imagined I saw a shadowy image move across the surface of the bowl, but when I tried to bring it into focus, it disappeared. An illusion caused by moving light and tired eyes, I thought.

The room was dark. Way too dark. There should be moonlight coming in through the windows. My hands were icy cold, and I wished I could disentangle my fingers and blow some warmth into them. Although I tried to act nonchalant, I didn't like this type of thing at all. The memory of an encounter with something evil in the Mark Twain house in New York was still fresh in my mind. Intellectually, I knew there were no ghosts, spirits, or evil entities, but something deep inside the darkest reaches of my mind told me differently.

Suddenly, Praxythea's long bloodred fingernails dug into my palm. "I'm here," she said, only it wasn't her voice that emitted from her mouth. "Mommy, I'm here, and I'm cold and scared. Where are you? Why don't you come, Mommy?"

A frisson of fear chilled my spine. What I was hearing was a small child. A frightened child. A child who was now crying.

A tear trickled down the psychic's cheek as the child continued. "Why don't you come? I've waited so long. Please, come get me. It's so dark. Please . . . please . . . please . . ." The voice deteriorated into pathetic sobbing that nearly broke my heart. I kept trying to remind myself that it was only Praxythea being dramatic, but damn, she truly did sound like a child.

"Where are you, darling?" Praxythea's speech was back to normal. She sounded like a concerned mother, talking calmly, trying not to alarm her frightened toddler.

The child's voice answered. "It's so deep . . . and still . . . something's holding me down . . . I'm cold . . . here . . . by the edge of running water . . ." The voice faded, and the room suddenly felt twenty degrees warmer.

"Lights, please, Luscious," Praxythea ordered.

Luscious leaped to do her bidding. I pried Praxythea's fingers off my hand and rubbed the painful dents in my flesh. When the lights came on, I saw she looked dreadfully worn. The dark purple of old bruises circled her eyes, and her cheeks were pale and sunken. I could actually see her heart pounding through the soft silk of her suit.

My heart pounded, too, with fear that she might have a stroke or something equally awful. I fetched a glass of water from the kitchen, and she accepted it wordlessly. Luscious helped himself to something from the bar, and we sat and waited.

After a few minutes, Praxythea regained her usual, glamorous demeanor with no apparent ill effects. "He's trapped," she said. "I saw a deep, still pool of water surrounded by cliffs. There's running water nearby. A spring or maybe a small creek. Can you think of any place that fits that description, Luscious?"

Now that things were back to normal, I couldn't refrain from expressing my disbelief. "You ought to be ashamed of yourself, Praxythea. Every time you try to locate someone psychically, you come up with the phrase 'by the edge of running water.' It's getting to be a bit much."

Luscious interrupted. "Sounds like the old limestone quarry on Seven Springs Road. But it's about five miles west of where the kids say Kevin got lost."

"They might not have told the truth," I pointed out. "If Kevin's cousins did something to hurt him, it's quite possible they'd try to throw the searchers offtrack by lying about where they'd last seen him."

I knew there was the off-chance possibility that Prax-ythea was right about the quarry. No matter what I thought about Praxythea's psychic ability, the quarry had to be checked out. And, much as I hated to admit it, she'd had some amazing successes with police depart-ments in other parts of the country.

"The child in your vision—he was dead, wasn't he?" I asked.

Staring deep into the fire, she nodded.

Luscious jumped to his feet. "I'll get divers out there right away. We'll know by morning."

He placed several calls. For once, he sounded sure of himself and in control of the situation. Garnet would have been proud of him.

"I'm heading out there now," he said. "You two try to get some rest."

"No way!" I protested. I was now wide awake. "I'm going with you."

"So am I," Praxythea said. "I can help you locate the exact spot to dive."

By four that morning, the area on the limestone cliffs above the quarry was lit by the flashing lights of dozens of emergency vehicles. Whoever wasn't searching the mountain near Stinking Spring was here to help.

Television crews from Hagerstown, Harrisburg, and York stretched out their cables and set up floodlights and cameras. I spotted the Poffenbergers being inter-viewed by a reporter who couldn't have been more than three days out of college. Although I couldn't hear him, I could imagine the dialogue: "Tell me how you feel . . ."

Teams of divers, trained in scuba techniques and body recovery, took turns diving into the still, black depths of the water below.

Praxythea and Luscious had their heads together, studying a map. Since there was nothing I could contribute, I sat down on a rocky perch overlooking the rescue scene. Ginnie Welburn and Oretta Clopper, bearing doughnuts and paper cups full of steaming coffee, soon joined me.

"I thought you two were up on the mountain," I said, moving over to make room for them on my rock. Oretta lowered her bulk with a grunt, making me wonder how she was ever going to get back on her feet.

"We thought we could be of more use here," Oretta said.

"Besides, nothing's happening up there. This is where the action is," Ginnie said as she squeezed in between us.

Even in the dim light, their drawn faces showed the stress we'd all been under for the last seven or eight hours. I wanted to say something light and clever to relieve the tension. I settled for "You two appear to have become best friends." Not exactly a bon mot, but at least it brought a trace of a smile to Ginnie's lips.

"We had a lot of time to get acquainted tonight," Ginnie said. "We discovered we're practically neighbors."

"I know Oretta lives on the other side of Moon Lake, but I didn't know you lived nearby," I said.

Ginnie nodded. "At the end of your street. I've always harbored a secret desire to live in a grand Victorian mansion. Finding one I could actually afford was a dream come true."

"They are fun to live in," I said. "Especially in the summer when you don't have to heat them. I've heard mine's haunted."

Oretta, who had been sipping coffee and listening to the conversation, broke in with a sniff. "They all are, Tori. If you believe local legend, Moon Lake has even more ghosts per square inch than Gettysburg."

I was disappointed to learn my ghost story wasn't unique, particularly when Ginnie said, "Mine is supposed to be haunted by the ghost of a woman who died in childbirth."

Oretta began a long, complicated commentary describing the play she planned to write someday about a haunted house, when a shout from below captured our attention. We waited for a few minutes, but nothing more happened.

"Do you really think Kevin's down there?" Ginnie asked with a shudder.

"Praxythea could be right," I said. "She has been in the past."

"This is awful!" Ginnie said softly. Oretta took her hand, and we watched the divers go down, again and again.

The dark night sky was brightening to the gray light of dawn, when we heard a shout from below. "Found something."

As people rushed past us to look down at the water, Ginnie and I pulled Oretta to her feet. From our vantage point, we watched a diver hoist himself out of the water onto a yellow rubber raft, where his diving partner waited. He laid a small item on the floor of the craft, then tumbled backward into the water.

"What is it?" someone called.

The man in the raft waved his arms and yelled something that was swallowed up in the noise of the crowd.

The diver reappeared on the surface, passed another object to the man in the boat, and disappeared beneath the surface once more.

So many people were calling out questions that there was no chance of hearing the answers. Luscious stepped forward with a battery-operated bullhorn and commanded the crowd to be quiet. An eerie stillness settled over the quarry. "What did you find?" he asked through the horn. His words bounced off the cliff face.

The man below cupped his hands and shouted back, "Bones! Looks like a child's skull."

Skull . . . skull . . . skull . . . The word echoed from the limestone walls of the quarry. Mrs. Poffenberger's screams shattered the still air, and Oretta Clopper exhaled sharply and dropped at my feet in a dead faint.

CHAPTER 4

Glad tidings we sing

SUNSHINE STREAMED IN THROUGH MY BED-room window. What time was it? Where were my cats? And who was cooking bacon in my kitchen? The events of last night and early this morning flooded back into my mind as I sat up in bed.

After finding the skull, the divers had brought up several more bones. They'd made a dozen more unproductive dives after that. Finally, they abandoned the search and carried what they'd found to the top of the cliff. The white bones lay obscenely on a flat rock for all to see.

Mrs. Poffenberger and Oretta Clopper had been taken away by ambulance, so Mrs. Poffenberger wouldn't learn until later that the coroner immediately determined the skeletal remains couldn't possibly be Kevin's. Even to a layperson like myself, it was obvious that the bones had been underwater for a long, long time.

Luscious suggested that everyone return to Stinking Spring and continue searching for Kevin in the mountains. The spectators and the television crews left; the divers remained, to look for more bones in the daylight.

Sometime in the pearly predawn hours, Praxythea and I had returned to the mansion. I'd pulled some sheets from the linen closet, handed them to her, and suggested she take any one of a dozen empty bedrooms. So much for being a gracious hostess. Then I removed my shoes and fell into bed, still wearing my slacks and sweater.

Wide awake now, I flung covers to the floor. Since no one had called with good news, I was sure Kevin hadn't been found. I needed to get in touch with Luscious to learn how the search was going. I also had a borough council meeting to cover, and I had to get to the office to write up my account of last night's tragic discovery.

I showered and dressed quickly, then, thinking I looked pretty damn good in hip-slimming navy slacks, white Irish fisherman's sweater, and red paisley scarf, I followed my nose down the curving staircase, through the foyer, the billiard room, the two front parlors, the dining room, the butler's pantry, and into the kitchen.

There, Praxythea, in a silky emerald-green mini-something-or-other, with her red curls escaping from the large comb that held her hair off her face, was pouring coffee into two bone-china cups. Fred sat pressed against one long leg, gazing at her with the adoration he usually reserved for a large helping of Tasty Tabby Treats.

"I had to run out to the supermarket, Tori. There wasn't anything in the fridge except diet soda, cold pizza, and Snickers bars. Want to nibble on some bacon while I scramble the eggs? Or are you on a diet?"

She was smiling sweetly as she said it, but suddenly, I didn't feel quite as attractive as I had a few minutes ago. "Yes to the bacon, please. It smells wonderful. Any word about Kevin?"

"You know I'd have wakened you if there was."

I drank the strong coffee and watched Praxythea whip the eggs in the Pyrex bowl that last night had served as her crystal ball.

"You really goofed this time," I said.

"What do you mean?" She didn't miss a beat, but her back stiffened.

"During the séance, you said you had a vision of Kevin being in the quarry."

The eggs sizzled as they hit the melted butter in the heavy cast-iron skillet. "I never said it was Kevin." She gave the eggs a quick stir and emptied the skillet onto a platter she'd heated in the oven. "Something's odd, though . . ."

"What?" I helped myself to a heap of pale, golden eggs and added a toasted English muffin.

"Those bones have been in the quarry for a long time. Why did the vision come to me now? I wonder if it had something to do with another child being lost?"

"I won't hazard a guess, since I don't believe in this psychic stuff." I spread butter on the muffin and watched it melt into the holes.

She went on as though I weren't there. "That must be the reason. I think the dead child wants to help me find Kevin before it's too late. That's why he contacted me."

I wiped butter off my chin and muttered, "Good grief—what are you going to come up with next?"

She smiled. "Be skeptical. I don't care. I'm used to it. You do realize that the good news is I wasn't contacted by Kevin's spirit."

"Why is that good news? More coffee?" She nodded, and I poured.

"It means Kevin's still alive," she said. "I didn't think so at first, because I had a vision of a dead child underwater—I misunderstood and thought it was Kevin, but it wasn't. To locate Kevin, I need an object that belongs to him, preferably metal."

"Why?"

"Because when I touch something of his, I'll feel the vibrations he's emitting, wherever he is. Don't try to understand, Tori. I don't, myself. Just bring me something when you go to visit his family today, won't you?"

"What makes you think I'm going up there?"

She threw me one of those mysterious smiles of hers. "I don't have to be psychic to know a good reporter will follow up on a story."

"I hope you're right about his being alive." I put our breakfast dishes in the dishwasher.

"There is no doubt in my mind . . . What's that noise coming from the front of the house?"

"Sounds like the mailman . . . he drops stuff through a slot in the door."

"Shouldn't he stay off that porch? I saw your warning sign last night."

"I've told him a dozen times. He says he's been delivering mail to the front door for twenty years and he 'ain't about to start trekking around to the back.' I'll be back in a second."

Miles from the kitchen, in the front hall, the mail lay scattered on the red Oriental rug. Hoping there'd be a letter from Garnet, I eagerly gathered it up and ran back to the warm kitchen. Praxythea studied the Draper's & Damon's catalog, while I tossed out the credit card solicitations and offers to try one issue of a magazine absolutely free. When the trash can was full, only two real letters remained. Damn! Neither was from Garnet. I hadn't had a letter from him in weeks. Was it too soon to wonder if I'd been dumped by another almost-fiancé?

The first was from Murray Rosenbaum, my next-door neighbor and best friend in New York. He missed me, New York missed me, and so did Con Ed. He enclosed the power company's third and final notice, which I dropped in the trash. With the salary I was earning at the *Chronicle* and no expenses except the horrendous heating bill, I'd be able to pay off most of my bills when I got back to New York. Until then, there was no point in worrying about them.

The long row of foreign stamps on the second envelope meant it was from my father, the ambassador to whatever country was lowest in importance on the State Department's list of third world nations. I ripped it open, glanced at the letter, and gasped.

Praxythea stared at me with her wise emerald eyes. "What's wrong?" she asked.

"He married his girlfriend!" A tear sneaked its way down one flaming cheek. "And he actually has the gall to say there's no need for me to worry about Mother. Says she'll qualify for Medicaid now and can move to a good state facility. Didn't tell me about the divorce sooner— wasn't sure how I'd take it."

I balled up the letter and threw it on the table.

Praxythea smoothed it out. "Do you mind?" she asked and proceeded to read it without waiting for my answer.

For the first time in a long time, I thought of my mother as she'd once been: tall, blonde, and elegant, handling the rigors of foreign service life and my father's infidelities with the stiff upper lip that was expected from women of her generation and social class. Now she hovered in a gray zone, her brain pickled from years of alcohol abuse, in a warehouse called the Willows, where she would stay until she was reclassified as a welfare patient, or whatever it is they call impoverished divorced women.

Praxythea handed me a tissue.

"He's had plenty of Bambi-bimbos over the years," I

sniffed into the Kleenex. "Why did he marry this one?" That he might actually be in love didn't occur to me.

"This might explain it," Praxythea read aloud, " '. . . baby's due near Christmas. I hope you'll find it in your heart to accept Tyfani and your new brother or sister.' "

I laughed, then, at the absurdity. Ambassador Grantham Livingston Miracle, age sixty-two, new bridegroom and father-to-be. The old goat's philandering ways had finally caught up with him!

My laughter stopped suddenly. I was going to be a sister to someone, once again. I was going to have a second chance—and this time I was going to get it right. It was a powerful and sobering thought.

My reverie was interrupted by a combination of strange sounds—hissing, scratching, and screeching—coming from the enclosed back porch that served as a laundry/mudroom. I immediately feared one or both of the cats had gotten into trouble, and leaping to my feet, I cried, "Fred . . . Noel?"

They meowed fretfully from under the table. "Okay, you scaredy-cats," I muttered. "Let's see what's out there." I grabbed a carving knife. "Maybe it's our ghost," I joked, trying to settle my frazzled nerves.

"No, it isn't," Praxythea said seriously.

I should know better than to joke about ghosts with a psychic.

"Stand back," I ordered and opened the door about an inch. Through the little crack, I saw a large and very angry animal trying to burrow through the back door.

"What is it?" Praxythea asked.

I slammed the door shut. "Damned if I know. Looks like a giant rat." The "rat" threw itself against the door. "Good grief," I gasped. "What should I do?" My back was braced against the door, just in case the creature tried to force its way into the kitchen.

We stared at each other; two city females confronted with a country problem, and with no idea how to resolve it. Then the front doorbell rang.

Praxythea went to answer it, while I stayed at the barricades. When she returned, she was followed by Oretta Clopper.

It didn't take long for our deus ex machina, moving at a surprising speed considering her bulk, to shoo the frightened animal away from the back door and replace the dryer exhaust hose.

"Just a little possum, looking for a warm hidey-hole," she said with a sniff. "More afraid of you than you were of it."

I doubted that.

It suddenly occurred to me to ask Oretta Clopper, who had never before visited me, why she had dropped by on this particular morning. I hoped she wasn't bringing me a copy of the play she'd told me about.

"I'll show you," she said. "It's in the living room." As I followed her out of the kitchen, Praxythea made a strange sound, which I would have interpreted as a giggle if she were the giggly type.

"What the heck is it, Oretta?" I asked softly, so as not to disturb the large, prehistoric-looking creature lying in a huge, rectangular glass box.

"It's an iguana. A man brought it to the Humane Society this morning. It belonged to his kids, but it grew bigger than they expected. They don't have room for it anymore." Her frown told me exactly what she thought of people who didn't accept proper responsibility for their pets.

"I need someone to care for it until I can find it a

suitable permanent home." She smiled brightly. "Naturally, I thought of you, since I know you're an animal lover."

"Cats," I muttered. "It's cats I love. Fuzzy, warm animals you can snuggle up to."

Praxythea peeked at it over my left shoulder. "Does it have a name?"

"No names," I pleaded. Once you name an animal, it assumes a personality and becomes a member of the household.

"It's called Icky," Oretta announced.

I groaned.

"How cute," Praxythea murmured.

Oretta launched into a long, involved description of what it ate, and I relaxed a little upon learning it was a vegetarian. As long as it wasn't interested in eating cats or people, I figured I could live with it for a while. We moved it into the kitchen because that was the warmest room in the house and plugged in its heat lamp.

"It should only be for a few days," Oretta promised. "Be sure and wash your hands after you touch it—they can carry salmonella."

Salmonella—just what I needed in my kitchen!

Oretta accepted my offer of coffee, and we sat down at the kitchen table. When I questioned her about last night's fainting spell, she said she was feeling just fine.

"Doctor said I must have been overexhausted to faint like that. It's all the work I've put in on the pageant and, of course, supervising the food tables for the search parties up in the mountains. The strain was just more than I could bear." She sighed deeply, worn out from her martyrdom. "But I'm not one to back down when a job needs done."

"It *was* quite a night," I said. "To start out hunting for

one lost child and find another. Do you have any idea who it might have been in the quarry?"

Oretta's eyes widened with surprise as she said, "Why of course, it's Eddie Douglas. Everybody there knew that."

CHAPTER 5

'Tis the season to be jolly

"OH, SURE, EVERYBODY KNEW THAT!" I MUT-
tered to myself as I pulled out of the driveway,
spraying gravel in my wake. "Everybody but me.
You'd think someone might have mentioned it to
me—for the newspaper." I sighed as I wondered if I was
ever going to be accepted here in Garnet's hometown, or
would I always be an "outsider"?

At the end of the lane, I spied Ginnie Welburn sweeping a light dusting of snow off a porch. So that was
where she lived. In typical New York fashion I'd been
oblivious to everyone who lived around me. She saw me,
raised one arm, and stepped forward as if she wanted me
to stop and chat. However, I was already late for the
borough council meeting, so I merely waved and continued on my way.

Outside Lickin Creek's historic borough hall, delicate
snowflakes dropped lightly onto the redbrick sidewalk.
Caught by sudden gusts of icy air, they swirled like con-
fetti around the picturesque gaslights, settled like talcum
powder on the shoulders of the little mermaid bathing in
the empty fountain on the square, and persistently struggled to enter the charming, but very old, municipal building through the cracks around the doors and windows.

Shortly before Thanksgiving, the borough council, acutely in tune with the concerns of its constituents and aware of upcoming elections, had voted to set the central heating system at an energy-saving sixty-two degrees. Despite the sheets of heavy plastic nailed over the inside of the ten-foot-tall windows, this afternoon the council's meeting room was only slightly warmer than a meat locker. Notice I said *slightly* warmer.

A wood-burning stove, dating back to the late eighteen hundreds, was lit to raise the frigid temperature, but all it accomplished was to fry those who sat directly in front of it, while the people seated at the far end of the long table had to keep on their coats, hats, and gloves.

I was late, as usual, but apparently I hadn't missed anything. The council was still enjoying its premeeting coffee break.

"Bless you," I said to Buchanan McCleary, the town solicitor, when he brought a cup to me. I hadn't been sure of the propriety of helping myself. I took a sip and was pleased he'd remembered I like my coffee with lots of artificial creamer and sweetener. As the hot liquid rolled down my throat my body commenced to thaw from the inside out.

"Any news about Kevin?" I asked Buchanan as we stood in front of the stove stamping our feet as though participating in some primitive dance ritual.

"I'm afraid not," he said. "Luscious called in a few minutes ago to say there are no leads."

"Damn!"

I looked up at him. Way up. Buchanan was about six-six, with a sixties Afro that added another four or five inches. "Did you know that the remains they found in the quarry last night could be a boy named Eddie Douglas?"

"Of course," he said. "Who else could it be?" He

must have caught something on my face, because he added, "I guess you wouldn't have known—not being from around here."

"Coming into a town where all the residents seem to be first or second cousins, I don't know lots of things."

Our fronts were thoroughly toasted. We turned our icy backs to the stove. "Don't let it worry you, Tori. Time will take care of it."

"Who was Eddie Douglas?" I asked.

"A little boy who wandered away from his house about thirty-five years ago and never came back. Nobody knew what happened to him—until last night. I was just a kid, myself, but I remember my mom wouldn't let me out of her sight for months."

I repressed a shudder. "I hope Kevin's story has a happier ending."

There was no sign that the council meeting was ready to begin, so Buchanan refilled our coffee cups. He handed mine back to me and said, "What's the latest word from our illustrious police chief? Has he finished his Spanish classes at the Foreign Service Institute?"

I was too proud to admit I hadn't heard anything from Garnet in weeks. "He graduated first in his class. And he's been in Costa Rica for nearly a month. As I'm sure Greta has already told you."

The smile that split Buchanan's dark brown face could have warmed the room. He and Garnet's widowed sister, Greta Carbaugh, had become an item over the past several months. United, they were going to save whales, rain forests, spotted owls, and Chesapeake Bay. They even seemed to enjoy the minor controversy caused by their interracial relationship.

Whenever I saw them together, I couldn't help but feel a tiny twinge of envy. They made me wonder how other people managed to meet, fall in love, and have uncomplicated relationships.

My romance with Garnet Gochenauer was a perfect example of how things always seemed to go wrong for me. As I'd plotted a surprise move to Lickin Creek to be near Garnet, he'd decided there was little job satisfaction to be found as a small-town police chief and took a year's leave of absence to work in Central America. There was a local Pennsylvania Dutch saying that seemed to describe me perfectly: A person who could screw up a one-car funeral.

Marvin Bumbaugh, president of the council, called for the meeting to start, and the council members took their places at the long oak table. Buchanan was on Marvin's right, Jackson Clopper, the borough manager, on his left. Next to Jackson sat Primrose Flack, described last night by Ginnie as "the council's token woman." Across the table from Primrose was "almost-a-doctor" Matavious Clopper. I wondered what effect the Clopper family feud had on council business. Several visitors joined the council members at the table. When everyone was seated, I took the last empty chair, black and sticky like the others from generations of council meetings.

After the reading of minutes by Primrose and the treasurer's report by Matavious (the borough was still solvent . . . barely), Marvin turned to Jackson Clopper and asked him what was happening with the search for Kevin.

"No news is good news," Jackson said. His face was lined, and I guessed he hadn't gotten much sleep last night.

"Nice attitude," Primrose muttered.

"I'll bet Garnet could find him," a woman said. It was

Bernice Roadcap, once again wearing her politically in-correct, full-length mink coat. She wasn't a council member, but she often attended the meetings to protect her business interests.

After her crack about Garnet, everyone turned to glare at me, as if I had chased Garnet away by moving to town. I ignored them and gave the blank page in my notebook my full attention.

"Let's talk about the downtown Christmas preparations and get the hell out of here," Marvin said. His breath, warmed by the coffee, was visible in the frosty air.

"What about my cold-storage building?" Bernice interrupted shrilly. "I need an answer, and I need it now."

"We can't just jump into this, Bernice," Marvin said. "We need to look at the remodeling costs. Having a center for the arts sounds great, but it might be more than the borough's budget can handle."

"Not to mention the environmental impact on the Lickin Creek," Buchanan added. "Your idea of having small boats travel from Moon Lake into the arts center sounds attractive, but we mustn't forget the native brown trout in the creek."

"A museum and creative arts center with a tasteful shopping mall attached would create a point of interest in the downtown area," Bernice protested, "where now there is nothing. You're always talking about bringing in the tourists, but once they're here, there's nothing for them to see or do."

This brought a flood of objections from the others. "Not true . . . the fountain . . . courthouse . . . municipal park . . . Civil War cemetery . . ." Their voices faded as they ran out of tourist attractions.

"Look at what San Antonio did with the River Walk," Bernice said. "We could do something like that here."

Marvin snorted rudely. "If you think Lickin Creek's gonna turn into another San Antonio . . . you got another think coming. For one thing, we got a creek here, not a river."

"Not to mention the trout," Buchanan added.

"I can't afford to pay taxes forever on an empty building, and I have to know what's going to happen to it before my divorce is final. So, I'm warning you, if you don't make a decision in the next six weeks, I'll tear it down. I don't need to remind you it's the last large historic building in the downtown area. Once it's gone you won't have another opportunity."

"We'll appoint a committee to—you know—ya dee ya-dee-ya-da," Marvin told her.

"How reassuring," she sniffed. "A committee . . . wonderful!"

"The Christmas decorations are literally on the table. Let's do something about them," Marvin said with a grim smile.

"I think you mean figuratively on the table, not literally," Buchanan whispered.

"I mean whatever the hell I think I mean," the council president snapped at the attorney. "We've had some complaints about the Christmas decorations in the square. Fifteen people called or wrote in to say they want colored lights, not the white lights we use each year. Here's one what says, 'We've lost the meaning of Christmas with them cold white lights. Colored lights is the traditional way to say Merry X-mas.' "

"X-mas!" Jackson Clopper stabbed the air with his ever-present pipe. "He wrote *X-mas*? A person can talk about tradition while abbreviating our Savior's name as an *X*?"

Murmurs of disapproval fluttered around the table.

"Who wrote it?" Jackson demanded to know.

"It's anonymous," Marvin said. "Just like last year and the year before."

"Actually," Buchanan said, "there is historic accuracy in using an X. X is the letter *chi* in Greek, which stood for *Christ,* and that, of course, is where the custom originated."

"Thank you, Mr. McCleary, for that scholarly explanation. I suppose we'd all know that if we was Rhodes scholars like you," Marvin said. "Let's try to stay on task so we can get out of here by lunchtime."

He looked at his list and continued. "Other complaints deal with where we're putting Santa's Workshop, if we really need to place an electric menorah in front of the courthouse, the small size of the red bows on the lampposts, and the 'environmental incorrectness' of killing a tree for decorative purposes." He paused and glared at Buchanan. "I think we all know where *that* came from.

"So, if it's okay with you'uns, I'll have Jackson deal with the complaints in the usual manner—a nice letter saying 'Thank you for your interest, ya-dee-ya-dee-ya-da.' By then, Christmas'll be over.

"What we *do* need to worry about is the living Nativity scene in front of the fountain. Yoder Construction built the barn and manger free of charge, and Foor's Dairy Farm is lending us some animals. Ten local churches will supply Marys, Josephs, angels, and wise men in four-hour shifts from ten A.M. to six P.M., beginning this week."

"Sounds fine to me. So what's the problem?" Primrose Flack asked.

"The baby Jesus. That gal who's the new director of our child welfare agency says it's too cold to let a baby lie in a manger for four hours. Says she'll charge us all with child abuse."

"Great, just great," came a snort from somewhere inside the mink coat. "What the hell good is a Nativity scene without a baby Jesus? It's no wonder this town doesn't go anywhere, with attitudes like that." Bernice adjusted her collar and scowled at Marvin, who scowled back at her.

"Stuff it in your sock, Bernice, I've got everything under control. My daughter's saved the day."

"Dakota's too old and the wrong sex to be baby Jesus." These were the first words I'd heard from Matavious Clopper since the treasurer's report.

Marvin ignored Dr. Clopper's comment. "Dakota is gonna loan us her favorite doll to use in the manger. It's one of them exact replicas of a real baby." He groped for something out of sight under the table. "Ah, here it is." From one large hand dangled a large, naked, blond doll with staring blue eyes. "Ma-ma," cried a voice from deep within its plastic tummy. "Ma-ma."

"Baby Jesus was a boy," Jackson muttered around the pipe stem clenched between his teeth.

"It'll be wrapped in swaddling clothes, whatever they are. Nobody's gonna know the difference. I'll see you'uns next week. Same time, same place, ya-dee-ya-dee-ya-da. Good-bye." Marvin scooped up his papers and was out the door before any more objections could be voiced.

I put down my pencil and tried to blow life back into my numb fingers. What on earth could I report about this meeting? They'd completely dropped the subject of turning Bernice's cold-storage house into a shopping center, which sounded like a fairly good idea to me, and had managed to absolutely ignore the wishes of the people who'd voted them into office. I finally made a notation on my blank page: "Dakota = Baby Jesus."

Bernice Roadcap, adjusting her furs, advanced on me.

"Toni, I've had a terrible shock. I wonder if you can help me."

"Tori," I corrected with a smile. "I'm sorry to hear that. What's happened?" As a foreign service brat, I'd been trained to smile politely and express interest where none was felt.

She threw a furtive glance over her shoulder to see if anyone was listening, leaned close, and whispered, "I've received a death threat!"

The odor of vodka hit me hard, and I realized her words were slightly slurred. There are some people who actually think it can't be smelled on their breath. Ha!

"Tell me about it," I urged, taking a step backward.

"It was a letter—an anonymous letter. Pasted up out of words cut out of a newspaper, probably one of your *Chronicle*s." She stared keenly at me as though she suspected me of having personally committed the cutting and gluing.

"What did it say?"

"See for yourself." She pulled a folded envelope from her Gucci bag, but before handing it to me, she again looked over her shoulder. Only Primrose, Buchanan, and Jackson were left in the room, and none of them was paying any attention to us.

I straightened the envelope and extracted a piece of ordinary white typing paper. Words and letters of different sizes, definitely cut from a newspaper, said "WHICH ONE DROP THE SAN ANTOINIO MALL OR ELSE."

"I don't see that it's a death threat, Mrs. Roadcap. It appears to be a poorly spelled attempt to change your mind about developing the cold-storage building."

Her voice turned louder, imperious. "You don't see it as a death threat? What about that 'or else'? My death will be on your conscience forever if you don't check this out."

"If you're worried, why don't you go to the police with this?" I asked.

Suddenly, the lofty manner disappeared, as she blinked her eyes and looked at me like a frightened child. "Who? That alcoholic idiot who's acting chief? Or that kid from the junior college who's the part-time patrolman? Or should I say *patrolperson*? Political correctness confuses me. Anyway, it's obvious there's nobody there who can help. You will check it out, won't you, Toby?"

She looked so frightened, I agreed to help. There really was no way in the world to identify the author of the letter, but if it made Bernice feel better to think I was helping, then let her think so.

She smiled gratefully and left. I studied the plain white business-size envelope the letter had come in. The type sold in boxes of one hundred at any store. The postmark was Harrisburg. That meant nothing. All local mail was sent to Harrisburg for a postmark; locals considered it to be a diabolical federal conspiracy to slow down delivery time. Naturally, there was no return address. Buchanan, standing by the door, cleared his throat. "Time to go, Tori," he said.

I looked up from the letter and realized the room was empty except for the two of us. "Sorry," I murmured. I folded Bernice's death threat and jammed it in my purse.

I pulled up to the solitary pump at Hoopengartner's gas station/police headquarters and signaled to the teenage boy on duty to fill the tank. He gestured at the new sign that said SELF-SERVICE, but I put on my New York face—the one that says I have no patience with losers—and he hustled right over. The look had long ago lost its effectiveness in the city but was new to Lickin Creek.

In the back room, I found Luscious sitting at Garnet's

gray metal army-surplus desk. The black phone he was using predated the Korean War. He hung up, smoothed his thin hair over his forehead, and smiled wanly at me. "Nothing," he said. "No signs of him anywhere."

I smelled garlic and onion on his breath as he spoke, and I was glad to note that was all I smelled. Maybe he'd taken my advice to lay off the bottle during the search.

The phone rang, ignored by Luscious, then stopped abruptly. I guessed someone in the front room answered it. Garnet had once explained the advantage of renting office space from Mr. Hoopengartner was that the garage was open twenty-four hours a day for towing service, so there was always someone available to take emergency police calls. Not exactly 911, I thought, but it worked for Lickin Creek.

"You look tired," I told him. "Can I do something for you? Run errands? Anything?" I'm not usually so solicitous, but the youthful and vulnerable policeman brought out my maternal instincts.

"You could pour me some coffee," he said. "I'm too tired to walk across the room."

I poured out some thick black goop and was surprised it didn't dissolve the paper cup. Luscious drank it without complaint, while I washed the glass container and started a fresh pot brewing.

Satisfied I had prevented a future case of poisoning from rancid coffee oil, I sat on one of the two folding chairs reserved for guests.

Luscious said, "Coroner says those bones we found last night have been in the quarry for more than thirty years."

He noticed my skeptical look. Caven County coroner was an elected position, and since Doc Jones's death it had been held by Henry Hoopengartner. Yes, the same Hoopengartner who owned this garage. Even though

Henry had attended coroner school somewhere in the state, I still had doubts about Henry's ability to figure out anything and get it right.

Luscious guessed what I was thinking. "No special knowledge needed for this one, Tori. The divers found most of the bones under the wreck of a '59 Chevy—belonged to Chucky Fowler, what owns Fowler's Flowers now. He was pretty wild as a teenager, I hear. The car got rolled into the quarry back in '65 during a keg party. So Henry's pretty safe in guessing the skeleton was down there since before '65.''

"Could Henry determine the age and sex of the child?"

"Henry guesses about five years old at time of death. He said he couldn't tell the sex because little kids' bones all look pretty much the same. He sent them to the medical examiner's office in Harrisburg.''

"Oretta came by my house this morning and told me it was a child named Eddie Douglas. Is that what you think?"

Luscious nodded and held up a manila folder. "I do. I've got his folder right here. He was the right age. And it's not like we've had dozens of kids go missing. There've been a few lost over the years—kids tend to wander—but Eddie was the only one that never turned up.''

"How long ago?"

Luscious wiggled his fingers in the air for a minute before coming up with an answer. "Thirty-seven years, last summer.''

"Have you contacted his parents?"

He shook his head and opened the folder. "According to what's in the file, his parents, Herman and Miriam Douglas, moved to Texas about a year after Eddie disappeared. I called Information, but there's no listing.''

"If you can't find them, who'll be responsible for burying him?" I asked. I hated the thought of the child being buried in the Lickin Creek equivalent of Potter's Field.

"No need to worry about that. Lickin Creek takes care of its own."

I was waiting for the traffic light to change at the square when I realized I hadn't mentioned Bernice's letter to Luscious. However, since I didn't regard it as a real threat, I didn't think it was important to go back. Instead, I made a mental note to show it to him when next we met.

Cassie's rolltop desk was covered with folders and papers, piled high. I hung my ski jacket on the hook by the door and, as I turned, stubbed my toe on the box from the Home Shopping Network I'd asked Cassie to move yesterday.

"Sorry," she said with a grimace. "Haven't had time to get to it. I've been collecting background information on Eddie Douglas's disappearance. It's all right here."

I stifled a grin. Even Cassie had immediately known who the child was. Apparently, I was the only person in town who'd been out of the loop.

She gestured toward her desk. I was sure that even though it appeared to be an unorganized mess, Cassie knew exactly where everything was.

"You're an absolute wonder," I told her. Her face flushed; the only sign that my remark pleased her.

I could tell by her appearance she now had her emotions under control. She wore an impeccably tailored tweed suit, in a color I would have described as *heather* during my short-lived career as a fashion reporter, her hair was pulled smoothly into a chignon, and a dramatic amber necklace accented the jewel neckline of her beige blouse.

I sat at my own rolltop desk and quickly wrote down my observations of last night's quarry search. "Can you fill this out with what you've found in the files?" I asked her.

"No problem." Cassie smiled. She knew and I knew that this was part of the me-editor-you-assistant game we played. Cassie could easily do the whole edition without me.

"How was the council meeting?" she asked. "Let me guess, 'Nothin' says Christmas like colored lights,' and 'We'll deal with it the usual way, ya-dee-ya-dee-ya-da.' "

I grinned. "That was about it. Except Marvin Bumbaugh's daughter is saving Christmas by lending her baby doll for the manger scene."

"I'll write it up with a straight face," Cassie promised.

"Cassie, do you think it's possible that there could be a connection between Kevin's disappearance and the dead child?"

She appeared taken aback. "A connection? Why do you ask?"

I shook my head. "I really don't know. Praxythea suggested it. I don't suppose there was any mystery around Eddie's disappearance, was there?"

Cassie looked through her folder. "Not that I can tell from the clippings in here. Apparently, he went out to play alone and didn't come back."

Like Kevin Poffenberger, I thought. No, not exactly, for Kevin hadn't been playing alone. His cousins had been with him. I needed to talk to them again.

"Okay, then," I said, standing. "If you'll take care of writing the council report and the quarry discovery, I'll go up to the mountain and see how the search is going."

CHAPTER 6

Over the hills and everywhere

As I DROVE TOWARD THE MOUNTAINS, I thought of how I'd seriously underestimated the work required to put out a weekly newspaper. I'd thought it would be a snap, leaving me with plenty of free time to finish up my second novel. Instead, I seemed to be working twenty-two-hour days and was never caught up with anything. I hadn't even looked at my half-finished manuscript in two months.

P. J. Mullins never worked that hard—I'd been told that often enough—and I was well aware of that fact. She'd earned new respect from me, and I couldn't wait until she was well enough to come back and take over again.

There were times, when I was snowed under at the *Chronicle*, I questioned my journalistic ability, and I had to remind myself that I'd often felt overwhelmed when I was working on the paper in New York. Although I'd won a couple of prizes for my investigative reporting, I'd never really felt comfortable with what I was doing there. What I need to do, I thought, is finish my novel and hope it's a best-seller. Then I'll never have to worry about working again. With pleasant thoughts of movie contracts and TV series drifting through my head, it seemed only a short time until I reached Corny's Corner.

The Iron Ore Road was still clogged with vehicles, but the parking situation at the crossroads was now better organized. A man in his youthful eighties, wearing a Day-Glo orange vest with black letters that said FIRE POLICE on the front, directed me to an empty place in the field. There were few media vehicles visible. I assumed they'd moved on to the latest tragedy du jour.

Walking was treacherous; the depth of the plowed furrows was hidden by the light dusting of snow. Wary of twisting an ankle, I slowly made my way to the area where the headquarters tent had been set up. I didn't recognize any of the women at the coffee and doughnut table, although one of them waved at me, which made me feel good.

Since Luscious was back in the borough, I wasn't sure whom I'd find inside the tent. The freckle-faced youngster in a Lickin Creek police uniform, studying a map, had to be the force's latest part-timer. One of a nonstop parade of recent graduates of the nearby junior college's criminal justice program. Once they had a little experience under their police belts, they moved on to "real" jobs elsewhere.

He recognized me immediately. "Hi, Tori. I've been looking forward to meeting you. My name's Afton Finkey." He extended his hand, which I shook.

I thought I'd grown accustomed to the odd names Lickin Creekers gave to their defenseless children, but Afton was a new one. I couldn't resist commenting, "I don't think I've ever met an Afton before."

"Thank you," he said, with a smile that revealed braces. "My mother heard the song 'Flow Gently, Sweet Afton' while she was carrying me and thought it would make a nice name. I really am glad you're here to help us, Tori. Luscious says he wouldn't know what to do without you."

All I could think was: Now I've got two Lickin Creek policemen to play nursemaid to. However, after talking to Afton for a few minutes, I realized Luscious had left a competent person in charge.

Unfortunately, there was still no sign of the missing child. More volunteers had arrived from all over the tri-state area, and Afton told me he was expanding the search area.

"Trouble is," Afton said as he showed me the enlarged area on the map, "a little kid like that could be easy to miss. If he fell into a cave, and there's lots of them out there, or got knocked out, he wouldn't hear us calling for him."

"What do you think his chances of survival are?" I asked.

"Pretty good, if he's conscious. The temperature's stayed above freezing. And he's a mountain boy; he should know how to take care of himself—for awhile anyway."

A cellular phone rang, and Afton picked it up. His boyish face turned grim as he listened. After a few moments, he disconnected, snatched up his coat, and jammed his arms into the sleeves.

"Gotta get up to the Poffenbergers'," he said.

"What's wrong?" I asked, trailing him outside.

"The kids—seems they've changed their story." His long legs had already carried him halfway across the field.

"Wait for me," I said, trying to keep up with him.

I drove behind the cruiser, as fast as I dared, to the Iron Ore Mansions Trailer Park. At the entrance to the park, I groaned, "Oh, no." Just inside the gate, media vans lined both sides of the narrow street. I saw television crews from as far away as Baltimore and the District of Columbia, as well as many from the tristate area of Pennsylvania, Maryland, and West Virginia. What had happened? I parked and leaped from the truck, fearing the worst.

Mr. Poffenberger, dressed in an ill-fitting blue suit, was standing in front of his trailer, talking to a female reporter who looked vaguely familiar to me.

Several people stared at me as I approached, as if trying to decide whether or not I was worthy of being interviewed. Most decided, correctly, I was not worth bothering with, but one young reporter, who must have been desperate, thrust a microphone in my face. "Would you care to make a statement?"

I brushed him aside with practiced scorn—I hadn't been in the news business for ten years for nothing—and he backed away.

Through the open door, I saw Afton standing in the living room with his back to me, so I squeezed past Kevin's father and went inside. Mrs. Poffenberger sat on the sofa, nursing her yellow-bundled baby. Her hair hadn't been combed today, and her puffy nose was nearly as red as the drooping Christmas poinsettia on the coffee table.

"Are you all right?" I asked.

Her eyes opened wide, as though she were surprised someone would care how she felt. "Uh-huh. They told me in the emergency room it weren't Kevin in the quarry." She wiped her nose with the milk-stained diaper that was draped over her shoulder.

"You should have stayed in the hospital," I said.

"Yeah, sure. You going to pay the bill? 'Scuse me. The baby needs changed." She left the room with the baby.

"What did the kids say?" I asked Afton.

"Now they're saying a man in a black sports utility vehicle took him."

My jaw dropped. "Kevin was kidnapped? Why the hell didn't they tell us that before?"

"Let's ask them," Afton said, his face grim. He reached through the open front door and tapped Mr. Poffenberger on the shoulder, interrupting his interview with an anchorman from NBC. "Get the kids in here. Now!" he ordered with surprising authority.

Within a few minutes, an assortment of Poffenberger children had been rounded up and sat in a semicircle on the orange shag carpet before us. Kevin's parents sat side by side on the couch. Another couple, parents of Kevin's cousins Pearl and Peter, took the recliner—he, seated, she, perched on an arm.

"Now," the young policeman said sternly, "let's hear what happened. And I want the truth!"

As one, the little towheads turned to Pearl. With her eyes downcast, she began her tale. "It was a guy in a big black boxy kind of car," she said. "We was walking along the road, and he stopped and said he needed some directions. Kevin went over to him, even though I told him not to, and the guy grabbed him and pulled him into the car and drove off."

"Which way?" Afton asked.

"Down the mountain. Toward town."

"This man—what did he look like?"

Pearl appeared to be thinking. "We couldn't see his face very good, because he was wearing a ball cap pulled down real low. But he had a beard. Didn't he, Peter?"

Her brother Peter nodded. "Yeah, a beard and a ball cap."

"What team?" I asked.

"Huh?"

"You said he was wearing a ball cap. I wondered what team?"

"It wasn't a *real* ball cap," Pearl answered. "Just one of them hats that look like ball caps. It advertised tractors or something."

"Yeah," Peter said. "Tractors."

"Did you notice anything else? How old do you think he was? How tall was he? What kind of clothes he was wearing?" Afton had his notebook out.

Pearl scrunched her forehead as if she were working really hard at remembering something. "He wasn't a real young guy. Maybe as old as her," she said, jerking a thumb in my direction. "He never got out of the car, so I don't know how tall he was. Wait! I remember he was wearing a red-plaid flannel shirt."

A bearded man, about thirty years old, wearing a cap advertising tractors and a plaid flannel shirt. Pearl had just described half the men in Lickin Creek!

"Why didn't you tell your parents right away about this man?" Afton asked. "Why did you let us believe Kevin had wandered off by himself?"

The little faces all looked at Pearl, waiting for her to answer. "The guy told us he'd come back and get us if we told," Pearl said.

"You were afraid, is that right?"

The heads nodded in unison.

"How about the vehicle? Did you catch a glimpse of the license plate?"

The forehead scrunched again. "Texas," Pearl said. "I think it was a Texas plate."

Afton asked a few more questions, with unsatisfying results, and finally told the children they could leave.

"Can we sleep over?" Pearl asked her mother.

The woman looked at Kevin's mother, who gave a

slight nod. But one of her children began to whine. "I don't want to sleep with Peter. He always pees the bed."

The scathing look Pearl directed at her brother should have immediately cured his enuresis problem.

"I'll call Luscious and the state police," Afton said to me as he pulled on his coat. "We need to put out an APB for that sports utility vehicle."

"You're not going to call off the search on the mountain, are you?" I asked him.

He shook his head and glanced into the kitchen, where the adult Poffenbergers had all adjourned. I could hear them popping the tabs off beer cans. The children had turned on the TV and were enthralled by an incredibly violent cartoon. He lowered his voice so only I could hear. "I don't really believe anything that Pearl says. This abduction story doesn't ring true."

"Exactly what I thought," I said. "I'd sure like to get that girl alone for five minutes. See what I could get out of her."

Afton sighed. "I know how you feel, but for the time being I have to follow up on her story."

Pearl, in front of the TV set, was watching us with a thoughtful expression on her face. I wondered what she'd overheard.

Afton opened the front door and jumped back, startled, as the press began shouting questions at him.

"You coming?" he asked me.

"You go ahead," I said. "I need to talk to Mrs. Poffenberger for a minute."

I'd just recalled that Praxythea had asked me to bring her something, preferably metal, of Kevin's. It couldn't do any harm, I thought, so I went in search of Mrs. Poffenberger. I found her in the bedroom with the baby.

She handed me a tiny pocketknife, saying it had been Kevin's birthday present. Although I wondered about the family's judgment in giving a small child a knife, I accepted it with only a word of thanks.

"They're going to find him, Mrs. Poffenberger. I know they will." I wanted to offer her some encouragement, some hope.

"Yeah, sure." Her voice was flat. I could tell she'd already given up.

I drove through late-afternoon shadows back to the borough. As I approached downtown, a volunteer traffic cop in a yellow vest signaled me to stop. I rolled down the window and asked, "What's the matter? Water main burst again?"

"Nah, they're setting up the Nativity scene in the square so the traffic needs detoured. You can take a right on Oak, a left on Elm, another left, this time on Maple, and then—"

"Thanks, I'll find my way." Lickin Creek isn't very big, but its one-way streets could have been the inspiration for Dante's circles of Hell. Why the borough council chose rush hour to close Main Street was beyond my comprehension.

After circling aimlessly for about fifteen minutes, I ended up where I'd started, only this time the traffic cop took pity on me and let me through. As I drove past the fountain in the center of the square, I saw Yoder Construction Company workers busily turning it into a manger.

Because of the time I wasted being lost, it was dark when I pulled through the gates into the Moon Lake compound, but my house was illuminated by floodlights like a Broadway theater on opening night. Trucks and vans lined the dirt road and filled my circular drive.

More media people, I realized. Cables lay coiled in the grass like a nest of pythons.

Praxythea stood on the front porch in a black bodysuit that covered her from neck to toe but hid nothing. Didn't the woman own underwear? She was speaking into a microphone held by a beautiful, raven-haired Asian woman.

As I approached the house, I recognized some faces from the tabloid news shows, and I heard snatches of predictable phrases: "—astounding new developments— search for bearded man—tristate area—possible connections with children abducted in Florida and Texas— noted psychic's vision directed police to a deserted quarry where . . ."

"Be careful up there," I called to Praxythea and several familiar talking heads. "That porch roof is liable to cave in."

They ignored me, as did the news crews on the lawn, so I took my life in my hands, climbed the steps, and entered the house through the front door. I gathered up the mail that lay on the carpet and flipped through the envelopes while I hiked to the kitchen. Damn! Still nothing from Garnet. I tossed the envelopes on the table to look through later.

I refilled the cats' bowls with Tasty Tabby Treats, and while they happily and noisily chewed their food, I checked the iguana to make sure it had water and some of the lizard food Oretta had left with it. As far as I could tell, he was all right, but I tossed in a little lettuce as a treat. Then I prepared two cups of instant coffee and doctored mine with the powders that represented sugar and cream.

Praxythea entered and sank into a chair across the table from me. "How did you know I wanted this?" she said with a smile, picking up one of the cups.

I didn't return her smile. "Maybe *I'm* the psychic."

"You're upset with me," she said.

"It doesn't take a psychic to know that."

"Publicity is very important. Without the media attention, the people who need me most wouldn't know about me."

"And it sells books."

"Of course. Money is important, no doubt about it. It gives me the freedom to go where I'm needed."

"Okay, Praxythea, you're a saint." Before the protest could burst from her parted lips, I took Kevin's pocketknife from my handbag and handed it to her. "See what you can do with this."

It was a small knife, just the right size for a child's hand. I could imagine how excited Kevin must have been when he first saw it. Would he ever see it again?

Praxythea held it between the palms of her hands, closed her eyes, and bowed her head over it. I refilled my cup and waited.

Her eyes popped open, and she laid the knife on the table.

"What do you think?" I asked.

"He's still alive."

Despite my disbelief, I experienced a surge of hope. "Can you tell where he is?" It was baloney, I was sure, but it couldn't hurt to check every option.

"You'll make fun of me if I tell you."

"Come on, Praxythea. Tell me."

She stroked the blade of the knife with her emerald-clad finger. "You're not going to like this, but here goes. I saw him . . . by the edge of running water."

I groaned. "I should have known you'd say that. It's always something about 'the edge of running water.' You should be ashamed of yourself."

"I was right last night," she said defensively. "They found the child exactly where I said he'd be."

"But it was the wrong child, Praxythea."

"There had to be a reason why I was sent those images when I was concentrating on contacting Kevin," she said. "I'm sure there's a connection."

"Like a serial killer who strikes every thirty-seven years? Give me a break!"

In the terrarium in the corner next to the stove, Icky squeaked. I think he was staring at me, but it was hard to tell. "I don't need your editorial comments," I muttered to the reptile.

Fred jumped onto my lap and I stroked his soft orange and white fur. Medical testing has proved having pets is good for your health. I agree that petting a cat is soothing, but I wondered what on earth an iguana could do for anyone?

CHAPTER 7

We'll tak' a cup o' kindness yet

THE VOICE ON THE OTHER END OF THE TELE-phone line said, "Tori, dear, how are you?" I noticed this time Oretta had my name right. That alone should have warned me that she wanted something.

"Weezie had a little accident today and won't be able to make it to the pageant rehearsal tonight." Her tone of voice spoke myriads about the kind of "accident" poor Weezie had experienced. I recalled what Ginnie had said Jackson would do to his wife when he found out she was in Oretta's pageant.

"So, I thought you could stand in for her. It's a dress rehearsal. Wear a black leotard and tights. I'll supply the rest of your costume."

"But I—"

"Don't be modest, Tori. Of course you can do it. You were there last night, so you know what the part entails."

"I have plans—"

"But everyone else I called has something important to do tonight. Besides," she wheedled, "you're our town's only famous author, and people would love to see you up there. It'll show the town you don't *really* think you're better than the rest of us. See you at seven-thirty. Don't be late."

"I've never thought I was—" My protest came too late. She'd already hung up.

"Why on earth didn't you say no?" Praxythea asked me.

"I couldn't get a word in edgewise," I said. My hand still rested on the receiver.

She smiled wisely. "You're still hoping to be accepted into the community, aren't you? You'd do anything anybody asked if you thought it would help you fit in."

Wishes don't come true. Otherwise lightning would have struck her right then and there. She was right, of course. That's what was so irritating.

An hour later, wearing one of Praxythea's black bodysuits stretched to its Lycra limits, I rushed down Trinity's basement steps two at a time, with Praxythea trailing behind me. I'd been surprised when she'd asked to come along to the rehearsal, but I was glad for the company.

Many people were there working on decorations for the upcoming greens sale, just as last night. Marvin Bumbaugh greeted us as we entered the auditorium. "Let me take your coat." He was speaking to me, but he was drooling over Praxythea. Before I could protest, he'd slipped my coat off my shoulders and hung it on a metal rack. Feeling practically naked, I sucked in my stomach and looked around for Oretta, who'd promised to bring the rest of my costume.

"I'd like you to meet my two daughters," Marvin said. "Dakota and Cheyenne."

The two oddly named girls giggled.

I couldn't resist saying to Marvin, "I'm surprised you're not on the mountain with the search parties."

"I hate not being there, but someone had to stay in town and keep an eye on things here."

The girls couldn't take their eyes off Praxythea, so I introduced them. The older girl, Cheyenne, surprised me by saying to me, "I liked your book a lot."

"Why, thank you," I said, thinking how rare it was to find a fifteen-year-old with such good taste.

"I like Dean Koontz better, though. He's sort of local. Went to college at Shipp, you know."

I bared my teeth at her. If she wanted to think it was a smile, that was okay with me.

I looked around the room, searching for Oretta and my costume. I didn't see her, but I did see clusters of people making wreaths, tying bows, and sprinkling glitter on pinecones. Not so many as there'd been last night—I assumed most of the men and many of the women were still on the mountaintop searching for Kevin.

The kitchen brigade had outdone itself tonight; the top of the divider between the rooms was covered with dozens of home-baked pies to be sold at the greens sale. The rich fragrances of cinnamon and mincemeat mingled in the air and flooded my mind with nostalgic memories of Christmases past—Christmases that were actually far more prosaic than those of my wishful imagination. For us thespians, there was plenty of hot coffee, tea, spiced cider, and platters of cookies.

No sign of my costume. I looked around to see if anyone was watching, then tugged at the miserable bodysuit.

"You're going to stretch it all out of shape," Praxythea warned.

"I certainly hope so," I said, giving the rear end another jerk.

I needn't have worried about anyone staring at me. Not with Praxythea there. Lickin Creek wasn't used to

TV celebrities—which I found refreshing—and she was immediately surrounded by a crowd of admirers. I was rather surprised to learn that so many members of the Trinity congregation watched the Psychic Network.

The Reverend Flack and his wife, Primrose, broke away from a mound of holly branches to greet me. "Any word about the boy?" the minister asked. He tried to keep his attention focused on my face, but his gaze kept drifting down to my hips. I noticed his lips twitching as if he were repressing a smile, and my cheeks flamed with embarrassment. Why had I let Oretta talk me into wearing this horrible outfit?

Was he assuming I'd know something because of my position as the town's newspaper editor, or was it because my relationship with the ex–police chief gave me a quasi-official position in Lickin Creek's law enforcement circles? I'd probably never know.

"I suppose you heard that Kevin's cousins are now saying he was kidnapped," I said.

Primrose gasped. "I didn't know. That poor little boy. How could his mother ever have left him out of her sight?"

I remembered what Mrs. Poffenberger had said to me last night—something about not being able to watch all of them all the time—and repeated it to Primrose. Perhaps I sounded as if I were an apologist for the mother, because Primrose grew rather huffy.

"The other kids should have taken care of him. Do you have brothers or sisters?" she snapped at me. "If you did, you know you would have done everything in your power to keep them safe."

The ever-present guilt over Billy's death that I had carried with me for nearly twenty years threatened to overwhelm me. I pretended I hadn't heard the question.

"Kids don't really think about things like that. They assume nothing bad will ever happen to them. What about you, Primrose? I'll bet when you were a youngster you didn't spend much time worrying about your siblings."

"I have to check the oven," she said quietly, then turned and walked away.

I looked questioningly at the Reverend Flack. "I said something wrong, didn't I?"

He patted me on the shoulder. "Not your fault, my dear. Primrose was orphaned when she was seven. Her adoptive parents never had any other children, and she's always felt something was lacking in her life. Our not having children of our own has made it worse. Uh-oh, Oretta Clopper's coming this way. I wonder what I've done wrong this time."

Oretta Clopper was an awesome sight in a purple chiffon toga draped over an enormous leotard. She made me feel positively svelte. Her face was scrunched into a scowl as her high-pitched voice berated him. "Really, Reverend, I have told your kitchen volunteers over and over how much cinnamon to put in the cider, and they . . ."

Someone behind me coughed delicately, and I spun around to see Ginnie bearing a tray of paper cups and cookies. "Have some cider," she suggested. "It's quite good." Her eyes twinkled as she added, "With just the right amount of cinnamon."

I took a cup and introduced her to Praxythea. For a few minutes the three of us chatted while we munched on cookies.

"Look," Ginnie said, "there's no rehearsal tomorrow because the Boy Scouts meet here in the church auditorium. Why don't the three of us play bingo?"

Praxythea begged off, mentioning something about speaking to the Kiwanis Club, but I agreed to go.

"And it wouldn't matter to me if there's a rehearsal

scheduled or not, because I am not going to be in this pageant," I said firmly. "I'm only filling in tonight for Weezie."

Ginnie smiled. "That might be what Oretta told you, but you'd better be prepared to perform."

The door burst open and Bernice Roadcap entered the room. She paused just inside the doorway and made quite a production out of shrugging off her fur coat. A rather good-looking man, with the usual Lickin Creek beard, received the offering before it fell to the floor and carefully draped it, inside out, over his left arm. Hanging from his right shoulder was a thermos in a sling. Remembering the smell of alcohol on Bernice's breath earlier that day, I was pretty sure I knew what was in it.

Bernice's companion appeared to be ten or fifteen years younger than she, but I always find it difficult to guess the age of men with beards.

"Is that her husband?" I asked Ginnie.

"She wishes," Ginnie said with a laugh. "But she's got to get rid of Stanley first. According to local gossip, most of the Roadcap money is tied up in property and businesses, and she's afraid to go through with the divorce until she's got the cash in hand."

"So that's why she's pushing the council to buy her cold-storage building."

"Most likely," Ginnie said. "That's Stanley over there. He's one of the church trustees." She pointed to a folding chair, where a thin bald man with rimless glasses, who didn't seem to notice the arrival of his almost ex-wife, was busy applying glitter to a pinecone wreath.

Bernice, on her unsteady march toward the stage, spotted Matavious Clopper in the front row. "There you are," she called out, attracting the attention of nearly everyone in the room. "I've been trying to get in touch with you all afternoon. My back is killing me." She kept

up a steady stream of complaints as she tottered down
the center aisle.

Matavious put his glasses on and looked up from the
tape recorder, searching for the source of the noise. His
wince upon recognizing her was nearly imperceptible.
"See me after the rehearsal, Bernice. I'll do a quick ma-
nipulation for you."

"I should think so. I knocked and knocked. Nobody
answered. The very idea."

"We're always closed on Wednesday afternoons."

"You were in there. I heard you moving around."

"You must have been mistaken, Bernice."

Bernice dismissed him with a "Humph."

"Places, people. Places," Oretta ordered, rushing
toward the stage. She stared at me, as if trying to figure
out why I was there. Perhaps I could escape, I thought,
but unfortunately she recalled she'd invited me.

"Toni," she gushed. "I'm so glad to see you take your
responsibilities seriously. Now that you're a member of
the cast, I'm sure you'll feature our rehearsal photo
prominently in the *Chronicle*. Come, come, everyone. We
must begin."

"Now that I'm a member of the cast? That doesn't
sound good," I said to Ginnie.

Ginnie made no reply, her attention caught by something happening behind me. She grabbed my arm.
"Look," she whispered. I spun around and saw two people by the door.

"It's Jackson and Weezie Clopper," she said. "I hope
he's not going to make a scene."

Jackson took a seat in the back row, while Weezie, her
red jacket still on, disappeared into the kitchen. I didn't
have time to see if she had any visible bruises.

"Your muse beckons," Ginnie said, nodding at Oretta,

who was tapping her foot and glaring down at me from the stage. "See you later."

I climbed the four steps to the stage where Oretta met me with several hundred yards of pink tulle. "Your costume," she said. Looking critically at me, she added, "I recommend wrapping it around your hips."

My cheeks burned, more from anger than embarrassment, and I bit my tongue to keep from making a nasty crack about the size of her own ample hips. Swathed in pink, I took my place on a stool next to Bernice, a yellow-draped sugar plum fairy reeking of gin.

"Hold your heads up high," Oretta said. "Remember you are goddesses." And the rehearsal began. I was the only actor with a script—the ladies had really been working.

With nothing to do but read an occasional plagiarized phrase, I amused myself by watching the people in the hall. Jackson Clopper leaned back in his folding chair and glowered directly at Oretta. At least I hoped it was Oretta he was glowering at and not me because he truly looked frightening. I wondered why he'd come.

Looking over the kitchen counter, I could see Ginnie removing pies from the ovens. I also caught a momentary glimpse of red and guessed that it was Weezie's jacket. I hoped the poor woman wasn't in for a beating when the Cloppers got home.

Stanley Roadcap occupied a seat near Bernice's fur coat, with a half-made holly wreath apparently forgotten on his lap. Praxythea stood in the back of the room, distributing signed eight-by-ten glossies.

There were other people present, their faces familiar but names unknown. Perhaps by the time I left Lickin Creek, I'd have all its citizens straight in my mind.

I suddenly realized the two other goddesses were staring at me. "Excuse me?" I said.

"Hail to the great mother," Oretta cried, with a touch of impatience in her voice. I realized I'd missed my cue.

"Hail to the great mother," I said with enthusiasm.

"Hail to the wycann," came from Bernice.

"Hail to the—" I stopped and looked at my script. Was *wycann* a misspelling of *wiccan*, another word for *witch*? Lots of New Age witchcraft was going around in feminist circles in New York, I knew, but here in Lickin Creek? And in a Christmas pageant? I hardly thought so.

"Hail to the goddess," they chirped in unison.

On the other hand, maybe it was possible.

Matavious cranked up the volume on his portable player and the music to the "Dance of the Sugar Plum Fairy" filled the room.

"I drink from the Goblet of Life." Bernice raised the Styrofoam cup to her lips and drank deeply.

More likely it was the Goblet of Martinis, I thought cynically.

It was time for the dance of the muses, and Oretta groaned her way down from her bar stool. But before the dance could begin, Bernice dropped the cup, opened her mouth, and uttered a noise that was a cross between a belch and a gurgle.

"What, dear?" Oretta said. "Bernice! Are you all right?"

A stream of greenish-yellow bile shot from Bernice's mouth and splattered Oretta's chiffon-covered bosom.

"Ohmygod!" Oretta screamed.

Bernice's eyes opened wide as if she had seen something that surprised her, then she doubled up, clutched her stomach, and crashed to the floor.

I ran across the stage, pushed past the stunned actresses who were frozen in their spots, and dropped to my knees next to the woman a second or two before Matavious Clopper scrambled onto the stage. I moved back a little to give Matavious room to work, but not before my nose was assaulted by the nasty smell of gin, cinnamon, and something else—almonds.

"Call an ambulance, somebody, quick!" Stanley Roadcap yelled frantically. "For God's sake, Matavious, you're a doctor. Do something!"

"I'm trying," the chiropractor snapped. His fingers were on Bernice's throat, trying to find a pulse.

Bernice was frighteningly still, her mouth bright red.

Speculations began to fly. "Heart attack . . . stroke . . . too much estrogen . . . not enough . . . my doctor says . . . ptomaine . . . stomach flu . . . like when my appendix burst . . ."

The white cup lay on the floor where Bernice had dropped it. I bent over and sniffed it. It had most definitely contained spiced cider laced with gin. And there was that other smell, too. Almonds. "Don't anyone drink the cider," I yelled, as I struggled to my feet. I moved quickly to the front of the stage. "Please, people, don't drink the cider!" To prevent panic, I added, "It might be spoiled."

My warning was picked up by the people gathered below and carried to the back of the room. Those people who held cups quickly put them down and stared up at me with anxious eyes.

"Somebody call the police," I urged.

"I already did," Ginnie said, at my side.

It occurred to me that nothing could have been added to the cider urn, since so many people had drunk from it without ill effect. It must have been something she brought with her. "Where's Bernice's thermos?" I asked.

Her gentleman friend stepped forward, holding it up. It was seized from his grasp and passed from one person to another until it reached me. No point in worrying about fingerprints now, I thought, and quickly un-screwed the lid. I sniffed, expecting the same odor I'd smelled in the cup Bernice had drunk from, but as far as I could tell, the liquid in the container was straight, un-adulterated gin. Whatever had sickened Bernice hadn't come from her thermos.

The ambulance arrived in only a few minutes, but it was too late for the EMTs to do anything for the poor woman.

People stood around in small groups, talking quietly to each other, until Luscious Miller and the county coro-ner arrived. While I watched Henry Hoopengartner open his black bag, I couldn't help but wish he was more like the last coroner, who, despite all his faults, had at least been a doctor.

Hoopengartner pronounced Bernice dead, glanced at his watch, and added, "Time of death: nine-eighteen."

As Bernice's body was placed upon the stretcher, I took Luscious by the arm. "I need to talk to you," I said softly, so as not to alarm the people around us. "I suspect Bernice was poisoned. You should get the dregs in her cup analyzed. Also the contents of her thermos and the cider urn. I don't think you'll find anything in them, but they should be checked."

Luscious looked shocked. "You don't think she was murdered, do you?" I could understand his astonish-ment; Lickin Creek's police force seldom faced anything more violent than domestic disputes and bar fights.

"It's quite possible, Luscious. Smell this."

I had picked up Bernice's cup with a pencil, and now I held it to his nose and let him take a whiff. He recoiled.

"I think it's cyanide. And it didn't get in there by acci-dent," I said. "I doubt very much that she chose to com-mit suicide this way. Also, I happen to know that a few days ago Bernice received a letter threatening her life."

"She did? How do you know?"

"She showed it to me this morning. I'm terribly afraid I didn't take it seriously at the time." I had to swallow my pride to admit this, but guilt was weighing heavily on me. I retrieved my purse from the corner, found the letter, and handed it to Luscious, whose lips moved as he slowly read it.

"The misspellings might help you identify the person who sent it," I suggested.

"What misspellings?" Luscious asked.

I sighed. This wasn't going to be easy. "Do you have any idea who might have wanted Bernice dead?" I asked him.

He shook his head. "Lots of people in town didn't like her, but I don't know anyone who'd want to kill her."

I watched Stanley Roadcap follow his wife's body out of the auditorium. "How about her husband?" I asked.

"Stanley?" Luscious looked truly shocked. "Impossible. I went to school with his younger brother."

Half the people who had been in the auditorium had already left, while the others milled around, destroying whatever evidence there might have been.

"Luscious, this is murder. You need to take charge," I told him.

Panic flared in his pale blue eyes. "I don't know what to do," he admitted.

He appeared to be defeated before he started. I stepped forward and raised my hands to silence the remaining onlookers. "Can someone tell us who put this cup on the stage? The one Bernice drank from."

Heads turned, voices buzzed, but nobody came forward.

"Maybe you saw someone near it?" I asked, but hope was fading.

A man pushed through to the front of the crowd.

"There was dozens of people up there before the rehearsal started," he said. "Some was making wreaths and had to move out of the way. I saw a couple of people with brooms, sweeping up—"

A woman interrupted. "Reverend Flack moved the Boy Scout flags."

"That wasn't Reverend Flack," someone shouted indignantly. "It was the custodian."

What it came down to was no one in the group had actually seen anyone place the cup on the stage.

Primrose Flack raised her hand, caught my eye, hesitated for a minute, then said, "I saw Bernice pour something into the cup from her thermos—right before the rehearsal started."

"Thank you, Primrose. Please, people, think about it," I insisted. "Perhaps after you go home, you'll remember something. If you do, please call Luscious immediately."

Marvin Bumbaugh climbed the steps to the stage. "I want to know why you'uns is asking all the questions," he demanded of me. "Where's Luscious?"

Luscious stepped forward to my side. "I asked Tori to help," he said firmly, "because with just Afton and me on the force, we don't have the manpower to do two things at once."

I would have been prouder of him if I hadn't smelled the brandy on his breath.

To my surprise, Marvin took Luscious's alcohol fortified outburst mildly. "Just find out what happened to her, Luscious," he said. "I don't care how you do it."

CHAPTER 8

I wonder as I wander

WHEN I ENTERED THE KITCHEN, PRAXYTHEA was bent over the terrarium, cooing endearments to Icky. She straightened when she heard me and turned, smiling. "He looked hungry," she said, gesturing at the iguana with a limp stalk of celery.

"How can you tell?" I helped myself to a cup of the coffee she had prepared and settled down at the table. Over the rim of the cup, I took a good look at my famous houseguest. This morning, she was a swirling cloud of lavender, purple, mauve, and rose. I suspected this was what Oretta thought she looked like last night in her ghastly black and purple getup.

The only thing marring Praxythea's perfection, in my opinion, was the mask of pancake makeup that covered her porcelain-doll complexion. I was pretty sure I knew why she was wearing it.

"May I assume you are going to be on TV?" I asked.

"My goodness, Tori, if you continue demonstrating psychic abilities I'll have to put you on my show. I'm going to be interviewed at noon on a York TV station." She smiled, endangering her makeup job.

We were interrupted by Fred and Noel strolling in looking for food and/or affection. Pretending the iguana wasn't there, Noel went straight to the Tasty Tabby Treats while Fred chose the security of my lap.

Praxythea looked critically at him. "How much does he weigh, Tori? Why don't you put him on a diet?"

"Nineteen pounds. And it's dangerous to put large cats on a diet. Fat cats can die in a matter of days when deprived of food. Besides, I like him this way. He's soft and cuddly."

"Noel's more to my taste," Praxythea said, as she picked up the dainty calico.

Over cats and Cheerios, we discussed Bernice's death.

"It could have been an accident," Praxythea pointed out after I'd used the word *murder* several times.

"I don't see how a poisonous substance could 'accidentally' get into a cup of cider on the stage. If it had, I'm sure someone would have come forward by now to say something like 'Gee whiz, I thought that funny bottle with the skull and crossbones on it under the sink was sugar water.' "

"If you're so sure she was murdered, you must have some ideas about who did it—or at least why."

"I don't know who did it, but I'm going to find out. I owe that to Bernice."

We each had a piece of toast, hers plain, mine buttered.

"How are you getting to York?" I asked, hoping she wasn't counting on me to take her.

"The station offered to send a limo. I'll be home late. Since it's so close to Pennsylvania Dutch country I thought I'd go look at the Amish."

"I could show you Amish right here in Lickin Creek," I said, gulping my coffee. "And not the touristy version, either. In fact, I'm heading over to the Farmers' Market this morning—there's lots of them there. Garnet's sister Greta has a stall at the market, and I want to ask her what she knows about Bernice's enemies. She's got a red-hot connection to the Lickin Creek Grapevine." I was referring to Lickin Creek's gossip chain, which spread the news about everybody and everything in town at warp speed.

"I didn't know the Gochenauers were Amish," Praxythea said.

"They aren't. Anyone can open a stand there. I think it's only in Lancaster that all the farmers are Amish—or at least appear to be."

"As long as you're going to a market, I have a little shopping list." Praxythea handed me a hundred-dollar bill and a list about a yard long. "Thought I'd make a fruitcake. I've got an old family recipe that's just wonderful. Do you think this will cover it?" she asked.

"You could make one out of solid gold for this much money."

The antique school clock on the wall chimed the hour, reminding me I had a lot to do today. I jammed the list and money into my fanny pack, swallowed the last of my coffee, said good-bye, and rushed out.

Although the Farmers' Market was open Thursday through Saturday every week of the year, the day to shop was Thursday, when the produce and baked goods were the freshest and the crowds the smallest. Outside the market, several beautiful horses, tied to buggies, waited patiently for their owners. I'd heard that the Amish often bought retired trotting racehorses. These looked hearty enough to still be in competition.

I parked my truck next to a black car, stripped of its chrome, which meant it probably belonged to a Menno-nite family. I had trouble recognizing the differences between the various groups of Plain People in the valley, and the only distinction I was sure of was that the Men-nonites drove cars while the Amish used buggies.

Plywood covered the window openings of the dilapidated brick building, and the wood canopy over the entrance was in danger of collapsing, somewhat like my own front porch. The first time I'd visited the market in the old railroad roundhouse, I'd been horrified. It reminded me of the primitive markets I'd seen in Asian countries, and I couldn't imagine eating anything that came from it.

But familiarity changes one's perceptions of a place, and now I raced inside without a single negative thought about its sanitary condition.

The vast interior was dimly lit by a few bare lightbulbs hanging from the ceiling. I paused in the open doorway and waited for my eyes to adjust. A young woman in a simple cotton dress, white apron, and starched bonnet looked up from a display of freshly baked bread and smiled at me.

"If you play with a door you'll start a family fight," she said, then added, "Or give me pneumonia."

"Sorry." I stepped inside, and the door banged shut behind me.

"Are you looking for Greta?"

It no longer surprised me when strangers knew who I was. I nodded. "But I need to buy some candied fruit and nuts for a fruitcake first."

"Aunt Emily has the best." She pointed to a booth at the back of the room.

I moved down the aisle, through a crowd of Plain People and townsfolk who knew where the best bargains in town could be found. Most of the stalls sold farm products such as cheese, milk, meat, and eggs. Some specialized in yummy-looking baked goods. Others carried odd items for unspecified uses like containers of goose grease, sheep tallow, and rings made from horseshoe nails that some local people swore cured rheumatism.

From Aunt Emily I purchased large bags of candied pineapple and cherries, dates, figs, a pound of pecans, and a dozen brown eggs. She looked askance at Praxythea's hundred-dollar bill and only decided to accept it after a lengthy consultation with several women from the next booth.

The sign over Greta's booth said THE FINE SWINE SAUSAGE STAND. It was named after the farm owned by Greta and her late husband, Lucky Carbaugh, who'd had a gruesome accident with a manure spreader last spring. While Greta waited on a customer, I stood to one side and watched her.

Greta was a tall muscular woman, whose face was all interesting planes and angles and deeply etched with wrinkles. Her waist-length gray hair was pulled back into a ponytail and tied with a green silk scarf. As usual, she wore a black T-shirt and long, multicolored skirt of Indian gauze, cinched at the waist by a silver concha belt. She was the last of a generation of flower children; more than an anachronism among the Plain folk of the market, but she still managed to be accepted by them by dint of the Gochenauer family having been in Lickin Creek forever.

When Greta saw me, she uttered an exclamation of pleasure and ran around the counter to hug me. "What a treat to see you, Tori! You look wonderful. And so skinny! Don't you ever eat? Let's grab a cup of coffee and talk."

I loved Greta for a lot of reasons, and one of them was because she always told me I looked skinny.

She led the way to the nearby Koffee Korner and showed me which redwood picnic table to claim. "I can watch my booth from there," she said. She stood in line at the window and came back in a few minutes carrying two sticky buns, hot from the oven and smelling of cinnamon, and two Styrofoam cups of coffee.

The white cup reminded me of last night and Bernice's death. I couldn't drink from it. Greta sipped her coffee with no problem, but, I reminded myself, she hadn't been there.

We chatted for a few minutes until she asked what I'd heard from Garnet. I really wanted to ask her how many letters she had received, but didn't, because that would mean I'd have to admit I'd had none. So I switched the subject to the real reason I was here—finding out who had a motive to kill Bernice Roadcap.

Greta spilled coffee down the front of her T-shirt. "You think Bernice was murdered?"

Was she putting me on? Greta usually knew about everything that went on in town—often, it seemed, even before the people involved were aware something had happened to them.

A voice behind me screeched, "Did I hear you say Bernice was murdered? Impossible. Now, if it had been Oretta, I'd understand."

I swiveled to see who it was. I didn't recall ever having seen the pudgy gentleman in a stained artist's smock and beret who had pushed his way into our conversation. He was Hollywood's idea of an artist, I thought, right out of a forties movie.

"Why do you say that?" I asked him.

"Oh, my dear, that Oretta is such a bitch!" He pulled a chair over from the next table and sat without being invited. "Greta, why don't you introduce me to your lovely friend?"

Greta rolled her eyes so only I could see. "Tori, this is Raymond . . . uh, Raymond . . . Zook."

"*Ray*mond alone is just fine," he said, accenting the second syllable of his name. "You two charming ladies seem to be having such fun with your gossip session. I hope you don't mind my joining you."

His snide reference implied we were just a couple of silly women exchanging neighborhood news over our morning coffee. His attitude irritated me, because I was only tapping into the Lickin Creek Grapevine in order to solve a crime—serious business, hardly a gossip session!

Because his lips were hidden beneath a handlebar moustache, I couldn't see them move as he said, "The line of people who'd like to see Oretta dead forms behind me." His eyes sparkled.

"What do you have against Oretta?" I asked.

"It's more like what Oretta has against me. Why, the woman actually had me arrested once. She called your brother, Greta, and insisted he raid my studio. He and Luscious kidnapped my darlings and took them to that hellhole she calls a shelter."

"I heard about that," Greta said. "Something about abusing cats you got from the shelter, wasn't it?"

He placed a soft white hand over his heart. "I have never—I repeat, never—abused a cat."

Up till then, I'd been totally confused by their conversation. But when I heard mention of cats, I perked up. There's nothing I enjoy more than talking about cats. "You're a cat lover? So am I. I have two. Fred and Noel. Noel's the quiet one, but Fred's quite a show-off."

"He's something of an artist, too," Greta said, laughing. "Didn't you tell me he tracked paint all over your apartment last year when you had it redecorated?"

"Indeed he did. I happen to think his little antique-white footprints have improved the otherwise drab linoleum."

Raymond turned to me, showing interest. "I'd like to meet him someday."

"He'd love that," I said. "He's a very outgoing cat."

"You'd better get over to your booth," Greta said. "I think I see an art connoisseur looking over your paintings."

"Oh, my!" He jumped up, hands fluttering, and ran down the aisle, calling, "Yoo-hoo. I'm here."

"Oh, my!" I said. Greta began to laugh heartily, and I soon joined in.

After we finally regained our composure, I returned to the subject I'd come to discuss—Bernice.

"Do you have any idea who might have wanted her dead?" I asked.

"Follow the money. Isn't that what they always say?" Greta said. "I'd take a long close look at that young boyfriend of hers. I've heard rumors that she bankrolled his new restaurant."

"What restaurant is that?"

"It's called the Fields of Glory."

"The one where the waiters and waitresses dress in Civil War costumes?"

"That's it. You can have your soup served by Clara Barton and your table bussed by George Custer." She sniffed. "Some people will go to any lengths to attract tourists. Maybe the payback she expected was more than he wanted to give, so he decided to get rid of her."

"I'll check him out," I said. "Also her soon-to-be-ex-husband. He might have been crazy with jealousy."

"Stanley? I hardly think he's the type." She appeared to think for a second. "But to get back to what I said about following the money—Stanley stood to lose a bundle in the divorce."

"Have you heard about someone threatening Bernice? Shortly before she died she showed me a note she'd received, warning her to drop her plans to create a San Antonio–like development along the Lickin Creek."

"I thought she'd given up on that wacky idea a long time ago."

"She was pitching it to the council this week."

"I wonder if she gave any thought to the environmental impact that would have on the river . . ."

Before she could climb on her soapbox, I steered her back to the subject by saying, "Buchanan is watching out for the river—and the brown trout in it."

"This town is only big enough for one mall," Greta said.

"Are there plans to build another?"

"Indeed there are. Ask Oretta. She and Matavious own part of the old Clopper tract on the edge of town. They've been trying to beat Bernice to the punch by selling their land to a mall developer before her project gets under way."

"Interesting. I'll have to talk to Oretta about that."

Greta was thinking out loud now, paying no attention to what I said. "Or maybe Bernice made some enemies when she left Trinity Church. I hear she had a shouting match with Reverend Flack and stormed out."

I smiled at the thought. "Are you suggesting Reverend Flack eliminates any sheep who stray from his flock?"

Greta laughed. "Put that way, it does sound silly. Forget I said that."

She stood. "I've got some customers waiting for me. Lots of folks believe eating sausage on New Year's Day will bring them luck." She hugged me. "You'll come for dinner Christmas Eve, won't you? That's when our family always has its celebration."

I accepted her invitation, although I had some trepidation about facing an evening of Greta's famous "down-home" cooking. I hoped she wasn't planning to serve one of her specialties like stuffed beef heart or hog maw.

She returned to her booth, and I picked up my packages and strolled down the aisle toward the exit. Suddenly, I spotted Alice-Ann, who at five feet eleven towered over most of the people in the market. Her streaked blonde hair gleamed in the light from an overhead bulb, and she was smiling warmly at a chicken vendor. My heart did a little flip-flop at the sight of the woman who'd been my dearest friend since we'd met on our first day at college. I wondered how she'd react if I dared go over and say hi. She glanced up, our eyes met for a moment, I took a step forward. She turned away.

I knew that Alice-Ann was not yet ready to reconcile, and for the time being it was best to let her mourn in her own way. But it still hurt. It hurt a lot.

On my way across town, I stopped at the state liquor store and bought a bottle each of port wine and brandy for Praxythea's fruitcake. Although I usually think of fruitcake as a close relative to a boat anchor, so far this one looked promising.

When I reached my office, I noticed the cleaning crew had again left the broom on the stoop. How careless! I really would have to speak to them. Inside, I discovered it was the twin of the first broom, which was still propped up in the corner where I'd left it. I placed the second broom next to the first, went to my desk, and began to write.

I had the *Chronicle* building to myself because it was Thursday—Cassie's regular day off. Usually, it was the day I fine-tuned my articles and typed the police blotter. Friday, then, was "panic day," when Cassie and I put the page proofs together and rush them and the computer disks to the printer in time to have the paper ready for distribution on Saturday morning.

Today, I had a murder to write about. A murder that was preying heavily on my conscience. If I'd taken her fears seriously would Bernice be dead now? The woman had turned to me for help, and I'd let her down.

I began my article. "Bernice Roadcap feared for her life, and, as it turned out, her fears were justified." Perhaps I did editorialize more than I should have in a news report about the sanctity of life and the cowardice of poisoners, but I rationalized that as editor I could do as I pleased.

I printed it out, corrected a few spelling errors, attached a file photo of Bernice, and carried the article to the front office to place in Cassie's IN box.

On the floor next to Cassie's desk was the package that had already tripped me twice, and that I'd twice asked her to unpack. It was still unopened. With a sigh of impatience, I grabbed an X-Acto knife out of Cassie's desk drawer, and slashed through the brown tape.

Beneath lots of crumpled paper were two stacks of books, all identical, all titled *Moon Goddess: The Magick and Rituals of Witchcraft.* Why would Cassie order ten copies of the same book from the shopping channel? I wondered. Gifts, maybe. I had another surprise coming; there was a letter from Llewellyn Publishers enclosed, addressed to Cassie Kriner, aka Golden EarthWoman, congratulating her on the publication of her new book!

It amused me to learn that solid, pillar-of-the-community Cassie had a secret life. It was the kind of thing I expected from acquaintances in the city, but in conservative Lickin Creek . . . ? I took the book into my office and thumbed through it. The little I read was well written. I couldn't wait to ask Cassie about her writing career.

When the phone rang, I reluctantly put the book

down. It was Luscious, calling from the police station with the weekly crime report.

"No news about Kevin," he said before I could ask. "We done put out an APB and had a couple of reports from West Virginia about a suspicious-looking guy with some kids in tow. I'll let you know what we find out."

Thirty-six hours. Kevin had been missing for thirty-six hours. Could a child survive that long in the cold of the mountains? And if he really had been kidnapped, what had happened to him during those long hours? I needed to put the possibilities out of my mind.

"What have you done about Bernice's death?" I asked. "Did you send that cup to the crime lab for toxicology testing?"

"Sure," he said. "But it'll be a few days before I hear anything back. The autopsy's going to take a while, too. Tori, I really meant it last night when I asked for your help. With only me and Afton here, I'm running in more directions than a chicken with its head cut off. Seems like the council's threatening to fire me every couple of minutes."

"I'll do what I can," I assured him. "Right now you should start interviewing the people who were on the stage. Find out if anyone noticed who put the cup on the pedestal—or even if they saw someone go near it."

"Thanks," he said with what sounded like a sigh of relief. "I'll get on it right away. Are you ready for the police news?"

"Fire away." I grabbed a pencil.

He gave me the details on two DUIs, a fight at Daisy's Bar-Grill-Laundromat, and a break-in that took place last night at the home of a noted Civil War historian, Dr. Cletus Wilson. I sat up straight when I heard the address, for it was in my own Moon Lake neighborhood.

"I hope this doesn't mean Lickin Creek's getting to be

like the city," I commented, thinking I was beginning to sound like a true Lickin Creek native.

"I hope not, too, Tori. But this was probably just teenagers out for a thrill. Not much was taken. Only a few flashy things, Wilson said. They left the most valuable stuff alone."

"How'd they get in?" I asked, thinking of my not-so-well-hidden key.

"Wilson said they got in through the servants' entrance in the basement, then came up the hidden staircase."

"Hidden staircase? Sounds like a Nancy Drew mystery—*The Hidden Staircase*. You're kidding, aren't you?"

"Of course not. Everybody knows that all the houses in Moon Lake were built about the same time, and all of them have hidden staircases and corridors."

"Even mine?"

"Probably. They were for the servants to use—so they wouldn't bother the rich home owners with their comings and goings."

I made a mental note to look for secret passageways when I got home tonight.

The next call was from Praxythea. Her limo had just arrived to take her to York, but first she needed to tell me that Ginnie had stopped by to remind me of our bingo date. "And she brought you a bingo kit," Praxythea said with a chuckle.

"What's that?" I asked.

"It's a little plastic bag with colored markers in it, and—let's see—a good-luck troll. How adorable!"

I groaned.

"She'll pick you up at five-thirty."

"Are you sure she said five-thirty? That's awfully early. I won't have time for dinner."

"She said to plan on eating there—they have good slippery potpie. What is that?"

"A local delicacy. One I don't care for. Have a good trip."

My hand was still on the receiver when the phone rang again. Thinking of the many articles I had to write, I almost chose not to answer, but I've never been able to ignore a ringing telephone.

"Hello," I said.

Nothing.

I tried again. "Hello, anybody there?"

Again, no answer.

"Damn computer-generated calls!" I muttered, almost ready to hang up.

Then I heard a faint, hesitant voice. "Miz Miracle?"

"This is Tori Miracle. Who is this, please?"

A pause. "It's me. Peter."

I jerked to attention. Was he going to tell me the truth about Kevin—despite his sister's bullying? This could be the break we needed. "What can I do for you, Peter?" I asked calmly. I didn't want to scare him off with my eagerness.

He mumbled something so softly I couldn't catch anything but Kevin's name.

"Do you know where Kevin is?" I asked. "If you do, please tell me."

"I'm scared," he whimpered.

"Of what?"

"Pearl."

My God, what has Pearl done? I wondered.

"Where are you, Peter?"

"Corny's," he said.

"Corny's Feed Store?"

"Yeah."

"Is Pearl with you?"

"I'm all alone."

"Is Kevin all right?" I asked. I couldn't bring myself to ask if he was alive.

"Don't know. I'm real scared." His voice quivered. "Can you come get me?"

"Peter, stay where you are. I'll be there in half an hour."

"Don't tell no one. I don't want Pearl to know I called you." I could hear sharp bursts of air and knew he was hyperventilating.

"Hang in there, kid. I'm on my way."

CHAPTER 9

Bless all the dear children

THE SNOW HAD MELTED, THE ROAD WAS NO longer icy, and I broke all the speed laws going up the mountain, arriving at Corny's Corner in record time. Fewer cars were parked in the field than last night, and I feared the search was winding down as people lost hope in finding Kevin.

Inside Corny's, the Friendly Feed Store, I discovered it was not only a feed store but also an old-fashioned hardware shop, dark and dusty, with shelves piled high with tools, bags of fertilizer, kitchenware, Christmas decorations, and many items I didn't recognize. Down the center of each aisle was a row of wooden barrels full of nails. Ceiling fans, high overhead, churned up dust motes, but did little to freshen the stale air. I looked around the cavernous old building, trying to spot Peter, but there was no sign of him.

A young man approached wearing black trousers, yellow suspenders, a bright-purple shirt, and a black hat too small for his head. A delicate golden peach fuzz bloomed on his rosy cheeks. With a thick Pennsylvania Dutch accent, he asked if he could help me.

I shook my head, since Peter was obviously hiding and I'd promised not to tell he'd called. I spent a few moments examining the store's selection of blue and white crocks and ceramic butter churns, while I tried to figure out what to do. It came to me that Peter would most likely be somewhere near the phone he'd called from.

"Do you have a public telephone?" I asked the young man. "I've got a little problem with my car." I don't know why I thought it necessary to throw in an explanation for wanting to use his phone.

The youth smiled, rather patronizingly, I thought, and said, "Ain't got no pay phone, miss, but you'uns can use the one in the office." He pointed down one of the long aisles, to a heavily varnished oak door. My helpless-female act had paid off. I stepped inside the small office, really not much more than a closet with a window, and closed the door behind me. "Peter, are you in here?" I whispered. "It's Tori—I mean, Miss Miracle."

From beneath the rolltop desk came a rustle, a grunt, and finally a frightened-looking, towheaded boy.

I stepped forward and wrapped my arms around him. I could feel the pounding of his heart right through his skimpy jacket and my quilted one.

"You didn't tell no one, did you?" he asked, still shaking. "Pearl don't know I called you, does she?"

I smoothed his tousled hair. "It's okay. There's no way she could know."

My words seemed to soothe him.

I watched through the crack in the door until the clerk left his position at the counter to wait on a customer. "Now," I said softly to Peter, and we scuttled, unseen, out the front door.

"Where to?" I asked him, once the truck had sprung to life.

Peter scrunched down beside me on the front seat. "Up the mountain," he said.

He and Pearl had told the police that Kevin's kidnapper had driven toward town—the opposite direction from where we were now headed.

"Keep going till I tell you to stop," he said. He appeared much calmer now. I reached over and patted his hand to reassure him, and he smiled wanly at me.

We passed the entrance to the Iron Ore Mansions Trailer Park. As far as I could tell, there were no media vans beyond the gate. The ghouls had moved on.

"Hurry," he urged. "She could be watching."

I knew he meant Pearl. Again, I wondered what she had done and why Peter was so terrified of her.

Shrouded by the evergreen forest, the road became so dark I could hardly believe it was still morning. It was now hardly more than a trail, and I feared I would round a bend and find it gone. As I drove higher and deeper into the forest, I realized I was also driving farther and farther away from the area on which the search parties were concentrating.

Peter was now sitting up, watching the passing landscape with intense interest. "Stop here," Peter said.

I braked, pulled onto the shoulder, and turned off the ignition.

He jumped out. "Come on," he said and pushed into the forest, where I could see no path. I followed him, not liking this one bit. The only sound to be heard was the faint crunching of dry pine needles beneath our feet. Low branches reached out, tangled my hair, snagged my jacket. I ducked to avoid one and came up with something unpleasant and sticky clinging to my face.

"Where are we going?" I panted after a few minutes. We'd been moving uphill at a brisk pace, and I was rapidly realizing I was in no shape for hiking.

"Shhh." He paused and looked around. "You hear something?"

"No," I snapped. I was growing impatient and, unfortunately, beginning to wonder if Peter was leading me on a wild-goose chase. For the first time I wondered if he and Pearl were pulling a trick on me.

"Let's go," he ordered.

At last, we stumbled out of the gloom into a small clearing. Directly in front of us was a crumbling tower of dark gray stones, rising at least twenty feet over my head. Behind it was a steep, rocky hill.

I bent over, gasping, and tried to catch my breath. Tomorrow, I vowed, I would really start my diet—and an exercise program, too.

When I'd pretty much recovered, I straightened up to see Peter climbing the hill behind the tower. What had at first looked like natural rock formations now appeared to be the ruins of a stone staircase.

"Come on," he urged. "Hurry." He was halfway up the hill, at the summit of the tower. A narrow bridge crossed from the hill to the tower, and Peter skipped across it. He leaned over the stone wall, looking down at something.

The tower, I realized, was similar to one I'd seen in Caledonia State Park—an enormous chimney, built long ago to process iron ore from the local mines. The large opening at the base, where the fire would have been built, was blocked now by fallen rocks. I suddenly knew Kevin was inside, and my heart pounded wildly as I scrambled up the hillside.

The rocks were moss covered and slippery, and many were loose. I stumbled, twisted my ankle, and had to grab a tree limb to keep myself from tumbling backward down the hill. At last, I reached the bridge. Trying not to look down, I hurried across it to where Peter sat on the edge of the chimney wall.

"Be careful," I warned. "Don't fall in."

I stood on tiptoe and peered down into the square opening. It was larger than my New York living room. Stones from the wall had tumbled in and partially filled the interior, and it was heaped with dead leaves, brown pine needles, and picnic trash.

"Kevin," I called into the pit. "Are you there? We've come to help you."

I listened, and at first I heard nothing, then came a faint crackling sound from beneath the debris. "I have to go down there," I told Peter as I climbed onto the wall. The height made me dizzy, but I managed to swing my legs over the side, get a good handhold on the ledge, and lower myself as far as my arms could stretch. It wasn't quite enough. Shutting my eyes and saying a quick prayer, I let go and dropped the remaining couple of feet.

I landed upright, then toppled over backward. The litter cushioned my fall. As I rolled over, my left hand came in contact with something soft and warm. I scrambled to my knees and began to dig through the trash.

It took only seconds to uncover the child's face. His eyes were closed, and his breathing was shallow and uneven, but he was alive, and that's what was important. I cleared some of the crumbled dead leaves and dirt away from around his lips and nose and made sure his breathing passages were open.

His eyes opened then, and he blinked several times, trying to focus. Slowly, he seemed to realize someone was with him, and this appeared to frighten him. He attempted to push me away with his frail arms. "Go 'way . . . go 'way."

"It's okay, Kevin." I tried to soothe him. "I'm going to get you out of here."

I began to scoop the rest of the trash away from his body. Suddenly he screamed, and I realized that one of his legs was twisted unnaturally beneath him. I gently uncovered it and saw a jagged, blood-crusted bone poking through the skin of his thigh.

"Peter," I called. "You'll have to hike down the mountain and find a phone. We need an ambulance—and emergency crew."

As if in answer, a rock tumbled off the ledge and landed in the pile of garbage next to me. "Careful!" I screamed. "That almost hit us."

Another rock fell, closer this time. I looked up and saw Peter peering over the edge. He was smiling, and I felt uneasy.

"What's wrong? Why don't you go?" I asked.

He giggled, and to my horror I saw him raise a large stone above his head.

"No!" I yelled. I threw myself over Kevin, hoping to protect him with my own body. The stone, when it landed, bounced off another and hit my right arm below the elbow. The pain was so severe I couldn't even scream. But Kevin could and did. I realized my weight was crushing him.

From above came one more high-pitched giggle. Another rock landed somewhere behind me. The next grazed my right leg. Lying facedown, on top of the screaming child I'd come to rescue, I knew we were both going to die, and there was nothing I could do about it.

I thought of Fred and Noel and hoped someone would give them a good home, and of Garnet, and the baby brother or sister I'd never get to see. "I'm sorry," I told Kevin, who seemed to have fainted. "I'm really sorry."

All was quiet for a moment. I tensed my back and waited for the next barrage of rocks—the one that would most likely prove deadly—when I heard a sound that was even more horrifying than Peter's laughter: the unmistakable blast of a shotgun.

Where had he gotten a gun? Would the end come

quickly? Would it hurt? I waited. Nothing happened. I rolled off Kevin onto my back and looked up. There was no sign of Peter. I feared he'd gone for more ammunition. I had to get out before he returned.

I started tossing rocks into one corner. The ledge was not too far above. If I could pile up enough stones, I might be able to climb out and get help.

I frantically continued working on my escape route, even when I heard approaching footsteps above me. I climbed to the top of the mound of rocks and reached for the ledge. Almost. Almost.

I had the feeling I was being watched. I looked up in dread and saw not Peter but Pearl staring over the edge at me.

"You two kids won't get away with this," I yelled at her. "Help me get out of here. Right now!"

"It's okay," she said. "I done tied him up. But you better hurry. He might get loose."

I quickly finished my makeshift staircase and climbed out of the pit. Behind me, Kevin moaned pitifully. The child needed help, and he needed it fast.

Peter was lashed to a nearby tree with gray metallic duct tape, tightly wrapped from his chest to his feet. More tape covered his mouth. Blood trickled from a wound on his forehead, and I guessed Pearl must have hit him with something. He writhed and twisted, but the tape held him fast.

Pearl stood a few feet away, cradling an enormous shotgun in her arms.

"You go for help," she said to me. Her voice was calm and confident.

"*You* go," I said.

"Uh-uh." She shook her head. "You wouldn't shoot him if he got loose." The coldness in her blue eyes said she would if she had to.

Somehow, I found strength I didn't know I had and ran down the trail to the road in only a few minutes. Luck was with me, for a pickup truck, with a dead deer strapped to the hood, came by almost immediately and stopped. I explained to the driver, in a rush, what had happened, and he called for help on his cell phone. He was familiar with the ruins of the old furnace and described to the dispatcher exactly where we were.

He grabbed his rifle from the window rack, retrieved a first-aid kit from the toolbox in the back, and followed me into the woods.

Pearl sat on a rock, gun on her lap, watching Peter, who had stopped struggling. The malevolent gleam in his wild eyes made me pray the tape held.

The kind stranger climbed down into the pit to look after Kevin. "I think he'll be okay," he called up to me. "Hand me my first-aid kit. I'll stay with him till the ambulance gets here."

I sat down next to Pearl.

"Well?" I said, not looking at her. "You going to tell me what this is all about?"

The story she told chilled me to the bone. The three children—Kevin, Peter, and Pearl—had been playing on the hill beside the furnace, when Kevin had tumbled into the chimney.

"He was hurt bad," Pearl said, "and scared, and crying. That's when Peter called him a crybaby and throwed rocks at him. I told Peter to cut it out, but he kept on. I pulled him off the wall, but Kevin was all bloody and wasn't moving, and I thought he was dead.

"I was afraid we'd get in trouble, so to make sure nobody would find him, we covered him with branches and leaves. Then we went home and made up the story about Kevin going home by hisself."

"But why didn't you try to get help for him?" I asked.

Pearl started to cry, and for the first time I remembered I was talking to a child. "We was real scared. I thought if we done told, they'd take Peter away and stick him in jail forever. I always done took care of him—nobody else does—and I knew if they took him away, then he wouldn't have nobody. Now, they'll do it anyway."

I put my arms around her. "Peter won't go to jail," I said. "There are people who can help him."

She sobbed into my chest. "Promise? I think there's something wrong with him. Ever since he was a little kid, he always liked to pull bugs apart and watch them squirm. And cut up mice and little animals." She cried, "I kept telling him to stop, but he wouldn't. Last summer he done poured lighter fluid on the neighbor's cat and set it afire. It was awful."

I shuddered and looked at Peter, who glared back at me. I wondered why I'd been unaware of the unadulterated evil in his eyes earlier. "He'll get counseling. He's just a child," I said to Pearl. "There are people who can make him better." I hoped this was true.

I got up and went to the edge of the chimney and looked down at Kevin and the helpful stranger. "How's he doing?" I asked.

"Well as can be expected. Hope the ambulance gets here soon."

I returned to my spot next to Pearl. "How did you find us here?" I asked.

"I caught sight of him sneaking out of our trailer, so I followed him to Corny's. He didn't have no business there, so I guessed he was going to call someone. Only phone they got's in the office, so I listened through the window. When you came and went in the store, I hid in the back seat of your truck, under all that junk you got there."

The junk was Garnet's. I hadn't even realized there was a back seat under it.

"The gun—where did it come from? And the duct tape?"

"The gun's my pa's—he don't lock them up. I took the tape from Corny's—just in case."

"Did you know Peter was going to hurt me?" I asked.

"I thought maybe he might. Didn't want him to hurt nobody else."

"Thanks, Pearl," I said, hugging her.

She wrapped her skinny arms around my neck and laid her head on my shoulder, and we stayed that way until we heard the distant wail of an ambulance siren.

Directly below us, water danced and sparkled in a small brook. "By the edge of running water," Praxythea had said. Once again she'd made a lucky guess.

CHAPTER 10

O come ye, O come ye

IT WASN'T LONG BEFORE SEVERAL EMERGENCY Medical Technicians and a state trooper arrived on the scene. With the help of the stranger I'd found on the road, the EMTs placed Kevin on a stretcher board and raised him out of the furnace. While they were fastening the straps to secure him, one said, "We gotta take him way over to Hagerstown Hospital, since the Lickin Creek clinic done closed down." The accusing look he gave me indicated he blamed me for the disastrous chain of events at the apple festival a few months ago.

I wanted to tell him it wasn't my fault, but I let it go.

Before they left, one man checked my bruises. "You'll be fine," he said with an unconcerned shrug. "Put some ice on when you get home."

The trooper, in the meantime, was listening to Pearl's story. When she was done, the officer came over to me, removed his Smokey the Bear hat, and fanned himself with it. "It's hard to believe a kid could do something like this," he said.

I thought of the many known serial killers who had started their careers as children, graduating from torturing animals to torturing people. Whether he knew it or not, Peter was following in their infamous footsteps.

"I just hope he can get some good psychiatric care," I said.

"I'll drop the little girl off at her house on the way into town," the policeman said.

Pearl let out a wail. "No! I ain't gonna ride with Peter! No way!"

He took off his hat again and scratched his head. "Can you take her home?"

I nodded, and put a sheltering arm around Pearl's thin shoulders.

"Tell her parents to come down to the state police barracks on Scalp Level Road. We'll need a statement from you, too."

"I can stop and tell the Poffenbergers Kevin's been found, if you want me to."

He looked doubtful, but then seemed to realize there was no other way to handle this situation. "Okay," he agreed, somewhat reluctantly.

I really didn't want to be the bearer of bad tidings, but neither did I want Pearl to have to ride in the patrol car with her brother. When I left with Pearl, the trooper was stripping the duct-tape bindings off Peter, who was screaming. Agony or anger? I couldn't tell.

Pearl wisely chose to stay in the truck while I went inside the trailer to tell Kevin's parents that he had been found. I could swear Kevin's father looked almost disappointed when he learned his son was safe. There would be no more media trucks in his yard, and most likely no TV movie. The mother, though, responded with a flood of tears and a gush of thanks.

As I started back to my truck, a voice behind me called out, "Miss! Wait up, miss!"

I paused in the small, tire-strewn yard and turned to face Kevin's mother. "Yes?"

Her shoulders drooped, and she looked as if she wanted to run away, but then she straightened up and said, "Thank you, miss. For saving my boy."

"I'm glad everything turned out all right."

"He coulda died."

"He'll be up and around before you know it."

"God must have something in mind for him to do with his life," she said.

I remained silent as I wondered what life held for any of her brood.

Almost as if she could read my mind, she said, "I know what you think of my husband. I done seen it in your face—the first time you'uns done come up here to our double-wide asking questions."

She continued her one-sided conversation. "You're right about him, you know. He ain't held a job in years. And when he gets drunk he hurts the kids and me. What do you think I oughta do, miss?"

I broke my silence. "I'd ask myself what was best for my kids, then I'd do it." Even as I said it, I knew it wasn't that easy.

"I don't know how I'd take care of them all by myself. I'm near thirty, you know, and I ain't never had a job."

Near thirty! I'd assumed she was much older than I. "Don't you have family? Someplace you could go until you can get on your feet?"

"I got a sister lives in West Virginia," she said thoughtfully. She turned and walked slowly back to her trailer. I wished there was something I could do to help her.

As I swung the truck around, preparing to leave, I saw the parents preparing to leave for the hospital by packing their kids into the back of an ancient pickup truck. I shuddered and headed toward Pearl's house.

⁓

Pearl clung to my hand for support, but she was strong when she told her parents exactly what Peter had done. Her parents were stunned—disbelieving—and angry. Angry with me for bringing them the bad news, with Pearl for not having stopped Peter, with his teacher for not having recognized his aberrant behavior, and with the community for not providing young people with enough to do. They appeared to accept no responsibility at all for what their child had become.

When they finally calmed down, they agreed to follow me to the barracks. The truck they drove was as old and disreputable as the one Kevin's family had left in.

The state police barracks was on Scalp Level Road, about half a mile outside the borough limits. It was a low, modern building of brick and glass, surrounded by barren fields. I'd been there before, wearing my reporter's hat, so I knew when summer came it would be nearly hidden among the cornstalks.

My legs shook as I got out of the truck. I was exhausted from the shocking events of the day: finding Kevin, the pounding I'd taken from the barrage of rocks, and the emotional meetings with both sets of Poffenberger parents.

A trooper whom I'd met a few times while covering stories there escorted Pearl and her parents into an interrogation room. While the door was open, I got a quick glimpse of Peter, who was behind a Formica-covered table. Across from him sat another trooper and an attorney I recognized from the public defender's office.

In another room, I was questioned by two troopers,

one male and one female, for nearly twenty minutes. After I'd described what had happened several times, the female officer asked, "Surely you must have some idea why Peter lured you there? Did you do anything to antagonize him?"

I shook my head, mystified. "I've only spoken to him two times. And I didn't even accuse him of anything, even though I sensed he wasn't telling me the whole truth. I gave him my card and asked him to call me if he thought of anything that might help us find Kevin. I thought he knew more than he was telling and might open up if he could get away from Pearl's influence. That's why I wasn't totally surprised to hear from him this morning."

While I spoke, the policeman who'd been in the interrogation room with Peter entered, sank into a chair, and sighed wearily. "I hate it when kids commit crimes. I want to believe people are basically good and learn to be criminals from others. But then I run into someone like Peter who seems to have been born bad. He not only admitted what he did, but told us how much he enjoyed doing it. The kid's a monster!"

"Did he say why he wanted to hurt me?" I asked.

He smiled wryly. "If it makes you feel better, Tori, it was nothing personal. He'd gotten warmed up killing Kevin—at least he thought he had—and found it a lot more exciting than torturing the neighbors' pets. He wanted to repeat the thrill. He figured it would be easy to get you to believe he was going to lead you to Kevin. He was looking for another victim, and you were available."

I pondered this for a minute. I'd always thought of myself as a wary person; that was how I'd survived for ten years in New York. But Peter was just a boy. It had never occurred to me I'd have anything to fear from a child.

"No wonder he was so secretive," I said. "I thought he was hiding from Pearl, but now I see he was avoiding being seen with me, so later nobody would connect him with my . . . disappearance." I shuddered to think what would have happened if Pearl hadn't followed us and rescued me.

"What will the court do to him?" I asked.

"Most likely, he'll be sent to a juvenile facility, where he'll get some counseling. It might help, but I doubt it. More likely, he'll come out at eighteen a full-fledged, hardened criminal."

With that gloomy statement, our meeting was concluded. As I walked into the waiting room, I saw the Poffenbergers, sitting apart from each other on wooden benches. I crossed over to Pearl and hugged her. "Thanks again, honey," I said.

She allowed herself a small smile. "They said I wouldn't get into no trouble since I helped you. But I guess Peter will."

"He'll be all right, I'm sure," I said.

Again, I wished I felt as optimistic about his chances for recovery as I tried to sound.

The late-afternoon sky was pewter-gray when I finally pulled into the circular drive in front of my house. I was exhausted, bruised, dirty, and emotionally drained. All I could think about was unwinding with a hot bath and an ice-cold Scotch and water.

As soon as I opened the back door, I knew something was wrong. The cats sat on the kitchen table, fur rumpled, golden eyes wide and indignant. Even Icky had edged forward an inch or two in his terrarium. For him that was practically aerobic exercise.

"What's wrong?" Even as I spoke, I began to notice

that my piles of books, catalogs, magazines, notes I'd written to myself, letters, and all the rest of the clutter that seems to accumulate wherever I am, looked messier than usual.

Someone had been in my house, searching through my stuff. Not Praxythea. I was sure of that. If she'd touched anything of mine it would have been to straighten it up, not throw it around like this.

Oh, no, I thought, what if they've stolen some of Ethelind's antiques! In a panic, I ran down the hall into the front parlor. The drawers of the antique walnut desk had been pulled out, upended, and tossed to the floor, but the valuable things, like the Staffordshire dogs on the mantel, the engraved silver boxes, and the Waterford crystal vases full of silk flowers were still in their places.

Upstairs, next to my bedroom, in the small room that I'd planned to use for a study back in the days when I thought I'd actually have time to work on my book, even more havoc had been wrought. My two-drawer, cardboard filing cabinet had been ripped apart, and my manuscripts lay scattered on the Oriental carpet.

The cats walked over and sniffed at the mess.

"Fine watchcats you are," I scolded. "If you can't do better than this, I'll have to take down my ATTACK CAT sign."

What on earth had anyone expected to find in here? I wondered as I stared at the mess. My secondhand laptop computer was the only semivaluable article I owned, and it was still on the desk where I'd left it.

I remembered Luscious telling me about a break-in at a nearby home. Teenagers, he'd suspected. I wondered if the same ones were responsible for this vandalism.

It took a while to check the entire house, but I could not see that anything had been stolen. Thankfully, none of Ethelind's antiques had been touched.

When I tried to call Luscious to tell him what had happened, the girl who answered the phone at Hoopengartner's told me he was "down to the state police barracks." I figured Luscious had enough to worry about without my adding something else to his list. Since nothing was missing, I told the girl not to bother paging him.

My filthy clothes were lying on the bedroom floor, and hot water was running into the claw-footed tub, when I heard a voice from downstairs call out, "Yoohoo, it's me, are you ready to go?"

A glance at the Seth Thomas clock on the wall told me it was five-thirty. I'd forgotten all about Ginnie and our bingo date!

I wrapped my terry-cloth robe around me and ran down the stairs. She wouldn't listen to any of my reasons for not going to bingo with her.

"You need to get out," she insisted. "You mustn't allow a home invasion to change your plans. That's what they want. You've got to show them you're not afraid. If you hurry, we'll only miss the early-bird games."

"Okay," I said reluctantly, "I'll go." I limped upstairs, drained the steaming tub, and took a quick and unsatisfactory shower, wishing all the time that I could learn how to say no like I meant it.

CHAPTER 11

See the blazing Yule before us

WHILE DRIVING TO THE WEST END LICKIN Creek Volunteer Fire Department, where the bingo game was to be held, Ginnie asked dozens of questions about my finding Kevin. Skipping over Peter's involvement, I told her I'd done it with Pearl's help. The notorious Lickin Creek Grapevine would spread the rest of the story soon enough.

Ginnie pulled her Subaru into the parking lot, where it looked out of place among the pickup trucks and SUVs. Just outside the entrance to the social hall, a dozen smokers, coat collars turned up against the cold, huddled in a small circle. Ginnie charged right into their midst and excitedly broke the news of Kevin's rescue. I was pounded on the back and swept through the door in a tobacco-scented cloud of congratulations.

My hand was shaken, my back thumped, and my body hugged by zillions of faceless people. We finally managed to break away from the throng and find two empty folding chairs, which Ginnie claimed by tipping them up against the side of the long table.

She slipped off her coat, revealing a T-shirt that said OUT OF MY WAY—I'M LATE FOR BINGO.

"Cute," I said.

"I can order one for you. Mine always brings me luck."

"Thanks anyway."

She shrugged. "Let's buy our cards and get some dinner."

We purchased bingo cards, three to a sheet, for the first game. Two sheets for me and four for Ginnie, then stood in line at the food counter.

Ginnie ordered the slippery potpie from a woman wearing a Santa Claus hat and Christmas-ball earrings. I chose French fries and an ox-roast sandwich that looked like barbecue to me. On Ginnie's recommendation I also selected a slice of Montgomery pie, which she assured me was "as near as you can get to heaven without dying."

While our food was being slapped together, I admired the holiday decor: an aluminum Christmas tree in one corner, paper garlands thumbtacked to the dropped ceiling, and red paper tablecloths on the long tables. We carried our food on orange plastic trays and claimed our seats.

When I tried to eat my sandwich, the flimsy plastic fork I'd been given snapped in two, and shreds of barbecued ox dribbled down the front of my sweater. I wiped up what I could with a paper napkin and tackled the pie, which was sweet and lemony and really very good.

Ginnie placed two grinning plastic dolls with purple hair on the table in front of us. "Good-luck trolls," she said.

The caller took his place on the platform at the front of the hall. "First game—fill the card. You'uns is playing for this here gathering basket."

I looked questioningly at Ginnie, who'd just taken the colored markers from our bingo kits. "Gathering basket? What kind of bingo is this?"

"Basket bingo," she answered happily.

I stared down at my cards. Baskets—with my luck I'd probably win one.

"First number is B-15," the caller shouted into his microphone. "Repeat, B-15." Above his head, B-15 lit up on a big wall chart.

Ginnie dabbed green spots on a couple of her cards and uttered a satisfied sigh.

Neither of us won the first few games. Ginnie purchased four more sheets of cards. I cut back to one. An evening of this could get expensive!

We used the time between games to get to know each other better. Ginnie shared with me several funny stories about her adventures as a substitute teacher at the high school, and I told her a few wild tales about my days as an investigative reporter.

We moved on to our reasons for living in Lickin Creek. She knew about Garnet, of course, everybody in town did. But she didn't know that I'd first visited Lickin Creek nearly ten years ago—to be in Alice-Ann's wedding.

"First time I saw Lickin Creek was five years ago," Ginnie said. "My husband was at the Pentagon, and we'd taken a week's vacation to visit Pennsylvania. We stayed in Gettysburg and made some side trips, and one day we drove across a mountain and stumbled onto this town. We both found it charming and on an impulse stopped into a realtor's office to see what houses cost here.

"Turned out the prices of homes here were about a fifth what they were in the D.C. area. I saw a picture of the house we eventually bought—it was the kind of place I'd dreamed about during all the years we'd lived on one Army post after another—a real home. We went to see it. It needed tons of work. We thought about it for a month, then made an offer. We worked on it every weekend for three years, getting it ready for the day Lem retired."

I knew there was no Lem in the picture now. She answered my unspoken question. "He had a heart attack at his retirement party. I moved into our dream home alone."

She didn't give me time to murmur sympathies. "Great," she said, "they've got a pantry basket coming up. With an eight-way divider! I've just got to win it."

She didn't, but it didn't seem to bother her. After purchasing another stack of cards, she came back to the table as full of enthusiasm as ever. "I just love bingo!" she said with a contented smile. "Guess it's the feeling that I'm getting something for nothing."

I mentally totaled up what she'd spent on cards. So far she'd got nothing for a whole lot of something—money.

She rubbed her troll's fuzzy head, "for luck." Its purple nylon hair was about the same shade as Oretta's pageant costume. I mentioned that to Ginnie.

She grinned wickedly. "It looks better on the troll." She unzipped the bingo kit and pulled out two brass pins that said I LOVE BINGO. "Nearly forgot these," she said.

"What did you think of Oretta's play?" she asked, as she fastened one of the pins to my lapel.

"The pageant? It's about as awful as a play can get."

"I meant the other play; the one she asked us to read."

I'd forced it out of my mind. "I haven't seen it. Told her I was much too busy. Did you read it?"

"She brought a copy by my house. Hard to believe, but it's so bad it makes the pageant look good. If there's a Broadway play in the last fifty years that she hasn't stolen from, I don't know what it was." As she spoke, she was oblivious of a man with a silver-white beard and moustache who was headed in our direction. "Oretta told me—Eeek!"

The *eeek* escaped as the man reached out and touched her right ear with one finger.

Ginnie's face turned red as she swung around and glared at the intruder. "Oh, it's you. Hello, Cletus," she said coldly.

He appeared to be a well-preserved sixty-five or seventy, and had a good-looking, if florid, face. "You don't sound happy to see me," he said, smiling. His eyes were now staring at me. "Who's your pretty little friend?"

Ginnie sighed. "Tori Miracle, I'd like you to meet another of your Moon Lake neighbors, Dr. Cletus Wilson. Cletus is a retired dentist."

I shook hands with Cletus, who held on a little longer than necessary while gazing soulfully into my eyes with his baby-blues. My mother had once said of an unpleasant visitor to the embassy, "I don't know why, but I dislike him immensely." That was how I felt about Dr. Wilson.

"May I join you ladies?"

"Bingo!" a woman shouted.

"Damn," Ginnie muttered and crumpled up her cards.

I recalled Luscious's police report from early this morning. "Are you the Dr. Wilson whose house was robbed?" I asked.

"I certainly am," he said. "Damn teenagers. It's got so a man can't even be safe in his own house. Back when I was a kid, we were taught respect for other people's property. Nothing like this would have—"

"Oh, stuff it, Cletus," Ginnie interrupted. "It wasn't all *Happy Days* back then. There's always been bad kids around. Always will be."

He didn't seem at all taken aback by her outburst. "You're right, my dear," he said with a smile, then leaned close to me so our shoulders were touching. I got a whiff of denture breath and turned my head slightly.

"I know who you are," he said, playfully touching my chin. I drew away, dislodging his finger. He smiled a white, false-toothy grin. "You're that girlfriend of the police chief's, running the *Chronicle*. Bet you're surprised I know that."

"Mmmm," I said, wondering how I could escape.

"You must be feeling lonely with that man of yours in Costa Rica. Since we're practically neighbors, maybe you'd like to come over for a drink some evening this week. Take a look at my Civil War collection. Ginnie can tell you it's well worth seeing." The leer he gave me indicated he had a lot more on his mind than showing me his cannonballs.

"I'm very busy," I told him. "The paper takes a lot of my time—"

"I'll call you," he said. "Excuse me, ladies, I see someone I need to talk to." The new object of his attention was a blonde woman with a disastrous permanent. She barely looked up from her cards when he sat down next to her.

"Charming gentleman," I remarked to Ginnie.

"Pond scum," she said cheerfully. "I actually made the mistake of going over there one night. I can tell you it was all I could do to escape with my girlish virtue intact. Oh, good—they're going to play inside-square next. That's my lucky game."

⌇

It was only a little past ten when Ginnie dropped me off, but it seemed much later. I'm not sure if that was because my bruises had been throbbing painfully for the last hour or because I'd been half bored to death all evening. Bingo was definitely not my thing, and I hoped Ginnie wouldn't invite me again. Perhaps now I'd get that hot bath and cold Scotch I'd been craving all evening.

Praxythea was in the kitchen, scratching Icky's chin.

"Get him off the table," I said sharply. "They carry all kinds of horrible diseases."

She stared at the pie basket I'd won, then tut-tutted when she noticed my bedraggled condition.

"I've spent the day with a child who's a wannabe serial killer, I've been pummeled with rocks, my house has been broken into—and don't even ask me what I think of bingo," I warned.

It was probably too late for ice packs to be effective, but I thought I'd give it a try. Since there was only half a tray of ice cubes in the refrigerator, I retrieved two bags of frozen peas from the freezer on the porch and positioned them on either side of my neck like bright green shoulder pads.

Praxythea gently placed Icky back in his terrarium and washed her hands. "He's so sweet," she murmured. She was still a vision of lavender loveliness, but her stage makeup had definitely seen better days. "I just got home, myself," she said. "It's been a long day."

"Amen to that," I agreed. "Did you visit the Amish market in Lancaster?"

"I never got there. While I was on camera, word came in that Kevin had been found, exactly where I said he'd be. I spent the rest of the afternoon giving interviews to the network newspeople. So exhausting!"

I retrieved my jaw from where it had dropped. "You took credit for finding him? I can't believe you."

She smiled sweetly. "He was by the edge of running water, wasn't he?"

"Yes, he was. But around Lickin Creek, it's hard to find any place that isn't near running water. You know that."

She sighed. "I'm used to disbelievers, Tori. Come see what I got for you."

I knew it was no use arguing with her; she was the mistress of illogical thought. I followed her out of the warm kitchen, through the cold interior rooms of the mansion, and into the large front parlor where a magnificent, long-needled Christmas tree dominated the center of the room.

"Isn't it beautiful?" she asked.

"It's gorgeous," I gasped. "How did you get it here?"

"The limo driver was kind enough to strap it on top of the car. He could barely see the road through the branches. It was like driving home through the forest primeval."

"Now I know stretch limos are good for something," I said.

"I thought we could decorate it tomorrow. Do something countryish—maybe make some popcorn and cranberry garlands, tie little red and white checkered bows on it."

"It's lovely, Praxythea. And I do appreciate it. But now that Kevin's been found, won't you be going back to New York?"

"I thought I might stick around for Christmas."

"Don't you have family or some close friends you'd rather be with?"

She shook her head and said softly, "Not really." She drifted over to the tree and pulled off a single dry needle.

I studied her back. It hadn't occurred to me that someone as rich and famous and beautiful as Praxythea could be lonely.

"Okay," I said cheerfully. "Neither one of us has family, so let's make it the best damn Christmas ever."

Her smile, when she turned to face me, was radiant.

"I'll fix us drinks," she announced. "We can toast the coming holiday."

"Sounds great. Make mine Scotch—a big one, please."

With a cat on each of our laps, we toasted the holiday and Kevin's rescue. As the first sip of Scotch hit my bloodstream, I felt a rush of warmth, and after a few minutes all my aches and pains were gone.

She refilled our glasses, and we toasted our continuing friendship. By the time I'd finished the second drink, I realized the alcohol was hitting me hard and fast. I was starting to feel weepy, and my speech was slurred as I said, "I wish I'd paid attention to Bernice when she asked for help. I might have shaved her."

"Shaved her?" Praxythea giggled. "I think it's time for us to go to bed."

Something woke me. I heard it again; a sound that wasn't loud, but was out of place. I remembered the possum in the laundry room and hoped we didn't have another unwelcome visitor. As I struggled to find the switch on the bedside lamp, the digital numbers on the clock radio told me it was nearly three in the morning. My mouth was dry from too much Scotch, and my head threatened to ache.

The bedroom door was ajar. I never left it open. Suddenly I realized something was missing. The cats!

I leaped from the bed and ran into the hall, calling for them. Maybe I was unnecessarily worried, but it was very strange not finding them in their usual places on the bed.

Praxythea's door opened, and Praxythea appeared in a sea-green chiffon negligee. Even at three in the morning, she managed to look glamorous. "What's up?" she asked. She grinned at the sight of my sleepwear, a Wizard of Oz T-shirt that said THERE'S NO PLACE LIKE HOME.

"Have you seen the cats?"

"Why, no. Not since they followed you to bed."

"Did you notice if I closed my door?"

"Yes. You did. Why?"

"It was open, and the cats are gone."

"It probably wasn't shut all the way. I imagine they're downstairs rustling up a midnight snack. Come on, I'll help you look for them."

I rushed down the front staircase, through the labyrinth of parlors and dining rooms to the kitchen, calling their names, "Fred. Noel. Here, kitty, kitty."

There was no answer. I was extremely apprehensive now. This wasn't like them at all. I opened the door to the back stairs, which led from the kitchen to the bedroom area above, and which was always kept closed because of drafts. "Kitty?"

A reassuring *meow* came from above. Without stopping to wonder how my cats had managed to open and close the door to the staircase, I ran up the stairs.

Noel was in the third-floor hallway, sitting on a priceless Oriental rug, cleaning a front paw. I scooped her up and hugged her tight. "Where's Fred?" I asked.

"If she answers, I'm leaving," Praxythea said, entering the hall from the stairs behind me.

"You don't understand cats," I said. "They communicate; you just have to learn their language. Come on, Noel, where's Fred?"

If ever there was a time for Noel to put on a show, this was it. But she chose this moment to put on her "stupid cat" act instead. She yawned, stretched, closed her eyes, and pretended to fall asleep in my arms. I ignored Praxythea's derisive snicker.

I searched the dusty bedrooms and survived a wild

attack of the sneezes, but there was no sign of Fred anywhere.

"Tori," Praxythea called from the hallway. "You need to come see this."

"What?" I asked, stepping out of the fifteenth or sixteenth bedroom I'd searched.

"Look." She pointed at an almost invisible break in the wall. "It's a door. If it hadn't been ajar, I'd never have noticed it."

I touched it, and it swung open as though it hung on well-balanced springs. Behind it was a spiral staircase with dangerously narrow treads.

Praxythea squeezed in next to me and peered up. "I thought we were on the top floor," she said. "Where do you think these stairs go?"

"Didn't you notice the turrets? I've never checked them out, because I don't like heights. I'll bet that's where Fred is. Come on."

Praxythea gamely lifted her chiffon skirts, and we climbed up, brushing aside some nasty cobwebs as we went. The last few steps brought us into a large, circular room, well lit by moonlight, and furnished with wicker furniture. Windows all around gave us a spectacular view of Moon Lake.

In fact, it was so spectacular I felt as if I were floating above the treetops and was immediately overcome with vertigo. I closed my eyes and grabbed Praxythea's arm to keep from falling.

"Tori, look!"

"Is it Fred?" Cautiously, I opened one eye.

Below us lay the dark waters of Moon Lake. On its smooth surface danced the reflected orange glow of the nearly full moon.

But as my eyes adjusted to the sight, I realized it

wasn't moonlight I was seeing. "My God!" I gasped. "That's a house! It's on fire!"

We clambered down the stairs as fast as we dared. In the kitchen I snatched up the telephone to call the Lickin Creek emergency number. "Already on the way," the girl at Hoopengartner's told me.

"You watch for Fred," I told Noel, who was fast asleep between the salt and pepper shakers on the kitchen table. I threw my jacket on over my nightclothes, grabbed the *Chronicle*'s camera, and dashed out of the house, headed toward the path that circled the lake. I could hear fire engines somewhere in the distance and Praxythea's footsteps close behind me.

When Praxythea and I reached the burning cedar-shingled mansion, I realized it was Oretta Clopper's home. The scene reminded me of the burning of Manderley in the movie *Rebecca*. I snapped a few pictures of the flames shooting out of the upper-floor windows.

A firefighter chopped down the massive oak front door and several others entered the building. They came out after a few minutes, forced back by the flames and thick black smoke.

I found the chief of one of the volunteer fire companies. "Do you know if anybody's in there?" I asked.

"At this hour they was probably fast asleep. Never knew what hit them."

I wrote his name in my notebook. Poor Oretta! Poor Matavious! How many tragedies could Lickin Creek handle?

All the firemen really could do was spray water on the fire and concentrate on protecting the houses on either side of the Clopper home. By this time, half the town was there, some of the people helping the volunteer firemen, others, like myself and Praxythea, simply watching helplessly.

The Clopper home emitted an almost human-sounding groan as the roof collapsed. Soon, the once lovely home was a steaming pile of black charred wood.

Someone grabbed my hand. "This is dreadful," Ginnie moaned. "Have you seen Oretta?"

"No, I haven't," I said, staring at the smoking ruins. "Nor Matavious, either."

"Dear God, I hope they got out."

Firemen were now working their way slowly through the remains of the house, methodically lifting smoking beams. I knew they were hunting for bodies, not survivors. I took more pictures.

When it was nearly dawn, Luscious, who had arrived with the firemen and had worked with them nonstop for hours, came over to me. His red-veined eyes peered out from a weary face, blackened with soot.

"Anything?" I asked.

He shook his head. "They gotta be in there. If they got out, someone would have seen them." He turned to Praxythea. "Do you think they're alive?"

I rolled my eyes, but he didn't notice. "I'm getting mixed vibrations," she began.

"Look for 'running water,'" I interjected. "While you two are doing your *woo-woo* thing, I'm going home to change. Then—into the office to write this up."

My attention was caught by the sudden commotion coming from the crowd of spectators, who had been very quiet for the past half hour. A car pulled up behind the fire engines, and people stood back, stunned, as Matavious Clopper got out. He stood in painful silence before what had been his home.

"Come on," I said to Luscious. We had to climb over

and around exhausted firefighters, sprawled on the ground.

When we reached Matavious's side, he was crying softly. "Oretta, I'm so sorry. Oh, my God, this is all my fault."

Reverend Flack and his wife, Councilwoman Primrose, reached him just as we did. Primrose put her arms around Matavious. "There, there," she soothed, "everything's going to be all right."

Looking at the disaster area before us, I wondered how she could be that optimistic. Maybe she'd learned it at ministers' wives' school.

I prodded Luscious. "Ask him where he was."

"Business trip," Matavious muttered. "Out of town." He pulled a handkerchief from his pocket and wiped his eyes. "Has anyone seen my wife?"

Business? What kind of business takes a chiropractor out of town in the middle of the night? "Wasn't she with you? Where did you go?" I asked.

Primrose glared at me. "Really, Tori. The man's suffered a dreadful loss. He's lost his home. And maybe his wife . . ."

Matavious lurched forward suddenly, ran a few steps, and dropped to his knees, his arms wrapped around a large dog. "Petula, you got out. Thank God. You got out."

Primrose put her hand on his shoulder. "I'm sure Oretta got out, too, Matavious. She's probably at a neighbor's right now."

He looked none too hopeful, but nodded. "Of course," he said. "You must be right."

Within a few minutes, Matavious found another of his dogs, two cats, and a Vietnamese potbellied pig. A cage containing a canary hung from a tree branch in the neighbor's yard. His delight was obvious. "They're all safe," he said. "Oretta got them all out of the house."

I was confused. If Oretta had let the animals out and even had time to rescue her canary, where was she? Something was dreadfully wrong.

And at that moment, a shout came from the ruins. "Found something!"

Matavious's face blanched. He staggered and would have fallen if Reverend Flack hadn't grabbed his arm.

CHAPTER 12

Away in a manger

THE FIREMEN EXTRACTED ORETTA'S BODY from the ruins of her home and placed her on a stretcher on the brick sidewalk. The crowd gasped, and I turned my head away from the gruesome sight. Henry Hoopengartner, carrying his black bag of coroner's equipment, officiously pushed his way through the spectators and dropped to his knees beside Oretta.

Jackson Clopper, trailed by his wife, Weezie, was close behind Henry. Jackson walked up to Matavious and extended his hand. "Real sorry, man."

"You son of a bitch," Matavious screamed. "You said you'd do anything to stop me. Even kill my wife!" He swung his right arm, strong from years of chiropractic manipulations, and slugged his distant cousin in the jaw.

Weezie uttered a shrill scream, while Jackson responded with several brutal chops to Matavious's midsection. Luscious needed the help of six bystanders to put an end to the fight.

Sweat and tears poured from Matavious's face, while Jackson's red face and throbbing neck veins made him look perilously close to a stroke.

If this was what a family Blue-Gray squabble was, I

was glad everyone in my family had been a Northern draft dodger.

"If you two don't stop this feuding right now, I'm gonna lock you both up," Luscious threatened.

They stopped glaring at each other and turned their fury on him.

"I mean it," Luscious told them, standing his ground. "I'm damned sorry about your wife, Matavious, but you can't blame Jackson for the fire. Now are you two going to shake hands, or am I going to have to take you both downtown and lock you up?"

After a long pause, Matavious stuck his hand out, and Jackson gave it a perfunctory shake. Weezie led Jackson away by the arm, and Primrose suggested to Matavious that he come with her to her house. He nodded, seemingly dazed, and let her and Reverend Flack guide him to their car.

"I'm proud of you," I said to Luscious. I couldn't help noticing his hand trembled as he pushed his hair from his forehead.

My Wizard of Oz T-shirt showed below my coat and my fuzzy pink bunny slippers were covered with mud and soot. "Guess I'd better go home and change," I said. "I need to get to the office." Before I left the scene, I got the names of the firefighters who'd found Oretta's body. Another tragedy to write about! Sometimes I hated being a reporter.

I looked for Praxythea, but she was nowhere in sight, so I walked home alone, calling for Fred and wondering, as I skirted the lake, why Oretta had gone back into the house after getting all her animals out. What was so important in there that she'd gambled her life and lost?

After showering and donning gray wool slacks and a Norwegian ski sweater I'd picked up for five bucks at the Goodwill, I went downstairs. Praxythea was waiting for me at the foot of the staircase with a strained look on her face. She'd exchanged her negligee for designer jeans and an expensive-looking rhinestone-studded sweatshirt from the Hotel Del Coronado in San Diego.

Alarmed, I asked, "What's wrong? Is it Fred?"

She shook her head. "No . . . I mean . . . actually, I don't know. Luscious walked me home, and we noticed a break in the bushes on the side of the house. There was a door hidden behind them, leading to the basement—you'd never know it was there, except for the broken branches."

I dreaded what I knew must be coming.

"It was open, Tori."

I sat down hard on the stairs. Fred had never been out on his own. All the traffic—the fire engines—the noise—

"Luscious checked it out and told me it was the old servants' entrance. Said all the old houses had them. The kids that broke in yesterday most likely live in this neighborhood and knew about the side door. They must have left it open."

I wiped a tear from my cheek. "And ever-curious Fred just had to investigate."

"Don't cry, Tori. I'm sure he'll come home. I made some fresh coffee. Let's have a cup."

In the kitchen, I automatically accepted the mug of coffee she handed me. It was delicious. "You're spoiling me," I told her.

"I enjoy doing things for people," Praxythea said. "Please don't worry. Most likely Fred's just out looking for a girlfriend."

"He wouldn't do that. He's been neutered," I said. "I'm a very responsible cat owner."

"I am sure he's all right," Praxythea said soothingly.

"He's never been outside by himself. What if he

gets hit by a car? What if he can't find his way back? What if . . ."

Praxythea took my coffee mug. "He'll be back. I know he will."

I left for the office, but only after Praxythea promised she'd keep searching for Fred.

She also promised to put the house back in order and to start preparing her famous fruitcake. She really was spoiling me.

As I approached the town square, I saw a crowd of shepherds, wise men, angels, sheep, and cattle gathered around the manger. Now what? I wondered. I parked in the vacant lot where the courthouse had stood before September's fire and hurried over.

I walked up to an agitated woman wearing a blue bathrobe and a lopsided halo, who I guessed was supposed to represent the Mother of God. A baby doll, wrapped in burlap, cried "Mama, Mama" every time the woman moved.

"What's up?" I asked, pulling out my notebook.

"We're the Friday-morning crèche people—from the Living Word Church—on the corner of Second and Maple," Mother Mary said. "Be sure you get that address right. We're not the Living Way people—they're out on Rabbit Road, and they voted not to help with the manger scene, so why should they get the credit? Anyway, when we got here we found the baby Jesus tossed right out of his manger bed. Look. It's full of trash!" She smoothed the baby doll's blond curls over its forehead. "Some people got no respect for religion."

"How true," I murmured. I saw Luscious, who was waving at me. "Excuse me, I need to talk to the police chief."

"He's an asshole," said the Mother of God. "Nothing like this happened when Garnet was here."

The people gathered around Luscious were all talking at once. His boyish face was more flushed than usual, and despite the chilly air, there were drops of perspiration on his brow.

"Press," I announced as I approached. "Coming through."

As the crowd broke apart, I heard murmurs of "What's this town coming to?" and "Damn teenagers."

I attempted to look official. "Can someone please tell me what's happened?" I directed my question at Luscious, as though I expected him to be in charge of the situation.

The ever-present councilman, Marvin Bumbaugh, stepped forward. "As president of the borough council, I believe it's my job to talk to the press."

Poor Luscious looked miserable. Once again, I wondered why any sane person would want to be the Lickin Creek police chief. No wonder Garnet had gotten out.

"Come on over here and take a look," Marvin said to me. He climbed over the iron chain that surrounded the fountain and pointed inside the shed. There, in the manger itself and scattered on the straw-covered floor, lay dozens of objects that I immediately recognized as Civil War paraphernalia.

"Could this be what was stolen from Dr. Wilson's house?" I asked.

"Damn right, little lady." The obnoxious dentist, himself, was breathing down my neck. "That's my stuff all right."

"Is anything missing?"

He rested an arm on my shoulder and surveyed the scene, then pulled a handwritten list from his pocket and checked the items off as he spoke. "Officer's sword, muzzle-loader, Colt 1860, flag and presentation plaque from the First South Carolina Volunteer Infantry Regiment, field glasses, Grand Army of the Republic Medal. Nothing's missing. Why the hell do you suppose they dumped it here?"

Luscious answered. "Probably got tired of the joke and didn't want to be caught with your stuff in their car. Why don't you pack it up and take it home, Cletus?"

"Don't you want to check it for fingerprints first?" Cletus asked.

"No point. Everything was handled by the Living Word people before I got here."

Dr. Wilson looked at Marvin for approval. When Marvin nodded, the dentist stepped over the chain and began to gather his treasures.

Marvin turned to face the people in the square. "You'uns better get the square cleaned up," he snapped. "Just look what those animals are doing."

Kings, shepherds, and wise men scurried to obey his command.

He then turned to Luscious, who seemed to shrink as the borough president directed his anger toward him. After blaming the policeman for just about every disaster to have occurred in Lickin Creek for the past decade, Marvin wound up by shouting, "And what have you done about finding Bernice Roadcap's murderer? Nothing, I'll bet."

Luscious spluttered. "Still waiting for the autopsy—"

"You've got till Christmas, Miller. Then I'm calling in the state police." He jabbed Luscious in the chest three or four times with his forefinger. "Five days."

Luscious waited until Marvin was gone, then turned to me with a groan. "I'm a dead man," he said. "If he calls in the state police, I might as well kiss my job good-bye."

I patted him awkwardly on the arm. Showing sympathy has always been difficult for me. "Five days is a long time," I assured him. I tried to ignore the memory of a New York policeman telling me that the longer an investigation took, the less chance there was of catching the perpetrator.

"Why don't you call the medical examiner's office and see if they can't rush the autopsy?" I suggested. "Explain to them how urgent it is."

"I'll try. Do you have any other ideas?"

"I do. There are some people I want to question. They might be more willing to talk to a reporter than to a policeman. I'll get back to you as soon as I know something."

I dropped off the film I'd taken of the fire at our regular One-Hour-Photo-Shop, and made the owner promise he'd send them over to the *Chronicle* as soon as they were ready.

When I got to the office, faithful Cassie was already at work, redesigning the front page to make room for news of the fire and Oretta's death. I sat down at the computer and quickly generated an article.

"This is going to be a great issue, Tori," Cassie said, when I handed her the paper. She glanced at it and corrected a spelling error with a red pencil. "More things happened in Lickin Creek this week than all last year."

"Let's go over the articles," I suggested. "Make sure we've covered everything."

Oretta's death was placed on the top of the front page because it was the most recent event. I ranked finding Kevin as the next most important news article. "Nothing wrong with featuring some good news once in a while," I told Cassie when she protested.

Bernice's murder moved down to third place. It had taken place two days ago and was now in the category of "old news."

Under a header that said PUBLIC SAFETY THREATENED, we put a warning about an outbreak of Hand-Foot-and-Mouth disease in a prominent box on the front page, to let parents know it had been found in two elementary schools, and listed the symptoms.

In last place came the announcement that the child's remains found in the quarry had been identified as those of Eddie Douglas, missing for the past thirty-seven years. Since the paper wouldn't come out until tomorrow morning, there was no need to mention that a memorial service for him would be held this evening at Trinity Church. We'd feature an article about the actual service in next week's paper.

I did a quick check of the remaining pages to make sure the regular columns were all there: social news; police blotter; farm agent's advice; church schedules (extra long this issue because of the Christmas season); real estate transfers; births, deaths, marriages, divorce announcements; comics; high school sports; and a very short column of national and world news. Anything we reported on would be old before the paper came out, and anyone interested in world events could watch TV.

Cassie looked over the advertising, including the classifieds, and announced everything was "fine and dandy." When the photos arrived, the issue would be complete.

I'd never win a Pulitzer here, I knew that, but I had to admit it was very satisfying putting this newspaper together.

Despite all the changes, the paper would be delivered on time, tomorrow morning. We celebrated with cups of coffee, mine liberally doctored with artificial cream and sugar to kill the bitter taste.

Our conversation turned, rather naturally, to Oretta's tragic death. "If only she hadn't gone back inside," Cassie said. "I wonder why she did."

"I've been wondering the same thing," I said. "I can't help thinking she might have gone in to rescue her manuscripts—that's what I'd worry about if my house caught fire."

Cassie nodded in agreement. "Me, too. Even though I always leave backup copies of my computer disks at my neighbor's house."

This was my perfect opportunity to ask Cassie about her book, *Moon Goddess*. At first, she was reticent about discussing it. "You'd keep it quiet, too," she said, "if you were a practicing wiccan, living in a small, religiously conservative town."

"*Wiccan* is another word for *witch*, isn't it?" I said.

From her pained expression, I realized I'd just displayed my ignorance of New Age neopaganism.

"I don't like that word," Cassie said. "It reeks of *satanism*, and that's not what we're about. We worship the Goddess, not the devil."

"Which goddess?" I asked.

"*The* Goddess, Tori. For crying out loud, I can't explain it in a few minutes." She reached into the bottom drawer of her desk and pulled out a book. "I was going to give it to you for Christmas," she said. "It'll tell you everything you want to know."

I opened it to the title page and saw she'd autographed it. "Thank you, Cassie. I really appreciate this."

Suddenly, I recalled a couple of lines from Oretta's Christmas pageant. "Hail to the Goddess. Hail to the wyccan."

"Was Oretta Clopper a witch—I mean one of you?"

Cassie shook her head. "She looked into it once, but didn't stay. I think she was afraid of being sky clad."

"Sky clad?"

"Nude. Naked. Bare."

"Well, do you? Do it . . . sky clad?"

"No way. Most of us are middle-aged or older. I know I've reached a point where I look a lot better with clothes on than I do with them off."

Oretta in a black leotard had been grotesque enough. No wonder she hadn't wanted to run around in the buff.

"What about the others in the pageant?" I asked. "Bernice and Weezie?"

"Bernice was a member of our coven," Cassie admitted. "In fact, she was recently elected high priestess. But Weezie? That would never happen. It was a stretch for her to even participate in something at Trinity. She belongs to a very fundamental church."

Bernice's death threat, which I had blown off as being harmless, now took on a new dimension. The anonymous writer had begun by calling Bernice *which one*, a phrase I now realized might have meant *number one witch*. The author had misspelled *San Antonio*, so why not the word *witch*?

"Could someone have wanted Bernice dead because of her involvement with your coven?" I asked Cassie. "Maybe you're in danger from a religious fanatic."

She gasped, then frowned. "I hope not. I really hope not. But I have been worried lately. There have been signs . . . like someone leaving a broom on the doorstep every night . . . that indicate someone's out to get me."

I glanced over at the corner where the two brooms I'd found on the stoop still stood. "What about the brooms?" I asked.

"There's a superstition that a witch can't step across a

broomstick to get into a building. Whoever laid the brooms on our top step must have believed that."

"Who else is in your coven?" I asked. "Do you know if anyone else has had a similar experience?"

"Not that I've heard," Cassie said. "And I'm not giving you any names, Tori. Even wiccans have a right to privacy."

"I wasn't being nosy," I protested.

"Of course not," Cassie said, turning back to her desk.

Our discussion was apparently over. To take my mind off my missing cat, I turned to the pile of letters in my IN box to determine which ones I would include in the next issue of the *Chronicle*. I couldn't help giggling over the first, a tirade at a supposed government conspiracy to put the farmers out of business by seeding the clouds to stop rainfall. The second was full of Bible quotes and dire warnings about the dangers of a nuclear attack in our own backyard: "us'uns being so close to old Fort Ritchie's secret bunker and all."

The third letter, handwritten and mailed the day before Bernice died, spoke vehemently against the borough's plans to construct a mall in downtown Lickin Creek. The author claimed Bernice's gift of her cold-storage building to the borough was self-serving, since she owned much of the adjoining commercial land and would profit tremendously from the mall. The last line caught my eye; in it the writer described the project as a poor man's "San Antoinio River Walk." It was the same misspelling of *San Antonio* that I'd seen in Bernice's anonymous threatening letter. Only this one wasn't anonymous. It was signed by Weezie Clopper.

CHAPTER 13

Please bring me a figgy pudding

CASSIE AND I WORKED QUIETLY AT OUR DESKS for another half hour or so. I would have liked to explain that my curiosity about whether members of the coven had been threatened came not from nosiness but from a concern that she and her friends might also be in danger. Tomorrow—I thought—tomorrow I'll smooth things out with her. Surely she'd understand.

A messenger arrived with the pictures, and I was pleased to see that several had actually turned out good enough to use.

"Either I'm getting used to the camera, or it's getting used to me," I said, hoping to provoke a smile from Cassie. It didn't work.

"I'm off for the print shop," Cassie said. "Don't forget the staff Christmas party tomorrow."

"Staff party? We have a staff?"

"Who do you think delivers the papers? And sells the advertising?"

I waited a few minutes until I heard Cassie's truck pull out of the parking lot, then I picked up the phone and called my friend Maggie Roy, Lickin Creek's head librarian.

"Have you had lunch?" I asked.

"Nope. I was just sitting here hoping someone would call and invite me out."

"I'll be there in five minutes."

I "outed the lights" as I've learned to say, gathered up my fanny pack and a notebook, and left the building. Maggie can usually tell me what I need to know, and her answers don't necessarily come from the reference section.

Downtown was coming to life. A few merchants were taking advantage of the day's unusually warm December weather and had set up sale tables in front of the stores. Christmas decorations brightened the shop windows, and carols rang out from loudspeakers. Hundreds of tiny white lights sparkled in the bare branches of the trees on the square.

The living crèche had been cleaned up, and Cletus Wilson's Civil War artifacts were gone. If I didn't know that there was a fountain, mermaid and all, in the center of the square, I could almost believe the manger had always been there, so well made was it.

A cow, a sheep, a Vietnamese potbellied pig, and a grumpy-looking llama stood watch over the baby Jesus. A small sign told passersby that the animals were provided by the Catoctin Zoo. A small charcoal grill kept Mary, Joseph, and the three wise men warm inside the shed.

Several people stopped me and congratulated me on having rescued Kevin Poffenberger. I basked in the warmth and felt well loved by the time I climbed the steps to the gracious old post office building, which had been converted into the public library in the fifties when the post office had moved to a newer and more efficient, but far less interesting, building.

Pausing just inside the door, I looked to my left where

the children's department was located, thinking I might see Alice-Ann. She'd returned to work as a children's librarian after the death of her husband. But she wasn't there.

Maggie was at the circulation desk and waved when she saw me enter. "Glad you came early," she said with a big grin. "Come see what I've done."

She handed her stamp pad to an assistant and came around the desk to take me by the hand. "Close your eyes and don't peek," she said.

I closed my eyes and let her lead me.

"Now," she said.

I could hardly believe my eyes. The top of the card catalog had been turned into a shrine to me! There stood my book, *The Mark Twain Horror House*, and next to it was my picture, taken on a really bad hair day. Finishing the display were several laminated newspaper articles about my adventures in Lickin Creek. One told of my involvement this past fall in uncovering the marijuana farm in Burnt Stump Hollow, another of my part in discovering who had killed Percy Montrose.

An older article described last summer's fire that had destroyed the historical society and mentioned at the end that I had accidentally set the fire while confronting the murderer of Alice-Ann's husband, Richard MacKinstrie.

"It's really nice, Maggie. Thanks so much." I would have preferred not to have the reminder there about the fire. Townspeople still unfairly referred to me as "that gal what burned down the historical society." It was a difficult reputation to shake.

"Come have some coffee. I can't leave for lunch until my assistant gets back," Maggie said, leading the way to the door marked STAFF ONLY. Inside the office, she wiped out a mug and filled it with the muddy black liquid she called coffee. It occurred to me I hadn't had a decent cup of coffee since I left New York.

"I'm so proud of you for finding Kevin," she said as she handed me the mug. "What a relief for his parents."

"Thanks. I'm glad he's okay, but I feel sorry for Peter's family. No telling what's going to happen with that boy."

Maggie nodded in agreement. "Always felt there was something funny about that kid," she said. "He and Pearl used to come in for story hour once a month while their mother shopped at Giant Big-Mart. Pearl never left his side. I thought she was kind of a control freak; now I think she was afraid to let him out of her sight."

We sipped our coffee and sat quietly for a moment or two, thinking about what the two Poffenberger families were going through right now. I also thought about Kevin's mother and what she suffered every day of her life.

Maggie roused me from my depressing thoughts with a question about Lickin Creek's latest drama. "What do you suppose made Oretta go back into her house last night?" she asked.

"Maybe she opened the door to let the animals out and was overcome by smoke before she could escape."

"But the canary cage was hanging in a tree next door, so we know she must have been outside," Maggie said. "She must have gone back inside to get something else."

"Cassie thinks she was going after her manuscripts," I said.

"Or computer disks. She told me once she backed everything up on floppy disks—ever since her hard drive crashed once."

I shuddered in sympathy. A hard drive crash is every writer's worst nightmare.

"It was her weight," Maggie said knowingly. "She

probably fell down and couldn't get up. I told her she ought to come to Overeaters Anonymous with me." She smoothed her tunic top over her bulging thighs. "Have you noticed that I've lost a few pounds?"

"Indeed I have," I fibbed. "I meant to mention it."

"You could come, if you like," Maggie said. "We meet every Tuesday night."

I was stunned she'd think I'd be interested in a diet group. After all, I was only a few pounds over the ideal weight for a big-boned female of my height. My cheeks flamed, but I managed to decline politely and quickly moved on to one of the subjects I needed to know more about: the coven of wiccans.

Maggie became unusually quiet and concentrated on fluffing up her already enormous beehive hairdo.

"Come on, Maggie. You must have heard something about them."

She put her mirror back in the desk drawer. "Of course I have, Tori. In fact, rumor has it that Cassie Kriner from your office is a big wheel in it. But to tell the truth, I'm just a little scared of them."

"Scared? Of Cassie?"

She looked sheepish. "Heard all kinds of funny things about witches. Devil worship. Blood sacrifices. You know . . ."

"I can't imagine Cassie involved in anything like that. And I am surprised a well-educated woman like you would even consider it."

"Underneath this elegant and sophisticated exterior, I'm still a local girl, Tori."

"Cassie didn't use the word *witch*, Maggie. She said *wiccan*, and she specifically called it a religion."

Maggie sniffed. "Religion, my eye. But I suppose I can find something about it. Be right back."

She soon returned with her arms full of dusty reference books and journals. We divided them into two piles, one for each of us, and dived in.

On top of my pile was *The Golden Bough*. It was too old to be helpful, but looked like it would be fun to read. I picked up a magazine, instead.

After about fifteen minutes, she looked up with her finger marking her place in one of the books, and said, "Hate to admit it, but it looks like you're right about wicca being a religion. I had no idea!"

"What did you find out?" I asked.

She held up a book by Gerald Gardner. "He calls it 'the Craft.' Describes it as a nature religion, worshiping 'the Goddess,' whoever she is. Oh, my—listen to this—'the coven often dances and chants in the nude.'" She began to laugh. "Can you picture that?"

I tried and couldn't. Not Cassie. Nude, never. She wouldn't even use the rest room in our office unless she was sure the front door to the building was locked.

We browsed through more books and magazines, and my head was soon full of unfamiliar names and terms: Valiente, Kelly, *The Book of Shadows*, the New Reformed Orthodox Order of the Golden Dawn, Old Dorothy, Buckland, Murray.

From one small booklet, I learned that Pennsylvania had a long history of belief in witchcraft, going back to Pennsylvania's first reported case, a trial presided over by William Penn himself. I was glad to read that the two women on trial got off with six months' good behavior.

"Apparently, there are as many types of Wicca as there are Christian denominations," Maggie said. "I *really* had no idea!"

I looked up from a journal and said, "Cool! Here's an ad for a correspondence school. Maybe I'll sign up for a class."

Maggie gasped.

"I'm not serious," I said, assuming she was shocked by the idea of my becoming a Witch by Mail.

"Not that, Tori. Listen to this. Says that for some covens the winter solstice is one of the most important 'sabbats.' Tori, that's tomorrow night. And it's full moon, too. Sort of a wiccan double whammy."

"I wonder where the coven meets?" I said, closing my magazine.

"Tori! You wouldn't!"

"If I'm going to take a correspondence class, I should know what I'm getting into."

"You're kidding . . . aren't you?"

"Of course I'm kidding. And I'm half starved. Can you leave yet?"

"Jeannie's back. I can go now. Where did you have in mind?"

"I thought it might be nice to try that new restaurant with the Civil War theme."

"The Fields of Glory. Isn't that the place that's owned by Bernice's boyfriend? Are you planning to investigate her murder over our lunch?"

"You got me," I admitted. "Perhaps we could ask him a few questions over hardtack and molasses."

"Thought that's what was served to sailors."

"Okay, goober peas, then."

"Sounds good to me," Maggie said. "In fact, anything sounds good to me. I'm starving."

As we were leaving the library, I noticed a sprig of mistletoe hanging above the front door. "Isn't that interesting," I commented. "I just read that mistletoe was used by the Druids in their solstice rituals. Did you realize that kissing under the mistletoe at Christmas is really part of an old Druidic fertility rite?"

"Stop kidding me, Tori."

"Sorry." I pushed the door open and stepped out into the brisk winter day.

Maggie followed in a few seconds. I glanced back and noticed the mistletoe that had been hanging in the foyer was gone.

We walked down the street to the restaurant. On the outside, it looked much like the other Victorian town houses on Lickin Creek's Main Street. The brick walls rose three stories high and were painted a soft shade of sky-blue. The front entrance was set to one side with two white-framed windows off to the right. Raised gold letters on a wooden sign above the door tastefully announced that this was the Fields of Glory Restaurant.

Inside, the walls between the rooms had been removed to create the long, narrow dining room.

Beside an antique walnut desk stood a short, rather stocky woman wearing a dark green watered-silk gown. Her face was framed with a white lace fichu. "Welcome to the Fields of Glory," she said with a smile.

"Mary Todd Lincoln?" I asked.

"Right you are. Table for two?"

She picked up two parchment scrolls and led us to a table in the back near French doors looking out over an enclosed courtyard.

The scrolls were menus, of course. The napkins and tablecloths were real linen, and the flatware and glasses all of good quality.

"Can't last," Maggie said, looking around the room at the rough-textured plaster walls, the framed Civil War prints, the exposed ceiling beams, and the crackling fires in the twin marble-faced fireplaces. "We local folks aren't used to such luxury."

A drummer boy filled our water glasses, and a Union

soldier brought us a basket of rolls—no hardtack. A Hessian in a splendid uniform stepped up, saluted, and said, "My name is Josh, and I'll be your server today."

I had to avoid Maggie's eyes, for I knew if we connected we'd have an embarrassing attack of giggles. With admirable dignity, we ordered Maryland-style crab cakes and Greek salads.

"Notice the prints?" she asked, after Josh marched toward the kitchen with our order.

They all depicted scenes from Lickin Creek's historic past. One was of General Lee in the square. Another showed Confederate soldiers in front of the old downtown hotel—now a seedy bar—threatening to burn down the town unless ransom was paid.

"Nice touch," I said.

"They're from the Lickin Creek National Bank," Maggie said. "About two years ago, they gave them out free to anyone who opened an account there."

"That must have been a very successful promotion," I said.

Maggie shook her head. "Bad. Lots of hard feelings. Old account holders got mad because only new customers got the prints. Some people even closed their accounts and went over to Gettysburg to do their banking. The LCNB's still suffering from that marketing fiasco."

Josh put our plates in front of us. "Bon appétit," he said, making it sound like *bone appetite*.

The crab cakes were perfectly prepared with huge lumps of crab held together with a small amount of binder and seasoned just right with a spicy seasoning. The Greek salad was even better, heavy on the feta cheese and with lots of black olives—just the way I like it.

Maggie added a dab of tartar sauce to what was left of her crab cake. "This is too good for Lickin Creek."

Josh paused at our table. "Is everything okay, ladies?"

Maggie glared at him. "Do waiters go to a special school to learn exactly when to interrupt a conversation?"

He blanched under his big hat.

"We'd like to talk to the owner," I said. "Could you get him for us?"

His hand went to his mouth, and his eyes grew as round as the shiny brass buttons on his uniform.

"It's a personal matter," I assured him. "Absolutely nothing to do with the food or service, both of which are excellent."

Mouth agape, our Hessian retreated, still looking worried.

"Hate it when they do that," Maggie said, buttering a roll. "Only thing worse is when they ask how everything is when I have a mouth full of food. What are you going to ask the owner about?"

"Rumor says Bernice bankrolled this restaurant for him."

"So?"

"What if she was demanding to be paid back, and he wasn't willing?"

"The restaurant's doing well. I'm sure he could get a bank loan to pay off his debts."

"I wasn't referring to a financial payback. I was thinking more along the lines of marriage."

Maggie spluttered into her iced tea. "You mean you think VeeKay killed Bernice because he didn't want to marry her?"

I looked around to assure myself no one was listening. "Not so loud, Maggie. I only want to learn if he had a motive for wanting her gone. That's all." Maggie called him VeeKay. It was the first time I'd heard his name.

"Do you really think VeeKay would be stupid enough to kill the golden goose?" she asked.

"Maybe—if the goose had stopped laying. Shhh. Here they come."

Maggie looked up and whistled softly. "What a hunk!" she sighed.

"Don't forget you're engaged," I said.

"Doesn't keep me from looking."

The bearded young man who followed Josh was the same man I'd seen with Bernice the night she died. Only today, for some reason, he looked better than I remembered. Unlike his employees, he wore modern clothes; a white dress shirt with the sleeves rolled up to reveal muscular forearms, and jeans riding low over his flat stomach and rising higher in the back, emphasizing a well-developed rear end.

"I understand you wanted to talk to me," he said with a smile. Pulling a chair from a nearby table, he straddled it and folded his arms on the back.

Maggie sighed softly, and I avoided her eyes for fear of acting like a teenage idiot, myself.

"I don't believe we've ever been formally introduced," he said to me. "I'm Vernell Kaltenbaugh, known to most folks around here as VeeKay. Welcome to the Fields of Glory. I hope your lunch was all right?" The two vertical worry lines appearing between his sea-blue eyes were all that marred the smoothness of his forehead, so summer-brown it could only have happened in a tanning bed.

I said softly, so as not to attract any more attention from the nearby diners, "I wanted to tell you how sorry I am about Bernice." My voice trailed away awkwardly. I'd never been very good at expressing sentiment.

"I really appreciate that." He blinked several times, but not before I noticed with surprise that his eyes brimmed with tears.

"Your restaurant is charming," I said inanely, trying to give him a moment to recover his poise. "What a clever idea to use a Civil War theme."

"It was Bernice's idea," he said. "We shared a dream of turning downtown into a cultural oasis. Our opening *Fields of Glory* together was a symbolic start." This time he was unable to blink back the tears, and several ran down his cheeks. He swiped them away. "I suppose it's a lost cause now . . . now . . . that she's gone."

If the tremor in his voice wasn't real, then he was putting on an act worthy of an Oscar.

Maggie retrieved a package of tissues from her purse and handed it to him. He wiped his eyes and dabbed at his nose.

"Sorry," he finally said. "Bernice was the best thing that ever happened to me. We were going to be married as soon as her divorce from Stanley came through."

Josh appeared at Maggie's side with a trayload of desserts.

"Good timing," Maggie snapped. But she went ahead and selected a piece of cherry-covered cheesecake. I shook my head and Josh left.

Maggie turned her full attention to dessert. I turned mine back to Vernell.

"You were going to be married?"

"You sound surprised."

"It's only that . . . how can I put this nicely? . . . Bernice appeared to be quite a bit older."

"Not as much as everybody liked to think," Vernell said, acknowledging that he was well aware of the local gossip. "She was only forty, and I'm twenty-six."

It seemed to me that a good many years had passed since Bernice blew out forty candles on her birthday cake, but I refrained from saying so.

"You look younger than that," I said.

"I work out."

I'd have bet my life on that! "This is such a nice place. Now that Bernice is gone, will you be able to keep it going?"

He sat back in his chair and stared coldly at me. "Are you implying that Bernice paid for all this?" His voice rose high with indignation, and several people turned to stare at us. "What do you think I am? Some sort of gigolo?"

There didn't seem to be an appropriate answer for that question, so I kept quiet.

"Since you're not local, you probably are not aware of the Kaltenbaugh Family Foundation."

"I can't say I am." Once again, my outsider status was being thrown in my face. Not only had I never heard of it, I couldn't even pronounce it.

Maggie looked up with interest. "Kaltenbaugh Foundation? Doesn't that own half of Pittsburgh?"

Vernell nodded. "It was established by my great-grandfather."

"I guess you're telling me that Bernice didn't back you financially," I said.

"Hardly. As a matter-of-fact, the foundation was looking into buying her property and building the cultural center she wanted so badly." He pushed up from his chair and glared down at Maggie. "You can tell your grapevine informants that they were way off this time."

When he was out of earshot, Maggie let out a little yip. "We sure were wrong about him."

"We don't know that he was telling the truth," I pointed out.

"I'll check out his story this afternoon," she promised. "As well-known as the Kaltenbaugh Foundation is in Pennsylvania, I'm sure I'll have no trouble finding out if he's really part of it. I'll let you know what I uncover."

"Even if Bernice's money wasn't the motive, there still could have been other reasons why he'd want her out of the way," I said. But my suspicions that Vernell had murdered Bernice were vanishing as fast as Maggie's cheesecake.

"Got to get back to work," Maggie said, looking around for Josh. "Where's a waiter when you need one? For goodness' sake, there's Luscious Miller—coming our way. Wonder what he wants here?"

As the deputy strode across the room, it was clear what Luscious wanted was me. Out of breath, he plopped down on the chair recently vacated by Vernell Kaltenbaugh and pulled off his hat.

"What's up?" I asked.

He tried to answer but only emitted a series of wheezes. "Sorry," he said at last. "Riding that bike in cold weather always brings on my asthma."

I handed him my untouched water glass, and he slowly sipped from it until the worst of the wheezing stopped.

"I wanted to tell you I just received the coroner's report on Oretta. She didn't die in the fire."

"Of course she did, Luscious. I saw her body."

"I know she's dead, Tori. What I meant is she didn't die *from* the fire."

"People often don't burn to death in a fire, Luscious. They suffocate."

"I'm not totally stupid, you know."

I was ashamed of myself for assuming he was always inept. "What was it, then?"

"Henry says she was shot in the head. And, Tori, there was no gun on the scene. Me and the firemen have gone over every inch of the ruins."

"Of course there wasn't," Maggie said. "Oretta was scared to death of guns. Wouldn't allow one in her house. Even made Matavious keep his hunting rifles at his office."

No matter what I thought of Henry Hoopengartner's lack of qualifications to be a coroner, I knew even he could recognize a bullet hole. "Was he able to say what kind of gun was used?"

Luscious shook his head. "Body's been sent to Harrisburg for an autopsy. I'll let you'uns know soon as I get the report."

"Luscious, have you found out where Matavious was last night?" I asked.

"He won't talk to me."

"That's terrible. Can't you make him?"

"You can't make people talk to the police, Tori. Even if we charged him with murder, he still has the right to remain silent."

Maggie looked up from wiping the crumbs off her blouse. "And Bernice was murdered, too! Tori, you could be in danger!"

"What are you getting at?" I asked.

"Don't you see? Bernice and Oretta played sugar plum fairies in the Christmas pageant. And they were both murdered. Tori, you were the third sugar plum fairy. You could be the next victim!"

CHAPTER 14

Sing, O sing this blessed morn

OUTSIDE THE RESTAURANT, MAGGIE HUGGED me good-bye as if I were sailing on the *Titanic* and she knew about the iceberg.

"Don't worry about me," I told her. "I really doubt there's a serial killer around with a grudge against sugar plum fairies."

After she left, I pulled up my hood against the cold wind and considered my options for the afternoon. Now that the weekly paper was on its way to the printer, my time was free—at least for the rest of the day.

Maggie's remark about my being in danger because of my part in the play had struck me as rather silly, but now, as I thought about it, it didn't seem quite as preposterous. However, it also occurred to me that I'd only been a substitute for the real sugar plum fairy—Weezie Clopper.

I needed to talk to Weezie anyway about her letter to the editor, with misspellings in it similar to the ones in poor Bernice's "death threat." I headed back to the *Chronicle* building to get Garnet's truck.

"What Cloppers is that?" asked the teenager at the gas station where I stopped for five gallons of overpriced gasoline and some free directions.

"Weezie and Jackson," I said, hopeful he'd know whom I was talking about.

"Oh, sure, the Jackson what's the borough manager." He painfully counted out my change and gave me directions in typical Lickin Creek style. "Take the Old Mill Road south for about three miles, look for the burnt maple tree. It'll either be on your left or your right. Turn there onto Orphanage Road, go about a mile to where the fruit stand used to be, then watch for the Hillside Mennonite Church. Hang a left at the cemetery, go past the Martin Farm—or maybe it's the Mellott Farm—till you get to the dirt lane. That's the Clopper place. You can't miss it."

To my great surprise, I found it, with no trouble. I was beginning to understand the local lingo!

A small, faded sign nailed to a fence post said ALTERATIONS and KNIVES SHARPENED. The winding lane was muddy from melted snow. I gritted my teeth and drove slowly down it to the two-story brick farmhouse nestled at the bottom of a hill.

A flock of Canadian geese who had taken up residence beside a partly frozen pond flapped their wings but didn't seem to be concerned by my presence. There was a general air of seediness to the property, from the white paint flaking off the wood trim of the house to the leaning red barn. A wheelless tractor was suspended on cement blocks next to the house. A scruffy German shepherd sniffed at my tires, then slunk back into the barn.

I knocked on the front door before noticing a handwritten sign saying COME IN. Pushing open the door, I stuck my head in and called out, "Hello . . . anybody home?"

From somewhere in the back, I heard the whir of a sewing machine. There was no answer to my question, so I went in, closing the door behind me.

There was no entrance hall. I stepped directly into the living room, furnished with the heavy red-plush furniture I associate with the Depression era. An artificial Christmas tree stood in one corner, but it did nothing to brighten the room. A gloomy Jesus looked down at me from several picture frames.

I passed through a dining room, crowded with the kind of enormous, dark oak furniture one would expect to find in El Cid's castle, and followed the sewing machine sound into a large kitchen.

Weezie looked up and nodded. "Have a seat. I'll be finished with this in a jiffy."

I moved a laundry basket full of clothes off a chair and sat down at the table. A hearty wail erupted from the basket.

"What the . . . ?" I exclaimed.

"It's my granddaughter." Weezie rose from her sewing and extracted a crying baby from the mound of clothes. "I sit her while my daughter works at the Giant Big-Mart."

She held the baby and stroked its back until the crying stopped, then gently replaced her in the basket and covered her with a towel. While she was busy with her grandchild, I had plenty of time to look around the kitchen and notice that it was a cheery place, unlike the gloomy front rooms. I found the red and white checked curtains at the windows and the Blue Willow china on the plate rail charming. Less charming was the purple shiner Weezie sported around her left eye.

"What happened to your eye?" I asked.

"Walked into a door." Her brazen stare dared me to argue with her.

"Sorry to hear that." She made me think of Mrs. Poffenberger, another abused wife. Didn't anybody have decent marriages anymore?

"Let's have a cup a coffee." Weezie filled two blue and white graniteware mugs from the coffeepot on the stove. "Sugar's on the table. Want milk?"

"Please," I said.

She took a plastic milk container from the refrigerator, dropped it on the table, and sat down across from me to watch me doctor my coffee.

"I don't often use real milk and sugar. This is a real treat for me," I said with a smile.

"Don't hold with that artificial stuff. It all causes cancer, you know. You like Christian music?"

"I . . . guess so. A long time ago when we lived in Okinawa, I sang with a Sunday school chorus. We did *The Messiah* at an Easter sunrise service on a cliff overlooking the China Sea." I stopped, because Weezie was staring at me as if I were speaking an unfamiliar language.

"Lived in Oklahoma, huh? Had a cousin went there once. But I didn't mean classical stuff. I'm talking about *Christian* music."

She jumped up and left the room for a minute. When she returned she was carrying a small electronic keyboard. She plugged it into the wall, hit a loud chord that provoked a fresh round of screams from the basket baby, and began to sing in a loud voice, "Neeeee-rer mah God, tuh thee, Neeeee-rer tuh thee . . ."

With a smile pasted on my face, I listened to what seemed like hundreds of hymns. The baby, thankfully, stopped screaming somewhere in the middle of "What uh fuh-rend we hey-vuh in Jeeee-sus." The wall clock must have stopped, I decided, or else it was running very slowly because that big hand only showed ten minutes had gone by when I knew several hours must have passed.

When she finally stopped, I applauded. Not too enthusiastically. I didn't want to encourage an encore.

"I get real pleasure out of my God-given talent," she said.

"And so must your family," I remarked.

"Jackson don't care much for music." She unplugged the keyboard and wiped the keys with a towel. "You want something altered?"

"Actually, that's not why I'm here."

She looked at me suspiciously.

"I've come regarding a letter you wrote to the paper. About the cultural center and shopping mall Bernice wanted to build downtown."

"What about it?"

"Before we print any letter to the editor, we always verify that the letter actually came from the person who signed it." That was the truth, but usually a quick phone call took care of the matter.

"I done wrote it. You gonna print it?"

"I'd like to," I said, "but I have to make sure you aren't trying to profit from it in some way."

She squirmed in her seat. "I don't catch your drift."

I took a chance and said, "Everybody knows you and Jackson want to sell your farm to a mall developer. Did you want to stop Bernice because she was a business rival?"

Weezie spluttered. "No way! Besides, our deal's off."

Sometimes the best way to get information out of people is to say nothing, so I waited.

"It's 'cause of Matavious. He went and sold his farming rights to the Conservation Bank. Now nobody can ever use his place for nothing but farming. The builder backed out of our deal, then . . . said he had to have both Clopper farms."

"Why would he have done that? Surely, selling the

farm would have been lucrative for him." She looked blank, so I added, "Would have made him lots of money."

"They don't need it. He's real rich, you know. Doctors always are. He did it out of spite . . . he hates my husband."

"Any particular reason? Boundary disputes or something?"

She shook her head. "Jackson's great-granddaddy fought on the wrong side in the War. Nobody round here lets us forget it. Especially them other Cloppers . . . they say our side of the family disgraced the family name."

"The Civil War was a long time ago," I said. "Do you really think people still hold a grudge over something that happened nearly a hundred and forty years ago?"

"I don't think . . . I know!"

"Perhaps he did it to preserve the land for future generations," I pointed out. "Farms around here are getting scarce, with all the new suburbs going in."

"That's what Oretta said . . . damn bleeding heart! Excuse my language. She cared more for them animals at the shelter than she did for people."

Her outburst against Oretta prompted me to ask, "Where were you last night . . . around one in the morning?"

"Home in bed with my husband, where a decent woman should be." Her eyes opened wide as she began to grasp what I was hinting. "Are you hinting I burned down her house? If anybody said so, then they're a damn liar. Excuse my language."

"I haven't heard any such thing, Weezie. But the authorities may be asking questions later, of anyone with a grudge against Oretta. You did know she was murdered, didn't you?"

Weezie's hands fluttered to her face, stifling a shocked whimper.

I moved quickly back to discussing Bernice. "If you weren't going to be involved with a rival mall, why were you so opposed to the downtown development?" I asked.

"I'm a good Christian woman," she sniffed. "I don't hold with that kind of stuff Bernice was into."

"What kind of stuff?"

"Satanism."

"Satanism? Could you explain?"

"I found out Bernice was into that witchcraft stuff," she said. "And I done read all about it . . . they have nekked sex, you know, and drink the blood of babies!" She touched the basket as if to reassure herself that her granddaughter was still there—safe from all things that go bump in the night.

"I have something I want you to look at." From my purse, I retrieved the letter Bernice had thought of as a death threat. "You wrote this, didn't you? You sent Bernice an anonymous letter threatening her," I said as I unfolded it.

"What makes you think so?" she said, glaring at me defiantly.

"You misspelled *San Antonio* the same way in the letter you wrote to the paper."

Her face turned guilt-red.

"You called Bernice 'which one.' You misspelled *witch*, too. With all the reading you say you've done about witchcraft, I'd think you'd at least have learned how to spell the word."

Weezie snatched the letter from my hand and tore it into tiny pieces.

"It's a photocopy," I said.

"She didn't have no right to make all that money. Her and her evil ways."

"That was enough of a reason to threaten to kill her?"

"I didn't say nothing about killing her. I only meant I was going to tell on her. I figured if decent folk knew what kind of person she was, they'd run her out of town—at least stop her from getting richer off the good people what lives here—and she wouldn't drink no more baby blood."

I was getting nauseous, and it wasn't from thinking about baby blood. If there were other "good" people like Weezie in Lickin Creek, I could understand why Cassie thought it wise to keep quiet about her wiccan activities. And thinking of Cassie, I asked, "You're the one who tried to scare Cassie Kriner, aren't you? By leaving the broomsticks on our door."

Her flushed face told me I was right. Religion and superstition are close cousins.

I picked up my purse and stood, preparing to leave. "I hope you realize you might be in danger," I said.

A look of panic spread across Weezie's flat face.

"Two Lickin Creek women who were playing sugar plum fairies have been murdered. You were the third fairy. There's a pretty good chance you could be the next victim." Scaring her wasn't very nice, I knew, but I felt some moral satisfaction at shaking up her narrow, self-righteous world.

Outside, ignoring the pungent odor of fertilizer in the air, I took a deep breath then headed for my truck. Weezie stood in the doorway and watched me back up. I couldn't help noticing her shabby cotton dress, so inappropriate for the winter. And the black eye, of course. And suddenly I felt sad . . . for her . . . for Mrs. Poffenberger . . . and for all the women like them living hopeless lives. Weezie needed to be hugged, not rebuked, but before I could make a move, she went back into the house and closed the door.

All the way back to town, I thought about Weezie and Jackson and their relationship. She could have been telling the truth about walking into a door, but I doubted it. During our conversation, Weezie had let me know she intensely disliked both Oretta and Bernice. Matavious, too. Was the mousy little seamstress fanatic enough to murder two people?

Back in the borough, the streets were once again torn up for repairs. This time the detour took me through the old section of town, where many deserted commercial buildings spoke of more prosperous times. Ahead of me was the enormous redbrick building that Bernice and Vernell Kaltenbaugh had hoped to turn into an oasis of art and culture. I stopped the truck to take a look at it.

Size was one of the only two things going for it. The place was definitely large enough to contain a lot of stores and art studios, and even the theatre Bernice had hoped would bring music and drama to Lickin Creek.

What really made the site special was the Lickin Creek itself. The sparkling little river tumbled in a waterfall over a small dam, meandered through some underbrush and under a crumbling stone bridge, then disappeared into an archway in the side of the old cold-storage building.

Curious about where it went, I got out of the truck to take a look. Along the base of the building were several arches, about three feet high, covered with wire mesh. To look through one, I knelt on the cracked macadam parking lot and saw that beneath the building the creek spread out into a huge tar-black lake. There was no way to tell how deep it was, but the water was so still and dark it gave the appearance of being bottomless.

My favorite childhood poem by Coleridge came to

mind, and I recited, " 'Where Alph, the sacred river, ran / Through caverns measureless to man / Down to a sunless sea.' " It was here that Bernice had dreamed of building her "stately pleasure dome." Could this deserted part of town really be brought to life again, as San Antonio had done with its River Walk?

As I stood up, dusting off my knees, I noticed a flight of rusted iron steps leading up to a doorway. And the door was slightly ajar. This was a siren call, urging me to climb the stairs and take a look inside the building. A NO TRESPASSING sign was tacked on the door, and beneath it someone had spray-painted a pentacle in a circle and written SATAN LIVES. I looked around to see if anybody was watching and pushed on the door. It creaked, rattled, and screeched as it opened just wide enough to allow me to slip inside.

At first, I found it too dark to see anything and was about to give up in disappointment. But my eyes soon adjusted, and I discerned that I stood on a concrete landing overlooking the mysterious lake. A flight of stairs to my right led to the upper floors of the building.

I soon wished I'd stayed home and minded my own business. The steps were of some kind of metal mesh that I could see through, straight down to the water below, and my vertigo kicked in. And even worse, the whole staircase was creaking and shaking, threatening to pull away from the wall. Realizing I was nearly at the top, I clutched the rail and kept going on wobbly legs until I stepped off the stairs and onto a blessedly solid concrete floor.

How was I ever going to get back down? There had to be another flight of stairs—just had to be! Hoping to find another way out, I looked around the cavernous room, dimly lit by the small amount of light filtering through the cracks in the boarded-up windows. I didn't see another exit, although the room was so large and dark that I realized there could be one somewhere.

What I did see, in the center of the room, was a long table, covered with black cloth. I walked over to take a closer look and saw on it several candles in a variety of colors, a brass bowl full of something smelling sweetly of dried orange peels and incense, a crystal goblet that looked like genuine Waterford, a ceramic statue of the Chinese goddess Kwan Yin, and a dagger with an ornately carved ebony handle. Without a doubt, this had to be where Cassie's coven met. Everything on the table was too expensive and too sophisticated to belong to a group of teenagers in a cult.

I'd discounted as nonsense Weezie's frightened statement that wiccans drank "baby's blood," but now, seeing the dagger on this makeshift altar, I wondered.

"Hands up, you little shit, or I'll blow your frigging head off." Although I'd heard nobody come up the creaky stairs, someone obviously had and was standing close behind me.

My arms flew up in the air, reaching for the ceiling.

"Don't shoot," I cried. "Please. I'm a reporter."

From behind me came a strangled sound I recognized as laughter. "Some'uns would think that was reason enough to shoot you. Turn around."

I did as ordered and immediately recognized Stanley Roadcap's melancholy face.

"I thought you were one of those teenagers that break in all the time. I should have known it'd be you."

Smiling innocently, I hoped, I said politely, "May I put my arms down, please?"

He pointed the barrels of the double-barreled shotgun at the floor, and I dropped my hands to my sides.

"What do you mean you should have known it was me?"

"I heard you'uns been running around town asking questions about my wife and Oretta. It was only a matter of time till you showed up here." He pointed with his chin to the altar, and a look of distaste crossed his face.

"That's true, Mr. Roadcap. I've been attempting to find out who killed them. I'd think you'd be grateful for that . . . unless you have a reason for not wanting me to learn the truth."

The gun barrel jerked up—for a moment I thought Stanley really was going to shoot me—then dropped once more toward the floor.

"What are you talking about?" he asked.

"I'm talking about murder, and you know it." I sounded brave, but my insides were quaking. If Stanley really was a murderer, he could shoot me inside this deserted building, drop me into the black water below, and nobody would ever know what had happened to me.

"Why on earth would you'uns think I killed my wife?" He managed to sound astounded that such a thought could cross anybody's mind.

"People say she wanted a divorce and you didn't."

"That's right. I loved Bernice enough to wait for her to come to her senses. This kind of thing's happened before with her."

"What kind of thing?"

"Rehab romance, they call it. Every couple of years, she decides to sober up, goes off to a place like Betty Ford, meets a young guy who's got more problems than her, decides she's in love, and asks me for a divorce. After a few months, a year once, she falls off the wagon and asks to come home. That's how she met this VeeKay character. He was into crack, heroin, meth, you name it. Bernice probably thought she was going to save him from himself. At Al-Anon, they say it's a mutual codependence that occurs fairly often with certain types of addiction. I think that's why she was into this kind of stuff, too."

I was sure "this kind of stuff" meant witchcraft. "Bernice had been drinking when I talked to her," I said. "And the night she died."

He nodded. "All part of her pattern. The next step would have been to break off her relationship with that young punk."

Perhaps she already had, I thought. VeeKay might have already received the bad news—that he was out and Stanley was back in. Was his dependency on Bernice so strong that he'd kill her rather than give her up? Was there any truth in what Stanley Roadcap was telling me?

"Were Bernice and Oretta Clopper particularly close?" I asked, still hoping to find the missing link—the one thing that would lead someone to murder both women.

"Not really," he said. "Bernice enjoyed working with the Little Lickin Creek Theatre and was in a couple of plays Oretta wrote. But she used to laugh with me about what a bad writer Oretta was. I don't think they saw each other much away from the theatre."

While we'd been talking, the afternoon light coming through the cracks between the boards on the windows had dimmed. "Come on," he said. "Let's go while we can still see."

The thought of going down that rickety staircase petrified me. "I'm afraid of the stairs . . . the whole thing nearly pulled away from the wall as I was coming up."

"Geez! You didn't use the iron staircase? It's liable to collapse any minute."

"That's rather dangerous," I said. "You could be sued if someone got hurt."

"Not with NO TRESPASSING signs pasted all over the building," he pointed out. "There's another way. Solid concrete stairwell. Nothing to worry about."

Although it was still afternoon, the sky was dark by the time I pulled into the circular drive of my Moon Lake mansion. The porch light was on, welcoming me home after my strange afternoon. Thankfully, all the media trucks and vans were gone. Lickin Creek was no longer newsworthy, and I was glad of it.

In the kitchen, Praxythea, who was stirring something in a mixing bowl, glanced up and asked, "Where have you been?"

"I spent half the afternoon on a farm interviewing a religious bigot, and the rest of the time I was held at gunpoint in a deserted building somewhere in Lickin Creek."

"That's nice," she said, obviously not listening. "Would you take the cookies out of the oven, please?"

I put on two oven mitts and removed three trays of cookies, while Noel watched with curiosity. I was doing something she'd never seen me do before. "What's with the domesticity?"

Praxythea was wearing a dainty white organdy apron. I wondered if she always traveled with one in her luggage, in case the urge to cook struck unexpectedly. "We agreed to have an old-fashioned Christmas," she said. "That means lots of cookies. And my special fruitcake, of course." Opening the refrigerator, she pointed at the huge ceramic bowl taking up an entire shelf.

"What is it?" I asked, peering at an assortment of brightly colored lumps floating in something that smelled of alcohol.

"It's the base for my fruitcake. All the candied fruit

and nuts need to soak overnight in a syrup of sugar, lemon juice, and port wine to absorb the flavors. It would be better to let it sit for at least a week, but this will have to do.

"Your mail's on the table."

I flipped through the envelopes and catalogs. By this time I'd given up expecting to get a letter from Garnet, so I wasn't disappointed. Well, maybe just a little, but I hid it well.

One of the envelopes, with a row of brightly colored foreign stamps, caught my eye because the handwriting was unfamiliar. Usually letters with that country's postmark came from my father.

I ripped it open and looked at the signature. "Tyfani Miracle. It's from my father's new wife!"

Praxythea said, "Yummy," but I think it was because she was licking cookie dough from her fingers, and not because I received a letter from the bimbo my father had married.

"She says she's going to be coming back to the States in the spring with the baby . . . can't wait to meet me . . . heard so much about me from my father . . . I can imagine! Wonder what he's told her about my mother?"

"Don't be bitter, Tori. He deserves to be happy."

"Shows what you don't know," I grumbled. Secretly, I was pleased to receive the letter. At least Tyfani had some of the right instincts. I folded it carefully, and put it in my purse, to reread later. The baby, she wrote, was due any day. Maybe even had been born by now. I couldn't wait to find out if I had a brother or sister.

"Call them," Praxythea said, as if reading my mind.

"Maybe on Christmas," I said. "My father gets mad if I don't wait for the holiday rates."

She smiled and resumed dropping dough onto the cookie sheets.

"Has Fred come home?" I asked, hopeful but fearing the worst.

She shook her head. "I've been all over the neighborhood, calling him." Catching my downcast look, she added, "Don't worry too much, Tori. I have a strong feeling someone has taken him in. I called the local radio station and asked them to make some announcements. I'm sure we'll hear from someone soon."

"I didn't get much sleep last night," I said. "I think I'll go lie down for a little while." What I really wanted was to have a good cry over Fred—in private.

"I'll wake you in plenty of time to get to the church," Praxythea said.

I looked at her blankly. "Church?" Then I remembered—tonight was the memorial service for Eddie Douglas, the little boy who'd drowned in the quarry so many years ago.

CHAPTER 15

Lullay, thou little tiny child

"TORI, WHAT HAPPENED TO YOUR FACE?" Maggie Roy's sly grin indicated she knew exactly what had caused the strange indentations on my cheeks.

"I did battle with a chenille bedspread and lost," I said. "Next time I'll remove it before taking an afternoon nap."

We were standing in the foyer of Trinity Evangelical Church, watching people arrive for Eddie Douglas's memorial service. Every stratum of Lickin Creek's society was represented, from farmers and shopkeepers to professionals. Many of them I recognized; some even came over to congratulate me for rescuing Kevin Poffenberger, and that made me feel really good—at last I was beginning to fit in. It didn't even bother me that Weezie Clopper, in dark glasses and accompanied by her husband, pretended she hadn't seen me.

We attracted a lot of stares from the more conventionally dressed people who streamed in. I assumed that most of them found us to be a strange-looking trio. Praxythea wore a floor-length, skintight cheongsam of white satin, slit to the hip on both sides. She looked something like a redheaded swan, with the mandarin collar exaggerating the length of her neck. White was the Chinese color for mourning, she'd explained when I questioned her choice of funeral garb.

Maggie and I had chosen to wear nearly identical navy-blue suits. Mine was left over from my working days in New York, where a tailored navy-blue suit had been a requirement for a reporter. When we were joined by Ginnie Welburn, we looked like a trio of uniformed security guards.

By the time we entered the church, the back pews were already filled. Praxythea, with a serene smile on her face, stepped forward and led us down the center aisle to seats in the front row.

A giggling middle-school girl handed us programs.

"I've never felt so conspicuous," Ginnie whispered to me.

"You'll get used to it if you hang out with Praxythea for any length of time," I told her, opening my program.

"What's it say?" Ginnie asked. "I didn't bring my reading glasses."

" 'Memorial service for L. Edward Douglas, Jr., son of the late Lemuel E. Douglas, Sr., and Miriam Hopkiss Douglas,' " I read. "I wonder what happened to them."

Maggie, as usual, knew the answer. "Moved to a little town in Texas. A few months later, Lem shot his wife and himself. Friends down there said they never recovered from losing Eddie."

My eyes brimmed with tears, and to hide my emotion I returned to reading the program. "Here's a surprise: 'Trinity Evangelical Church is grateful to Dr. Matavious Clopper for his generous sponsorship of this memorial service.' My goodness, how thoughtful of him to do this—especially with the tragedy he's just suffered."

Maggie, sitting on my other side, between Praxythea and me, uttered a derisive "Humph."

"What is it?" I asked.

"He didn't do anything. Oretta set all this up the day she died. Matavious couldn't exactly stop it. Not without looking like a real Scrooge."

Ginnie leaned across me to ask, "Do you know why she did it?"

Something I recalled made me answer. "Right after Eddie's body was found, Oretta said to me that 'Lickin Creek takes care of its own.' This must have been her way of showing how much she cared." Weezie Clopper had told me she believed Oretta liked animals better than people. This proved she was very wrong about the woman. The flowers alone had to have cost a fortune.

Reverend Flack entered the sanctuary from a side door, took a position behind the teddy-bear-covered altar, and held up his arms. His robe was splendid, a far cry from what I would have expected a Lickin Creek minister to wear.

The congregation hushed, and then, from the back of the church came the sound of bagpipes. I turned to Maggie with a questioning look.

"Reverend Flack's cousin," she whispered. "Lots of Scotch-Irish here. Plays at most of their funerals."

All heads turned as the piper, in formal Scottish garb, slowly walked down the aisle playing "Skye Boat Song." Behind him came pallbearers, carrying a tiny white coffin containing Eddie Douglas's remains. I had to press that special spot on my upper lip to keep tears from flowing.

"Carry the lad that's born to be king, over the sea to Skye." The music ended, and the piper stepped to one side of the altar and stood at attention as the coffin was placed on a stand before it.

The service was touching, even though no one there seemed to have actually known the child. One after another, members of the church came to the front to read prayers, and several added their personal thoughts about childhood in general.

As it went on, I thought about the world as it had been when Eddie died. The sixties: the Age of Aquarius and Vietnam, turmoil and violence on college campuses, flower power and drugs, Dylan and Baez, psychedelic clothing and love beads, children who "left their hearts in San Francisco" and, in many cases, their minds. It really had been the age of innocence, when young people still believed they could make a difference. Another time, another world.

Eddie would have been too young to participate in any of that, of course. A child's view of the sixties would be pretty much that of any child at any time. If he'd lived, Eddie would be in his forties now, I realized. Perhaps balding, a little overweight, in need of reading glasses, maybe even a grandfather. But Eddie had missed all the joys and sorrows that life could bring and would be forever five years old. My nose tingled, and I had to pinch my upper lip again.

Maggie nudged me, bringing me back to the present. "Wake up," she whispered.

"I'm not sleeping, just thinking."

The Reverend Flack gave the signal for us to stand, and the piper stepped forward. I was sure of what was coming next and rooted fruitlessly in my bag for a Kleenex. Maggie handed me one of hers. I was right—as the pallbearers carried the coffin out, "Amazing Grace" filled the church. Nothing in the world could keep me from crying when I hear that beautiful hymn played on the bagpipes.

In the foyer, everybody was sniffing and blowing noses. A red-eyed Primrose Flack came over to get a tissue from Maggie, who seemed to have an endless supply.

"How I wish someone from his family could have been here to know he's finally been found," Primrose said.

"I'm sure they're watching from heaven," Ginnie said.

This was so unlike her usual sarcastic remarks that I looked at her to see if she was kidding. She appeared to be serious.

"How awful to think of him lying there all those years in that cold, dark water." Maggie had a catch in her voice.

"But at least he was at peace," Ginnie pointed out.

"Is he going to be buried here?" I asked.

Primrose shook her head. "My husband found out his parents are buried in Jasper, Texas. The body's being shipped there tomorrow."

"It's nice they're going to be reunited, even if they are all dead," Ginnie said.

"This is getting too gloomy," Praxythea said. "I have an idea. We all need to be cheered up. Let's go back to Tori's house and trim her tree. We can make it a sort of old-fashioned all-girl party, late-night snacks and all. It will be fun."

"Praxythea," I whispered. "There's nothing in the house to feed them."

"Don't worry about it. I baked cookies all day, and I bought gallons of eggnog. We're all set."

So Praxythea's party invitation was not quite as extemporaneous as she expected us to believe. I didn't have any Christmas ornaments, either, but I was sure Praxythea had already taken care of that little matter.

Because it was late and everybody was so downhearted, I was surprised when Maggie and Ginnie immediately agreed to come over. Even Primrose accepted, saying she'd be along as soon as she could tell her

husband where she was going. However, since the reverend was very busy shaking hands and hugging babies,
that might be a while.

Driving Garnet's truck, with Praxythea practically
glowing in the dark beside me, I drove home to Moon
Lake with Maggie and Ginnie following close behind in
their cars.

Praxythea shed her white fur coat, covered her white
satin gown with her organdy apron, piled little moon-
shaped cookies on Wedgwood plates, and poured chips
into ceramic bowls. While I petted Noel, who was obviously depressed at being separated from Fred, Ginnie
poured eggnog and a bottle of brandy into the Waterford
punch bowl, and Maggie, following orders from Praxythea, searched for linen napkins in a drawer in the
pantry.

We carried everything into the front parlor, where the
giant Christmas tree stood. Oohs from Ginnie and aahs
from Maggie pleased Praxythea, who recounted the story
about bringing it from Lancaster strapped to the roof of
a stretch limo.

"Here we go," Praxythea said. "I made popcorn this
afternoon—for stringing. There's red construction paper
and paste for making garlands. Does everybody remember how from kindergarten? And," she said, pointing to
three enormous cardboard boxes, "I bought a few little
ornaments to fill in the gaps. Lights go on first, I think.
My household staff usually takes care of that part."

"Me, too," Maggie giggled. "My butler does it all."

We wound the strings around the tree and plugged
them in. After a few bulb replacements, the tree sparkled
with hundreds of tiny white lights.

Ginnie ladled eggnog into four crystal mugs, then settled down on a sofa with a bag of popcorn, a needle, and
a spool of plastic thread, while Maggie gravitated toward

the construction paper. "Just like the children's room at the library," she said.

Praxythea handed me a bowl of cranberries. "Why don't you string these?" she suggested before leaving the room.

It was an impossible task. The little red balls were as hard as rocks. I stabbed myself with the needle half a dozen times and only succeeded in staining my fingertips red.

"I give up," I announced. "Hand me a bag of popcorn, please."

It was much easier to poke a needle through the soft popcorn, and an added benefit was I could nibble on it as I worked. While my popcorn garland lengthened, I couldn't help thinking this was a sad little gathering, despite all of Praxythea's attempts at gaiety. I was feeling lonelier by the minute and missed my cat, Garnet, my mother, and my few good friends in New York. For the first time in many years, I thought about Nobuko, the Okinawan woman who lived with us from the time I was born and was practically my second mother, and wondered how she was.

Praxythea, despite her fame, also claimed to have no one in her life. Ginnie was a widow, who'd moved to a town where outsiders were rarely accepted. And Maggie? I wondered why she wasn't with her fiancé this evening.

"When are we going to have the snacks?" Maggie asked after we'd worked for twenty minutes or so. "I'm getting hungry."

"I thought we'd wait for Primrose," Praxythea said. "Have some more eggnog." She had returned, with Icky draped over her left shoulder. "He was lonely." She stroked the beast's head.

"Yuck!" Ginnie squealed. "It looks like a dragon. Keep it away from me—far away."

Maggie didn't say anything, but she quietly placed her scissors and paste on the couch cushion next to her so Praxythea couldn't sit there.

"I don't understand you three," Praxythea said. "He's a sweetheart. Iguanas may look frightening, but they are really very gentle. Why, just last night, he—" The ringing of chimes interrupted her. "What's that?"

"It's the front doorbell." I took off for the front hall at a run, praying that the person on the porch wouldn't be crushed to death by the roof before I got there.

I jerked open the door, dragged Primrose in by one arm, then closed the door gently so as not to disturb anything.

"Well!" Primrose said, shaking off my hand. "That was some greeting."

"I'm sorry. It's just that the porch roof is about to collapse. I guess you didn't see my sign."

"It would help if you turned on the porch light. A person could break her neck out there in the dark."

She placed the small paper bag she was holding on the silver calling-card tray next to the door. I assumed she'd brought something to eat, or maybe even an ornament for the tree. "Why, thank you, Primrose—" I began.

"Don't thank me. I found it next to your front door. It has your name on it."

As she shrugged off her coat, a burst of laughter came from the front room. I had the feeling the "girls" had dipped into the eggnog again.

"You've got to see what Maggie's made for us," Praxythea called.

"Come on in and have some of Praxythea's crescent cookies," I told Primrose. "They look wonderful." I led her into the parlor, where she was greeted with warm cries of welcome from the three women wearing red and green crowns decorated with popcorn "jewels."

Praxythea poured eggnog for Primrose and refilled Ginnie's and Maggie's cups. I declined, since I really don't care for sweet drinks.

"I found a tape player and some Christmas tapes in the dining room breakfront while I was looking for the punch bowl," Praxythea announced. She fiddled for a moment or two with the little black box until Andy Williams's smooth baritone voice filled the room with "O Come All Ye Faithful."

After several more cups of eggnog, our homemade decorations were complete—and only a little peculiar-looking. We danced around the tree, entwining the popcorn strings and paper garlands, while Bobby Vinton sang "Christmas Eve in My Home Town."

"It is beautiful. Really beautiful," Praxythea announced. "It looks as I imagined it would. So country. So homey. So old-fashioned. So—"

"So tacky," Maggie interrupted. "Let's put the store-bought decorations on. It might look better."

We unloaded Praxythea's ornament boxes. Everything was very lovely and very expensive-looking, although I thought she'd gone rather heavy on stars and moons. We loaded the branches and stepped back to admire our work.

"*Now* it's beautiful," Maggie said. "So elegant. So sophisticated. So—"

While she grasped for another adjective, Praxythea interrupted. "Let's toast the tree."

We switched off the lamps, so the only light in the room came from the tree. With arms entwined, we sang "Silent Night" with Perry Como.

I heard several sniffles. " 'Silent Night' always makes me cry," Ginnie said.

Maggie handed her a Kleenex, then blew her own nose. "Me, too."

Even Praxythea's eyes were moist, and Primrose kept her face turned away from us.

"What makes me cry is seeing a group of women who have had too much to drink acting maudlin," I said. "I do believe the party's over."

I wasn't about to let any of them drive home in that condition. Maggie accepted my invitation to sleep over.

"I'll walk home and pick up my car in the morning," Ginnie said.

"And I'll call my husband," Primrose announced.

It was about another half hour before Reverend Flack arrived and the party officially ended. At first, I interpreted Reverend Flack's frowning countenance as disapproval, but then I realized it was really concern. He helped his wife into her coat, propped her up against the wall in the kitchen, and went back to the living room with me to find her bag.

"You're a very understanding husband," I remarked as we hunted for her purse among the empty ornament boxes.

"I'm not one to throw stones," he said. "Christmas is a rough time of year for my wife. It brings back memories of her birth parents. They died in a car accident on Christmas Eve when Primrose was seven."

"I'm sorry. I didn't know that."

"It's not the kind of thing that would come up in casual conversation. Ah! Here it is." He held up Primrose's missing purse.

"Thank you for having her over tonight, Tori. Mostly, local people wouldn't think of inviting her to something like this. I believe they think a minister's wife has to be serious all the time."

We rejoined the ladies and the lizard in the kitchen.

"I'll drop Ginnie off at her house," Reverend Flack said.

"What a nice man," I said, after they'd left. "I wonder if I'll ever have someone like that in my life."

"You already do," Praxythea said, placing Icky back in his glass home.

"I wonder . . . Let's put the cookies and chips away and get to bed."

We went back to the parlor and gathered up the debris from our party.

"What about the paper and empty ornament boxes?" Praxythea asked.

"We can get all that in the morning. I'll just out the lights in the foyer."

" 'Out the lights'?"

"I'm speaking Lickin Creekese," I said as I went into the front hall. There I saw the paper bag with my name on it.

"What's that?" Praxythea said behind me.

"I don't know. Primrose said she found it on the porch." I opened the bag and peeked in.

"Odd. It looks like a stuffed toy." I pulled the little object out of the bag. It was one of those collectible bean-bag animals. Orange and white. Like Fred.

"Why, it's a little toy cat. How cute," Praxythea cooed.

"It's not cute at all." I held it so Praxythea could see there was a knife stuck in its belly, and some of the beans clattered onto the floor.

"Oh, my God!" I screamed.

"What?"

"A note. On the back of the tag." I couldn't bring myself to read the foul words out loud and handed it to Praxythea.

She read, " 'Stay out of our business or I'll do this to your other cat, too.' "

CHAPTER 16

Jolly old Saint Nicholas

THE BLUSTERING WIND THREATENED TO PUSH my truck into a barren field as I drove the very quiet Maggie home on Saturday morning. Her face was a ghastly shade of green, and she kept the window on her side open all the way despite the near freezing temperature.

Hangover-free, I felt really pure, having chosen for once not to overindulge.

"Oh, shut up," Maggie said to me.

"I didn't say a word," I protested.

"You were thinking I'm an idiot. Well, I am."

I couldn't argue with that.

"I'll never do this again."

"We've all said that, Maggie. Many times."

"This time I mean it."

Bill Cromwell, Maggie's fiancé, was waiting for us outside their small split-level home. As he walked over to the truck, I noticed he still walked with a limp, a painful reminder of our adventure last fall when he was injured while trying to help me trap a killer. He was wearing his Union Army general officer's uniform, plumed hat and all.

"Kinky," I said to him. "Do you hang around your house all weekend in that getup?"

He grinned and opened the door on Maggie's side.

Maggie looked up from her struggle to unbuckle her seat belt and laughed. "His regiment is going to be in the Christmas parade today. Doesn't he look glorious?"

Kind of young and skinny, I thought, but refrained from saying so. I still wondered why Maggie came to the funeral service alone last night, but if there was a problem between them, she kept it to herself.

I drove on to the Sigafoos Home for the Aged, where the *Chronicle*'s Christmas party was to be held.

"Why a nursing home?" I'd asked Cassie when she told me about the brunch plans she'd made there.

"Because the Holiday Inn's been booked for months. Besides, the Sigafoos serves good food and is really inexpensive."

Inexpensive was the magic word at the fiscally challenged *Chronicle*.

The parking lot behind the home was only half full. I pulled in between two black vans. From one came a swarm of little Amish boys, all dressed in identical black overalls, blue shirts, and little flat black hats.

" 'Morning, miss," the non-Amish driver said. "Brought some of your paperboys down from Burnt Stump Hollow. I'll be back to get them after the parade."

"What do you mean 'after the parade'? The brunch only lasts till noon. I can't baby-sit them all afternoon."

"You'uns wouldn't want the kiddies to miss the parade, would you? They don't get to town much—just for special occasions like this one." He tipped his ball cap and pulled out in a rush before I could argue with him.

"Okay, men," I said to the children, as we headed

toward the canopy-covered back entrance of the nursing home. "Let's party!"

The *Chronicle*'s "staff" consisted mainly of the delivery team: about fifty boys and girls under the age of twelve and ten retired men who drove the papers to places where the children could pick them up. The rest of the people present were the dozen men and women who sold advertising, six freelance writers, and the printer. Most were already seated, waiting eagerly for breakfast to be served.

Cassie greeted me with today's paper in hand. "Wait till you see the front page," she said, laughing.

I unrolled the paper and was smacked in the face with a headline that said PUBIC SAFETY THREATENED. "*Pubic* Safety! For God's sake, I know I typed *public*."

"Stuff happens," she said with a shrug. "Half our readers won't notice. The rest will say something like 'What do you expect from the *Chronicle*?' and then forget about it.

"It looks like everybody's here, Tori. Why don't you make your welcoming speech now?"

"Welcoming speech? Oh, dear. I never thought about—"

But Cassie was already tapping a water glass with a knife to attract everyone's attention.

"Sit down, please. Our editor has a few words to say to you."

"Very few," I promised, and was greeted with enthusiastic cheers from the group.

I thanked them all for their hard work. More cheers. Urged them to drop by the office any time for a visit. Cheers from the children, a frown from Cassie. Wished them a happy new year. Polite applause. Announced brunch was ready. Standing ovation, followed by a wild charge to the buffet table.

After everyone, including a few stray nursing home residents who dropped in to see what was going on, had filled their plates, Cassie and I helped ourselves to what was left: dry scrambled eggs, cold English muffins, and warm fruit cups. The coffee was good, though, and plentiful, since very few of the children drank anything but orange juice.

Everybody seemed to enjoy the party, especially when the waitresses came out with big trays of sticky buns. Everybody but me, that is, for I kept thinking about that dreadful stuffed cat with its stomach slit open that some sadistic person had left on my porch last night. *Please,* I thought, *please let Fred be all right. Who hates me enough to want to hurt my cats? What does anyone have to fear from me?*

As the waitresses cleared the tables, Cassie began distributing gifts. Apparently, I was the only person present who found it odd to have a practitioner of a pagan religion passing out Christmas gifts, but I decided it was quite likely that I was the only one who knew about her unorthodox beliefs.

Once the food was gone and the gifts were opened, it was time to leave for the parade. The logistics of getting everybody downtown could have been overwhelming, but Cassie had done it before and knew just what to do. After the children put on their coats and mittens, she had them line up side by side, flanked the two rows with the adults, stationed me at the tail end to round up stragglers, and led us out of the nursing home and out onto the sidewalk.

Four residents of the home, one man and three women in bathrobes and slippers, tried to follow us. One woman was tall and thin, and had silvery-blonde hair pinned in neat curls on top of her head. She looked something like

my mother, making me wonder how Christmas was celebrated at the Willows, where she was warehoused. Or if
she even knew it was Christmas.

When I led them back inside the home, they looked so
disappointed that I asked the nurse if I could take them
with me.

"They're going to be in the parade," she said. "But
thanks anyway."

I tried to say good-bye to my mother-look-alike, but
her attention was already on something else.

We had only a few blocks to walk, and we soon found
a place to stand in the square right in front of the ruins of
the burned-out courthouse.

"This is the best place to be because Santa stops here
at the end to pass out candy," Cassie said. "You'll be
able to get some good pictures here for the paper."

Our staff bounced up and down, screaming, "Candy.
Yay!"

Downtown was beautiful, from the white lights in the
bare branches of the trees to the red and white plastic
candy canes hanging from the streetlights.

"It's like fairyland," one of our papergirls said.

Someone behind me grumbled, "Nothing says Christmas like colored lights."

Cassie no longer seemed upset with me, and I was glad
for that. For one moment, I considered asking her if I
could come to her coven meeting tonight, but in the back
of my mind I kept hearing Weezie's voice repeating
"baby blood" over and over, and I just couldn't bring
myself to do it. We chatted amiably about nothing of
importance and thanked several people who came up to
us to tell us today's edition of the paper was the "best
one yet."

"I wonder why a paper full of tragedy is so popular?"
I asked.

Cassie shrugged. "After years of looking at our 'grip and grin' photographs and reading hot tips from the extension office about the latest developments in cattle food, they probably find it exciting to have something interesting to read about."

The sound of a band approaching on a side street caught the crowd's attention, and everyone pushed forward. I worried about my kids losing their places, but they all held their own quite nicely. The high school band came around the corner and was greeted with a rousing cheer. Their instruments were decorated with red ribbons and sprigs of mistletoe.

"They just won the district band competition," Cassie shouted over the din. "This week everybody loves the director."

I snapped several pictures.

"Don't use up too much film at the beginning," Cassie warned. "The best floats come at the end."

Behind the band came a yellow school bus with a Nativity scene on top. Screaming children hung out of the windows and tossed Hershey Kisses to the spectators. I was proud to see my staff got most of them. This was followed by a troop of Brownies dressed as Christmas trees, carrying flashlights that they flicked on and off to represent stars.

A group of middle-aged women, preceded by a banner that said they were the Silver-Haired Twirlers Association, marched in front of the junior high school band in little white tasseled boots and skirts that were much too short for them.

I heard a strange noise come from Cassie. She sounded like a strangling horse, and I couldn't look at her for I knew if I did I'd have the giggles for the rest of the day.

When the bus from the Sigafoos Home for the Aged went by, I saw the woman who reminded me of my mother sitting in the front seat wearing a Santa Claus hat. I waved at her and she returned my greeting with a Queen Elizabeth–style finger wiggle and a vague smile that really did look like my mother's. I suddenly realized I needed to visit the Willows.

The man who'd played the bagpipes at Eddie Douglas's funeral passed in front of me playing an explosive version of "Scotland the Brave." I noticed Buchanan McCleary, the borough solicitor, standing on the other side of the street beside Luscious, who looked quite official and almost handsome in his blue uniform.

I waved at Buchanan, who smiled back.

"I want to talk to you," I mouthed.

He tilted his head and moved his lips. I interpreted it as "What did you say?"

I cut through a troop of marching Boy Scouts to get across the street.

Buchanan greeted me with an enthusiastic hug. He and I had developed a kinship based on our both being outsiders in the small town and both being romantically involved with members of the Gochenauer family.

A Maryland high school band stopped in front of us to play a medley of Dixieland jazz. "What's up?" Buchanan asked loudly.

I didn't want my questions to be overheard by everyone nearby, so I stood on tiptoe and yelled in his ear, "I want to ask you about Stanley Roadcap."

"Like what?"

"Like what did Stanley have to gain by Bernice's death?" As I finished shouting out my question, I realized the band had stopped playing and everyone around us either heard me or was stone-deaf. I winced with embarrassment.

Buchanan laughed at my expression. Luscious turned

bright red, moved away a few inches, and pretended he didn't know me.

Taking my arm, Buchanan led me through the crowd to the semiprivacy of the covered entrance to the Sweete Toothe Candy Shoppe.

"I'm so embarrassed," I said miserably.

He shrugged. "If that's the worst thing you ever do, consider yourself lucky."

"I like your philosophy." I lowered my voice and made sure nobody was listening before I asked, "Is there anything you can tell me about the Roadcaps? I met Stanley yesterday, under rather strange circumstances, and he tried to convince me that he and Bernice were getting back together. I just wondered if this was true. Or if Stanley was trying to convince me that he didn't have any reason to want her dead. Do you know if he stood to gain a lot from her will?"

"I was Bernice's lawyer," Buchanan said. "So I do know quite a bit about their affairs. And since the settling of her estate is a matter of public record, I won't be breaking any confidentiality by telling you this. Bernice inherited her personal fortune from her father in a trust. The beneficiary of the trust is Stanley and Bernice's son. Stanley won't get anything—a fact that he was well aware of. And he doesn't need it. Stanley is fairly well-to-do."

"A son? Where is he?" I asked, thinking I had just acquired a new suspect.

"In the army, stationed in the Middle East. He's flying home right now for the funeral."

There went my suspect. I was vaguely disappointed. The idea of the killer being someone I didn't know was far more preferable to the alternative. I was also aware that the terms of the trust meant Bernice was more valuable to Stanley alive than dead. And for the same reason, it would have been to Stanley's advantage to keep his marriage going. How much of Stanley's patience with Bernice's history of rehab romances was due to his love for her, and how much was due to her wealth?

"At least no man's going to marry me for my money," I thought out loud. "I don't have any."

Buchanan looked seriously at me. "I'm not so sure about that," he said cryptically. "Sometimes I think you act like a rich kid slumming it."

"Where did you get that idea?" I asked, startled by his comment. "I'm no different from anybody else."

He smiled. "What about that preppy accent, the five or six languages you speak, the casual way you drop exotic places into your conversations, the way you assume everything will go your way?"

"It's my background," I protested. "In the foreign service, we tend to live 'rich' even when we're not. My father is a career diplomat who worked his way up, not one of those millionaires who bought his ambassadorship. And that accent you referred to comes as a result of my having lived in a dozen foreign countries when I was growing up."

Buchanan said, "Okay, Tori, you've convinced me. I didn't mean to stir up a tempest in your teapot."

The high school steel band drummed out my retort. He planted a kiss on the top of my head and moved on with a cheery good-bye.

"If you ask me," said a woman's voice behind me, "he and that galfriend of his done it."

I spun around to face Weezie Clopper, who was standing in the open doorway of the candy shop. How long she'd been there, I didn't know, but apparently she'd heard most of our conversation.

"Hello, Mrs. Clopper. How nice to see you again," I said, forcing a smile.

"I thought about calling you after you left," she said. "About that Gochenauer woman. She thinks she's so much better than everybody else because her family's been here forever."

As the poison dripped from her lips, I thought how untrue were her remarks about Greta. Garnet's sister was a true original, an aging flower child, who lived to help everybody and everything in the world.

"What is it you are trying to tell me, Mrs. Clopper?" I asked. My smile was gone now, and I was striving for cool and intimidating.

"You know how she and that—that black man"—she spoke with a sneer in her voice—"have been yacking about saving them brown trout in the Lickin Creek. And you know how they are. If you really want to find out who killed Bernice, you ought to look closer to home, rather than bothering us good Christians."

"Why don't you write an anonymous letter about it to the *Chronicle*? I won't publish it, of course, but you might feel better getting some of that venom off your chest." I turned my back on her.

"You better watch your tongue, young lady. It's liable to get you into big trouble someday."

I ignored her and pushed through the crowd.

Inside, I was seething at her snide remarks. Just because Greta sometimes used militant methods to further her causes, it was ridiculous to suggest she'd resort to murder to protect some fish. Smiling to myself, I recalled the time she bombarded the town meeting at the Accident Theatre with overripe tomatoes and another time when she chained herself to the fountain to protest the nuclear-waste dump. Yes, Greta could be extreme, even a little scary at times, but she was definitely not a murderess.

I found myself, once again, standing beside Luscious.

"Hi," I said cheerfully, but Luscious was too busy being chewed out by Marvin Bumbaugh to acknowledge me. Of course, being the mind-your-own-business type of person that I am, I tried not to listen and took several pictures of the Fogal Farms float going by stacked with mounds of beef sticks, or summer sausages as my mother called them. But, standing as close as I was to the men, I couldn't help but overhear their conversation.

Actually, it wasn't a conversation but a one-sided diatribe in which Marvin bombarded poor Luscious with accusations that he was incapable of doing his job and dire threats of having him fired.

"Yesterday, you said I had till Christmas," Luscious protested. "I haven't even got the toxicology report back yet."

"And what about Oretta Clopper? What have you done about finding her killer?"

"I'm waiting for the results of the forensic tests on the bullet that killed her."

"Christmas, Miller. If I don't have a report on my desk on December twenty-sixth, you can kiss your job good-bye."

Marvin leaned forward slightly to glare at me across Luscious's brass-buttoned chest. "This wouldn't have happened if Garnet was here."

"Why yell at me?" I snapped back. "I didn't make him go to Costa Rica."

"Maybe he wanted to get away from something—or somebody," Marvin said nastily, touching the very painful thought I'd been trying to push deep into my subconscious—the possibility that Garnet had left because of me.

When he left, I turned to Luscious and muttered, "I hate that man."

"That makes two of us," he said.

"We'll show him," I said. "We'll find his murderer for him."

"Sure we will." He didn't sound convinced.

I wondered if Marvin would have treated either of us so rudely if Garnet were still here. But, of course, if Garnet were here, he wouldn't have any reason to.

The *Chronicle* employees waved at me from the other side of the street, and I decided to rejoin them. Reverend Flack's cousin, the bagpiper, was accompanying a group of little girls in full skirts and clogs who stopped to perform a charming Irish folk dance in front of me. As I wove my way through them, a tall clown, carrying a bunch of helium-filled balloons, stopped in front of me and mimed an elaborate double take as if he were surprised to see me. He was taller than anyone around and wore a baggy yellow suit covered with black polka dots. A bright orange wig topped his creepy, white-painted face. When he bent down and patted me on the head, I heard laughter from the crowd.

I've never liked clowns. There's something eerie and disturbing about them, like a bin of broken dolls. I want to know what's under the makeup, yet I'm afraid of finding out.

For the sake of the children watching, I forced a smile. The clown slapped his pockets, as if looking for something, then with a theatrical gesture of relief, pulled something from his vest pocket and handed it to me with a low bow.

I took it, a folded piece of paper.

"Open it. Open it," the children cheered.

I smoothed it out and read the neatly printed message: MEET ME AT RAYMOND'S. SUNDAY AT TWO.

"Tori's got a boyfriend. Tori's got a boyfriend." That annoying little choral rendition came from the direction of my office staff.

"Who are you?" But the clown was gone when I looked up.

"Where'd he go?" I asked, but nobody seemed to know.

Besides, who cared, when Santa was coming down the street in an army Jeep with a deer head mounted on the hood? Red laserlike light beams blinked on and off in the dead animal's nostrils. Rudolph the red-nosed reindeer, I realized with a shudder. Or Bambi. This kind of thing could warp a little kid's psyche forever.

CHAPTER 17

In sin and error pining

LUCKILY, CASSIE HAD COUNTED OUR KIDS BE-
fore we left for the parade, because when she
lined them up to return to the Sigafoos Home we
quickly realized three were missing. After a brief
but panicky search we found the missing trio sharing a
cigarette behind Santa's Workshop.

I breathed a deep sigh of relief when the last of the
children was picked up. After only a few hours I was
exhausted. What an awesome responsibility full-time
parenthood must be!

Cassie said a quick good-bye to me and hurried off. I
was left standing in the parking lot, wondering what I
should do next.

"Meet me at Raymond's," the note had said. I assumed that meant Raymond's Art Studio and Gallery at
the low-rent end of Main Street. Since the One-Hour-
Photo-Shop was nearby, I could check out the studio on
my way to drop off my film.

Raymond's Studio was in an old building, once the
home of a dress shop. I knew that because the old sign
over the door still said TRISHA'S TOGS FOR TASTEFUL LADIES.
The door was securely locked. Black draperies behind the
large display window made it impossible for a passerby

to see inside, even though I pressed my nose against the glass, trying to find a crack to peek through.

The only thing in the window was an easel, and on it was a sign that said NEW SHOW OPENING SUNDAY AT ONE. REFRESHMENTS WILL BE SERVED.

I suddenly realized the clown had simply been passing out flyers for Raymond's art show. He hadn't been targeting me at all. It disappointed me that my mysterious assignation had turned into nothing more than an advertising gimmick.

I pulled the note out of my pocket and tossed it in the trash container on the curb. As it dropped into the mesh basket something caught my eye, and I reached in to retrieve it. A woman passing by eyed me curiously, probably thinking I was one of Lickin Creek's many collectors who constantly check garbage cans and bulky trash pickup sites for antiques and other treasures.

Pretending I didn't see her, I smoothed out the piece of paper. What had attracted my attention was on the back of the paper. My name, handwritten in pencil. This was no flyer. Someone had planned to hand this message to me and me alone.

I had almost twenty-four hours to wait for my mysterious meeting with the clown, and patience is not one of my virtues. I wanted to know who he was. Did I simply have a secret admirer? Or was there something more sinister involved? I thought of the mutilated bean-bag kitty I received last night and wondered if both incidents had something to do with my investigation of the murders of the sugar plum fairies. I'd know . . . tomorrow at two.

After I dropped off my film, a slight gnawing in my tummy let me know the Sweete Toothe Candy Shoppe snack bar was calling.

While enjoying the house specialty, an old-fashioned chocolate soda made with chocolate ice cream, I thought about poor Luscious, who was in danger of losing his job if he didn't find out who killed Bernice and Oretta. I'd promised to help, but so far I hadn't accomplished much.

As I slurped up the last of the creamy liquid, I decided the answer could lie with Matavious Clopper, the elusive widower who refused to be interviewed by the police and who hadn't been seen anywhere in town since his wife's death. At the fire scene Friday morning, I'd overheard him blaming himself, saying this was all his fault. I wondered what was his fault . . . and why? And why hadn't he been home that night? He'd offered no explanation of where he'd been. Since he'd done a disappearing act, I also wondered where I could find him.

When I stepped out onto the sidewalk, I realized the temperature had dropped considerably in a very short time, and the sky was darker than it should have been for this early in the afternoon. Several people rushed past me, their collars turned up against the wind. I pulled my hood over my head and walked back to the Sigafoos Home where I'd left Garnet's truck.

I'd decided the logical place to look for Matavious Clopper was at his chiropractic office. Even if he hadn't yet reopened, he might be staying in the old Victorian mansion in the historic district.

I had to drive past Garnet's home to get there. The large old home where the Gochenauer family had lived since the late 1700s brought back too many memories. It's over, I told myself, you've got to look ahead.

The street turned partly commercial in the next block. At one time, people had considered the gracious mansions too big for contemporary living and many had been divided into apartments. Now, one housed the VFW Club and another was a bed-and-breakfast.

The Clopper Chiropractic Clinic was a white Victorian with black shutters, by far the largest house at this end of the street, sitting on a low hill fronted by several acres of lawn. It was the kind of grand black-and-white mansion that was often turned into a funeral home in small towns. Most likely, the Lickin Creek Historical Preservation Society had fought that undignified intrusion.

A small sign on the wrought-iron fence announced there was parking in the rear. Below it hung an even smaller sign that said CLOSED. I circled the block and approached the building through a deserted alley.

The parking lot behind the business was also deserted. But just because the clinic was closed didn't mean Matavious wasn't in there.

A brick walkway led to a glassed-in porch, which I entered through an unlocked door, a good sign that Matavious was there, I thought, until I noticed the four mailboxes on the wall, which meant the upstairs had been divided into apartments. He wasn't the only one who used this entrance.

The clinic door was locked, and although I knocked loudly, no one answered. I decided to try the front door and walked around the house, through the garden.

I rang the doorbell several times. Because this was Lickin Creek, where people were not as careful about security as New Yorkers, I tried the doorknob. As I thought it might, the door creaked open. This was actually the clinic's back entrance, so most likely it had been years since anybody had thought to check on whether or not it was locked.

"Hello," I called, not too loud. "Anybody here?" My voice echoed in the dark hall, and I was sure I was alone.

As long as I was here and the opportunity was at hand, I decided carpe diem was the motto of the moment. Matavious had to have an appointment book. Perhaps I could find a notation in it that would explain where he was the night his house burned down and his wife was murdered.

The office, I assumed, would be in the back. Even though I was sure I was alone in the house, I tiptoed down the hall, past the open doors of several treatment rooms, and found the office in what surely had to have been the original kitchen. There was neither a stove nor refrigerator, but the old pine cabinets were still there, probably now holding office supplies.

A receptionist's desk faced the door, so I approached it from the back and had a good view of a well-tended plant, a ceramic snowman, and several photographs of a smiling man and two school-age children. Tinsel and strings of tiny white lights surrounded the windows and the door frame. And a real tree stood in one corner, covered with Christmas cards. I looked at a few of them; they all seemed to be from satisfied patients.

Good! No computer on the desk meant the reception-ist probably kept an old-fashioned, handwritten appoint-ment book. Her desk wasn't locked, of course. After all, this was Lickin Creek, where locking your door was considered an act of antisocial behavior! In the top drawer, I found what I was looking for.

I took the leather-bound book over to the window where there was more light, and opened it to Thursday, December 19, the night of the fire, and was disappointed not to find any mention of an evening engagement. When I turned to the next day, December 20, I was surprised to see that no appointments had been scheduled.

Most likely there's a good reason for that, I thought. Fridays could be the doctor's regular day off. But when I looked back at the past weeks, I saw that Fridays were especially busy days, with appointments scheduled until late in the evening.

Matavious's down day was Wednesday. A picture

crossed my mind of a tipsy Bernice weaving her way down the center aisle of the church and complaining to Matavious about her back—and Matavious saying that he was always closed on Wednesday afternoons—and Bernice saying, "But you were in there. I heard you moving around."

If he'd been closed on Wednesday, why had he also shut his office down again on Friday?

I noticed a car pulling into the parking lot, and I stepped back, away from the window. Probably one of the upstairs tenants, I guessed, but even so, I didn't want to be caught snooping through the office. I placed the appointment book back in the desk and closed the drawer. The footsteps were coming up the walk. I heard voices, one male and one female, on the porch. And the sound of a key in a lock.

Holy cow, they were coming in here! As I backed into the hallway, I heard the door open. No time to get out. I ducked into the first treatment room. Saw a door. Opened it and darted inside. Right into a supply closet with no other exit. I sank down on a pile of sheets, drew my knees up to my chin, and attempted to make myself invisible.

Something clicked, and light streamed through the crack between the door and the threshold. They'd come into this room. I was afraid to breathe for fear they'd hear me. I'd stirred up some dust when I ran inside the closet, and it was tickling my nose. I pressed my finger against my upper lip. This was not the time for sneezes!

Who were they? Did they know I was here? What on earth would I say if they opened the door?

All I could do was sit still among the mop buckets, brooms, sheets, and towels, and listen to what was going on. Something dropped softly to the floor, followed by whisperings, silky rustles, and finally several loud clumps. Then there were some other unidentifiable sounds. I didn't want to imagine what was happening out there.

A woman's voice gasped, "Oh, Mat, now . . . now!" I had a pretty good idea of what they were up to, and what Bernice must have heard on Wednesday when she had attempted to get in to see Matavious. I cringed with embarrassment and tried to do the Victorian thing of thinking of England, or something. Anything but what they were doing.

The examining table creaked. My face burned as I heard the unmistakable sounds of mounting passion: slurping kisses, moans, and rattles from the table. I was glad I couldn't see them; Matavious doing the nasty wasn't even an attractive thing to imagine.

Matavious paused in whatever he was doing to ask, "Debbie, where are the . . . you know?"

He didn't even want to say *condom*! What a guy.

"In my desk. Middle drawer."

"I'll get one." More rattles and groans from the table and the patter of bare feet on the wood floor.

She'd said *my desk*, so apparently Matavious was getting it on with his receptionist.

He returned in less than a minute. And I had to endure more of the kissy sounds. Lots more.

The mood changed suddenly, as the woman exclaimed angrily, "Damn it, Mat, what's wrong with you?"

"I don't know." Matavious sounded miserable. "I just can't seem to—"

"You'd better get yourself a prescription for Viagra!"

"Debbie . . . I can't help it. I keep thinking about Oretta."

"That's just great! The woman's dead, and she's still messing things up between us. I thought now she's gone, I could get a divorce and we'd get married."

"It's too soon to think of that."

"Too soon? After the years I've given you? Mat, you are a real SOB."

"If we hadn't gone away together that night, Oretta would still be alive. I don't know if I could marry you now, feeling that guilt."

The sharp crack I heard next had to be a slap.

"Ow," Matavious yelled. Something crashed on the floor and shattered. "Damn it, Debbie, you broke the massage oil. It'll stain the floor."

Before I realized what was happening, the closet door burst open, and a tall, skinny, naked man was staring at me with a horrified expression that would have been funny if it hadn't been directed at me. I could only imagine what I looked like to him.

The next moments, as I came out of the supply closet, were a blur. Matavious grabbing a towel and covering himself. The woman pulling on slacks and a sweater. Matavious looking for his glasses. The woman jamming her feet into her boots. Me looking in vain for a nonexistent escape route. Me finally slumping into a chair and waiting for the consequences.

"Call the police," the Debbie-woman screamed at Matavious.

"But, darling, we don't want people to know about us."

I breathed a little more easily. He had his reputation to lose if this got out. Maybe I'd be okay.

She glared at me, seized her purse, and slammed out of the room.

Matavious made his towel more secure around his waist. "Tori Miracle! What the hell are you doing here? How did you get in?"

"I was looking for you. The front door wasn't locked, so I came in, thinking you were here."

"And why were you in my closet?" He'd calmed down a little. Maybe I'd get away with it.

"I thought it was the way out. By the time I realized I was in a closet, you started—well, you know—and I was too embarrassed to come out."

He scratched his head, but he was smiling a little. I was winning him over, I thought.

"Why were you looking for me?" He sucked in his stomach. Now I knew I'd won him over.

"I only wanted to ask you some questions."

"What kind of questions?"

"About where you were the night your wife died. But I don't have to. You were with her, weren't you?" I pointed at the little pile of ladies' underwear Debbie hadn't had time to put back on.

He turned red all the way down to his towel and tried with one foot to push the silky pink things underneath the examining table.

"Were you going to ask your wife for a divorce?" I figured the best defense for my bad behavior would be to go on the offense.

He glanced toward the door and lowered his voice. "No," he said firmly. "I had no intention of divorcing Oretta."

"And what did your girlfriend think of that?"

"I'll answer that," Debbie said from the doorway. "She didn't know. She trusted him. She was ready to give up her husband and children for him. That's what his girlfriend thought!" She threw Matavious a look that would probably reappear in his nightmares for years to come. "I could kill you."

"Aw, Debbie . . ."

"Maybe I'd better go," I said.

"Like hell you will," Debbie said. "I called the police."

Matavious blanched. "I told you not to."

"And why should I care what you say?"

Caught between them, I was almost relieved when the police, in the person of Afton Finkey, arrived.

To give Afton credit, he didn't even crack a smile as he listened to the naked man and the half-dressed woman complain about me.

When they were through, he said, "Come on, Tori. I've got to take you down to the station."

I tried a little humor. "Are you going to put me in leg irons?"

He still didn't crack a smile, and I was beginning to realize he was taking this seriously.

He didn't even talk to me in the police car.

Leaving the cruiser by the gas pump, he led me through Hoopengartner's Garage office, into the back room where the Lickin Creek Police Department was located.

Luscious looked up from the army-surplus desk, shook his head in despair, and said, "Tori, I know I asked for your help, but I didn't think you'd do something like this!"

The next hour was really dreadful. Luscious actually took me to the old Pizza Hut building where Judge Fetterhoff had temporary offices until the courthouse was rebuilt. After a long wait, the judge listened to Luscious file a complaint against me, a court date was set, and I was released on my own recognizance. But not before the judge looked sternly at me over his half-moon glasses and said, "I've been hearing a lot of stories about you bothering people, young lady. I hope this puts a stop to it."

In the waiting room I asked, "Can I make my one phone call now?"

Still no smile from Luscious. "You're not under arrest.

You can make all the phone calls you want—if you've got enough quarters."

"What about my truck? I left it at Matavious's office."

"I don't want you'uns going anywhere near his office, Tori. Give me the key. I'll fetch it later."

I placed a call to Maggie Roy and shivered in the dark parking lot until she arrived.

CHAPTER 18

Still proceeding

"WHAT HAVE YOU DONE NOW?" MAGGIE asked, once I was belted into the front seat of her car.

"You might say I was caught somewhere I wasn't supposed to be."

Maggie gasped. "You were trespassing?"

"That's what the judge called it. He also charged me with breaking and entering." I described my ridiculous adventure to Maggie.

When I was through, she said, "There are two things you need to keep in mind about Lickin Creek, Tori. First, the Lickin Creek Grapevine spreads gossip faster than the speed of light, so you can't do anything wrong and not expect to get caught."

"I am fully aware that the news of my arrest is spreading through town, even as we speak," I said.

Maggie laughed. "Not to mention what the gossips are saying about Matavious's affair with his married receptionist. The other thing you have to be aware of is the extent of the old boys' network. All those good old boys who are descendants of the town's founders." She glanced sideways at me. "Like Judge Fetterhoff and Matavious Clopper and—"

"Let me guess . . . Stanley Roadcap."

Maggie nodded. "Yup. And Marvin Bumbaugh, of course. Even Jackson Clopper. They stick together against outsiders, Tori, no matter what they think of each other."

"When you say *outsiders*, you mean me, don't you?"

"Right. You've upset a lot of important people in the past few days. They aren't going to let you get away with it." She giggled and changed the subject abruptly. "Now, tell me what Matavious looks like naked."

"You really don't want to go there, Maggie." I tried to speak flippantly, but I was concerned. Not only had I angered the old boys' network, but someone was scared enough about what I'd been doing to leave the bean-bag cat on my door as a threat. Was it one of them? I was quiet for the rest of the short drive home.

"Here we are," Maggie said cheerfully. "Going to offer me a cuppa coffee?"

"Isn't Bill waiting for you?" I asked ungraciously. I really wanted to be alone with my thoughts.

"He left for the Poconos right after the parade. To set up a Christmas reenactment camp. I'm going to join him there on Christmas Eve, if the weather holds out."

"Then please come in." A cup of coffee was the least I could do to show my appreciation for her driving me home.

As we stepped into the warm kitchen, Noel came over to rub against my legs. I bent over to pat her and whispered, "Did Fred come home?"

I knew he hadn't. If he was home he'd be at the door to greet me.

A delicious aroma tantalized my nose. "What smells so good?" I asked Praxythea, who was once again in her domestic goddess role.

She looked up from dipping a piece of white cheese-cloth in a bowl and said, "I baked my fruitcakes this morning." She wrapped one of three loaves in a brandy-soaked cheesecloth, laid several slices of apple on top, and wound aluminum foil around the whole thing.

"Brandy?" Maggie asked.

Praxythea nodded. "Sometimes I use rum."

"It's her old family recipe," I said to Maggie, as I filled two mugs from the pot of coffee on the back of the stove.

"I never liked fruitcake very much," Maggie said. "Heard too many jokes about using them for door-stops."

"You'll like mine," Praxythea said, not at all insulted. "Even people who don't care for fruitcake rave about it."

I flipped through the day's mail. Christmas catalogs were still coming in. Who was disorganized enough to order gifts four days before Christmas?

"Anything interesting?" Maggie asked.

I shook my head and burned my tongue with the big gulp of coffee I took to hide my distress. The counterirritant was a good remedy for self-pity.

Praxythea handed me a plate of her homemade crescent cookies, saying, "The powdered sugar will cool your mouth."

It did, and I ate several, vowing to restart my diet immediately after Christmas.

At Maggie's insistence, I once again told of my afternoon's adventures. Praxythea listened with a bemused look, which turned to a small frown when Maggie told her about my having rankled the members of the old boys' network.

"I can't help worrying," Praxythea said. "I thought all day about that nasty stuffed cat. Someone is out to frighten you away."

"Or worse," Maggie said.

"Thanks to both of you for making me feel so good," I grumbled. "Does your psychic power tell you who that someone is?" I asked Praxythea.

"That's not the kind of thing I do," she said. Before I could make a snide remark, she added, "But why don't we look at what we know and try to figure it out?"

"Good idea." Maggie jumped to her feet. "Got some paper? I'll make notes."

It wasn't a bad idea, I thought. Two heads (or in this case three) are usually better than one, and I've always found that talking something out helps me focus in on what's important. I found a yellow legal pad in the drawer near the phone and handed it to Maggie.

"Okay," I said. "Who wants to start?"

"You're the one who's been doing all the snooping," Maggie said with pencil poised. "Tell us what you've found out."

"We know that Bernice and Oretta were murdered," I said.

They nodded.

"What we don't know is if they were murdered by one person or by two."

"I'm betting on one," Maggie said. "This is a small town. It's hard enough to imagine a murderer on the loose, much less two."

"Strong, strong vibrations tell me both murders were done by the same person." Praxythea finished wrapping the last of her fruitcakes and daintily wiped her fingers on a paper napkin.

I went on. "We do know Bernice was poisoned, most likely by cyanide, and—"

"What makes you think it was cyanide?" Maggie asked.

"Certain obvious signs. Her color, the smell, the speed with which it killed her. I've asked Luscious to have the lab check for it. And we know Oretta was shot, but the gun has disappeared. It would help to know what weapon was used."

I thought for a minute. "The disemboweled cat with its attached threatening note tells me the murderer is frightened of me. It means I'm getting close to the killer, even if I don't know yet what it is I know.

"Although I've talked to a lot of people, I can't see that I've learned anything. The boyfriend, VeeKay Kaltenbaugh, appears to be a logical suspect, at least in Bernice's death, but all I can tell you about him is that he's very rich and that his rehab romance with Bernice was on the skids."

Maggie said as she wrote on the legal pad, "VeeKay Kaltenbaugh. Could have killed Bernice in a fit of passionate rage over their relationship breaking up."

I repressed a grin at Maggie's efforts to solve the crime. VeeKay didn't look like the kind of man who'd get excited over much of anything except his restaurant and maybe his muscles, and although I'd seen little of Bernice she didn't strike me as a woman who could inspire passionate rage in anybody. Hiding my skepticism, I continued.

"Stanley Roadcap said he loved Bernice and was trying to save his marriage—"

"That's what he *says*," Maggie interrupted. "How do you know he's telling the truth?"

"For now, that's all I have to go on," I pointed out.

Maggie licked her pencil and wrote Stanley Roadcap's name. "I'll just put ditto marks under what I put for VeeKay."

"I guess that's all right." If we agreed that Bernice was capable of inspiring passionate rage in one man, then why not two? Or maybe even five or six? Who knows what kind of temptress lurked beneath that boozy, middle-aged exterior? "However," I pointed out, "neither Stanley nor VeeKay had a motive to kill Oretta, and we've practically decided both women were killed by the same person."

"I could be wrong about that," Praxythea said.

"You? Admitting you're wrong? I'm amazed."

"No need to be sarcastic, Tori. I sometimes get interfering vibrations that can cloud an issue. How about some more cookies?"

I was surprised to notice the plate was empty. I couldn't possibly have eaten them all, or had I?

"They're good brain food," Praxythea said, placing another heaping platter of cookies on the table in front of me.

"We're getting off track," Maggie said. "What about Matavious Clopper?"

"Before he caught me in his closet, I overheard him say he was with his receptionist the night Oretta died," I said.

"Couldn't he have killed her first, then joined Debbie for a night of passion?" Maggie asked.

"And his reason for murdering his wife was . . . ?" Praxythea asked.

"I dunno." Maggie looked at me. "What do you think, Tori?"

"From what I heard, I don't think he had any real desire to marry Debbie. But even if he did, there was no need to murder his wife. He could have simply divorced her."

"Unless there was something about their relationship you don't know," Praxythea pointed out.

"I'm sure there's lots of things I don't know about them, Praxythea," I responded. "Wait! I just thought of something else. Bernice overheard him and Debbie in the office last Wednesday. Maybe Matavious killed her to prevent her from telling Oretta about his affair."

"That makes about as much sense as someone murdering his wife instead of asking for a divorce," Praxythea sniffed.

Maggie scribbled as fast as she could, then read, " 'Matavious Clopper. Motive to kill wife—she wouldn't give him a divorce. Motive to kill Bernice—to hide his affair. Both motives—highly unlikely.' "

"Okay. Let's move on," I said. "There's Debbie, the receptionist. What if she wanted to marry Matavious so badly, she decided to get Oretta out of the way?"

Maggie looked up. "And she killed Bernice first, to keep her from blabbing to Oretta."

"Write that down," I said.

When Maggie was finished writing, she said, "You haven't mentioned the other branch of the Clopper family. Weezie and Jackson. They had reason to resent both Oretta and Bernice. Bernice, because the town's too small for two big shopping malls, and she was rushing to build her shopping center downtown before they could sell their land to a developer. And Oretta, because she persuaded Matavious to put his land in a conservation bank, making it nearly impossible for Jackson to sell his land to anybody in the future."

Since I really disliked Weezie, I agreed with Maggie that the Cloppers were likely suspects.

"What about that nutty group Bernice belonged to?" Maggie asked. "You know, the witchie-poos."

"What makes you think she was a member of the coven?" I asked.

"You're not the only one who can play Nancy Drew. Besides, it's hard to keep a thing like a witches' coven a secret in a gossip-loving town like Lickin Creek."

"I don't think they had anything to do with her

death," I said. I didn't want either woman to know I planned a sneak visit to tonight's coven meeting, for I knew they'd try to stop me.

"Okay, then. Here's the list." Maggie ripped the top page off the legal pad and handed it to me. I studied it and decided it was a good start, but that was all it was. There was nothing definite to go by, and there could be many other people we simply hadn't thought about. The clown, for instance. Who was he? And what, if anything, did he have to do with all this?

"What's missing is a connection between the two women," I announced. "Find that, and we find the killer."

"We can start another list." Maggie licked the end of her pencil. "I'll start with the Christmas pageant."

"I nearly forgot your hunch that there's a serial killer out there bumping off sugar plum fairies," I said with a giggle.

"Don't be so nonchalant about it," Maggie warned. "I still think you could be next."

The back door burst open, admitting Luscious Miller and putting a stop to our list-making.

Luscious tossed my truck keys on the table, then helped himself to coffee.

"Thanks," I said meekly.

"Don't mention it." He sat down without removing his jacket and sipped from his mug.

I figured he had something to say to me, and I hoped he wouldn't be too harsh in front of my friends. He surprised me, though, by not even mentioning my afternoon's escapade.

"I had a call from the medical examiner's office in Harrisburg."

"So soon?" Usually it took a week or more to hear anything from that busy place.

"I think they were trying to clear their desks before Christmas."

That I could understand. "Whom were they calling about, Bernice or Oretta?"

"Both," Luscious said. "You were right about the cyanide, Tori. Bernice drank enough of it to kill a horse."

"How could she?" Maggie shuddered. "Wouldn't it have a bad taste?"

"The cyanide was in spiced cider, which she laced liberally with gin," I reminded them. "And she was already looped when she arrived, so she probably didn't even notice the taste."

"That's true," Maggie said. "Once, not too long ago, I was at a party where Stanley accused her of drinking anything if it had booze in it."

"Many alcoholics will do that." I remembered a few times when my mother drank aftershave, mouthwash, and even vanilla extract after my father and I had emptied the liquor cabinet.

"I wonder where you can buy cyanide?" I mused.

"Lots of places, I should think," Maggie said.

"Name one."

"How about a drugstore?"

Praxythea laughed out loud. "I can just see someone walking in and saying 'Hello, Mr. Pharmacist, I'd like a gallon of your very best cyanide.'"

Maggie protested. "What I meant was it's probably used in mixing medicines or something."

I remembered when I was a kid living in some third world country, I forget which, the missionaries used to use a strychnine-based medicine as a dewormer, but I couldn't think of anything with cyanide in it. I could ask a pharmacist.

"And I think you can buy it in a garden shop," Maggie went on. "Isn't it used in bug killers?"

"Do you want me to check that out?" I asked Luscious. I would anyway, but I thought it would be good for his self-image if I involved him.

"Go ahead, do what you want. Just stay out of trouble, please."

"What about the bullet that killed Oretta?" I asked. "Was the lab able to determine what kind of gun was used?"

Luscious nodded and drained his coffee. Praxythea leaped up to refill the mug, earning an adoring smile from the young man. With the addition of a little tail, he'd make a perfect puppy dog.

"The bullet," I prompted.

"It was a forty-four caliber. You don't see many of them in use anymore. Ballistics said it came from an early Colt, probably the model 1860."

"Find any traces of black powder?" Maggie asked.

Luscious nodded in agreement.

I stared at her in awe.

"My fiancé's a Civil War reenactor," Maggie reminded me. "And he's taught me more about guns than I ever wanted to know. The Colt model 1860 was the most common sidearm used during the war. Reenactors use them a lot."

I grabbed Luscious's arm. "The Civil War items that were found in the manger yesterday morning . . . in the square . . . were there any guns?"

"You mean that stuff that belonged to Cletus Wilson? Sure there were guns." Luscious paused, and I could tell that he and I were thinking along the same lines. "Damn! I gave everything back to him. What if there were fingerprints?"

"I wouldn't worry too much about that," I assured him. "Everything there had been handled by the church group. Fingerprints wouldn't tell you anything."

"I'd better go talk to Cletus," Luscious said, standing. "Maybe he has some ideas about who broke into his house."

"Good idea," I said. "There's always the possibility he made up the story about a robbery as a cover-up." I tried to recall when he'd reported the burglary. Then I remembered—the dentist claimed his home had been broken into on Wednesday, the day of Bernice's murder.

CHAPTER 19

At the hour of midnight

ACCORDING TO THE CLOCK ON TOP OF THE Lickin Creek National Bank, it was half past eleven. I was alone on the dark streets; the bad weather had forced even the local teenagers off the "peanut circuit," their Saturday-night party route around the downtown area on its confusing one-way streets. From what I'd read at the library, I was pretty sure the coven would meet at midnight. I hoped I was right.

A block away from the old cold-storage building, I parked and walked the rest of the way, staying close to the deserted buildings to keep from being seen. That was an unnecessary precaution, for there wasn't a soul around. It was too cold for anyone to be out, a fact I was really beginning to appreciate. I pulled up the hood of the floor-length black velvet evening cape I'd found in Ethelind's hall closet and put my head down against the wind.

When I reached the parking lot, I paused for a moment in the shadow of a pine tree, knowing I was damn near invisible in my black getup: cape, slacks, sweater, gloves, and even blackface, for I'd burned a cork and smeared its soot all over my cheeks just as I'd seen some-one do in a movie. I could see no lights, but that didn't mean anything because the windows were all boarded up. There were a few cars there, and one of them I recog-nized as Cassie's BMW. It looked like I'd guessed right about the meeting time.

I crouched over and stepped forward.

Something grabbed my ankle and held on. I tumbled to my knees and was face-to-face with Lickin Creek's best-known homeless man, the notorious Big Bad Bob. He'd lived on the streets for years and constantly refused any and all offers of shelter, even on nights like this.

"Let me go," I whispered, trying to pull away from him. I wasn't afraid, because Bob was neither big nor bad, and he'd never harmed anybody but himself. His body odor, though, was enough to asphyxiate a skunk.

He stared intently at my face, then said, "Hey, Miz Miracle. Damn near didn't recognize you with that dirt all over your face. You one of them witches?" He lisped his question, due to the absence of all but his incisor teeth. With his wide face, low brow, receding chin, glassy eyes, and fanglike teeth, I thought he resembled a well-fed python.

"Not really," I said softly. I turned my face to the side to avoid his foul breath and asked, "Are they inside?"

"Yeah. Bet you'uns is writing a newspaper article 'bout them, ain't you?"

"Yes. Yes, that's exactly what I'm doing. So if you'll just let go of my ankle, I'll be on about my business."

"You want me to come with you? I can take care of you if they try to hurt you."

"Good God, no! I mean no, thank you. There's noth-ing to be afraid of."

He released my leg, then put his face very close to

mine and rasped, "I done hear they kill babies and drink their blood."

I scrambled to my feet and shot across the parking lot before he could share any more local folklore with me.

Thanks to Stanley Roadcap, this time I knew where the safe entrance to the building was located. The door was unlocked, and with one last glance around to make sure I was unobserved, I slipped inside.

It was reassuring to feel the solid concrete stairs beneath my feet as I slowly made my way up through the heart of the building. Although I'd brought a flashlight with me, I didn't dare turn it on, so I groped along in the darkness. From above, I heard music. A harp. It sounded more heavenly than sinister.

I reassured myself that I had nothing to fear. After all, these people were just local women who happened to have some rather unorthodox beliefs. One of them was my own employee, Cassie. There was absolutely no reason for them to harm me. So why was I sneaking in when Cassie probably would have invited me to come if I'd asked? Because, I told myself, if they knew they were being observed by an outsider they might do things differently. This way I'd learn how they *really* celebrated the winter solstice.

Up ahead flickered a dim orange glow. I moved silently through the open doorway at the top of the stairs and ducked behind a post. It was pitch-black here on the edge of the large room, and I knew the people around the altar in the center of it would not be able to see me. From my position behind the pillar, with my black hood nearly covering my face, I was in the perfect position to observe everything that went on.

About a dozen women, in long white gowns, held hands in a circle, while another sat on a stool and strummed a Celtic harp. Their faces were lit by the black candles on the altar, but I was too far away to identify any of them.

As the last chord of the melody I recognized from the Irish musical production *Riverdance* faded away, one woman stepped into the center of the circle, raised her arms over her head, and began a melancholy chant. I immediately recognized Cassie.

She stepped outside the circle of women, and began to walk clockwise around then, her arm outstretched, one finger pointing to the floor. Four times she stopped to chant words I couldn't hear, then moved back to the center of the circle and raised her arms. "Sisters, we stand between the worlds, where darkness and light, birth and death, love and hate, meet as one. Under the Cold Moon, we have aligned ourselves with the Goddess to celebrate the sabbat of the winter solstice." After some arm waving in the direction of the women, Cassie stamped the floor with one foot and called out, "As above, so below—this circle is sealed."

One after another, four women in the circle murmured something I couldn't catch. I edged forward a little closer, knowing I was still in the shadows.

"I, your priestess and witch, do call upon our blessed Lady of the Moon. Descend upon me now." A candle flared on the altar behind her, and Cassie's whole body seemed to glow from within. "I am the Maiden, I am the Great Mother. I am the Crone. I am Mystery, but I am known to all." Cassie lowered her arms and held them out as if embracing everyone in the circle.

"Tonight we will say good-bye to our dear sister Bernice and assist her on her voyage to Summerland."

"To Summerland." A bell rang three times.

"There she will rest, till she returns."

"Rest and return." More bells.

Cassie pulled something from the purple cord that circled her waist and held it above her head, where it glittered in the flickering candlelight. "Hold your athames high, my sisters, and send your energy through them to our beloved sister Bernice."

Now, I recognized the shiny articles all the women held as ceremonial daggers.

She began to chant again. "As the Moon waxes and wanes, so do the seasons flow, and so do we move from death to rebirth." The others joined in. The room filled with the eerie sound of panpipes. The heavy odor of the sandalwood incense burned my eyes and made them heavy. My vision became blurry, and I blinked my eyes several times trying to clear them. I wondered what was going to happen next.

"Dance!" Cassie cried. "Dance and raise the Cone of Power!"

One of the women accompanied the harpist on a small drum that resembled the bongo played by Desi on *I Love Lucy*. The rhythmical drumbeat was strong and hypnotic. On a bamboo flute, another woman played a haunting melody that wove in and out of the drumming. As I watched the women circle the altar, it became difficult to keep my eyes focused. I wanted to get out. To leave them alone with their ritual. This was a private place, and I didn't belong here.

I suddenly realized the huge room had fallen silent. The women had broken their circle and were looking in my direction. I knew there was no way they could see me, but even as I thought that I knew somehow they could. I turned to flee, and someone grabbed me around my waist. I screamed, pulled free, and ran toward the exit, but the door had closed, and I couldn't find it in the darkness. I crashed into the cold brick wall, almost knocking myself out.

Behind me, someone shouted "Get him," and I ran, as fast as I could, with one hand on the wall, hoping, praying, to find a way out before I was caught. At last, I reached an opening. I charged through it and down the stairs as fast as I could run, only to realize, too late, that I was on the rickety staircase I'd been warned about yesterday.

Above me, someone screamed. The staircase began to shake and groan. I clutched at the railing as if hanging on to it would save me. The whole thing leaned to my right, swayed back, then leaned again. With a terrifying screech, it pulled away from the wall in slow motion. As it started to drop, I had the presence of mind to fling myself off the steps before I could become entangled in the twisted metal. I plunged through the black air forever, although in retrospect it was probably only a second or two, and heard a scream that I recognized as my own. It was cut short when I hit the icy water and my mouth filled with water.

Down I went. Down into the frigid water. I held my breath as long as I could, until, at last, my feet touched the bottom. I pushed off with all my might and shot back up. Just as I thought my lungs were going to burst, I surfaced and gulped a mouthful of air and water.

A flashlight beam played the surface, then shined directly in my eyes. I couldn't see who was behind it. Something whacked me on the side of my head, and I again slipped beneath the surface.

I came up spluttering, and heard someone yell, "Can you see him?"

"Here," I gurgled.

The flashlight swung around. "There he is. See if you can reach him with that pole."

This time I ducked when the thing came round.

"Grab on," a voice called out. "We'll pull you in."

I already had a tight grip on it. "Got it," I yelled.

I was pulled rapidly through the water until I bumped into a solid wall. I could see by the glow of the flashlight that the landing was several feet above my head. Many hands reached down, took hold of my clothing, and tugged. Everything I had on was so heavily waterlogged, I thought I'd never be able to get out, but they finally managed to drag me onto the landing, painfully scraping my stomach in the process.

I gasped and choked, facedown on the cold pavement, until someone rolled me over and held a flashlight close to my face.

"Good grief, it's Tori Miracle," came Cassie's familiar voice. When she stopped shining the light in my eyes, I was able to see a dozen angels in white gowns and one creepy-looking python staring down at me.

I struggled to a sitting position. Cassie knelt down beside me and supported me with an arm. "What on earth are you doing here?" she asked. "We thought you were one of those teenagers that break in to smoke pot. You're sure lucky. If we'd had a gun, you could be dead."

"Real lucky," I said ruefully. "I'm half-drowned." It was all I could do to say that much through my chattering teeth.

"We've got to get you out of those freezing things and into some dry clothes," Cassie said. "Can you walk?"

With some help, I stood.

The python stepped out of the angel circle, and was transformed back into Big Bad Bob. "I'm sorry I scared you, miss."

"Go away, Bob," Cassie said, not unpleasantly. "You know you aren't allowed in here."

"I was only trying to make sure she was okay."

"She is. Now go."

He looked at me as if asking permission, so I said, "It's all right, Bob." Satanic rituals and baby blood didn't seem nearly as dangerous as sitting around in my soggy, freezing clothes.

With one last worried look, Big Bad Bob disappeared into the shadows.

Cassie and her friends led me up the safe staircase and into a small room adjoining the large hall where they held their meeting. Cassie handed me a soft heap of white silk. "Take off those wet things," she commanded, "and put this on."

She discreetly turned her back while I stripped. As I peeled off my sodden clothes, I wondered if I'd ever be able to wear any of them again. Certainly, I'd have to replace Ethelind's black cape. The dress Cassie had given me turned out to actually be two pieces, with a crinkly slip worn underneath several layers of transparent silk. Once I had it on, I announced, "I'm decent."

Cassie tugged on the sleeves, straightened the plunging vee-neckline, and wrapped a white cord around my waist. When she was finished, I felt like a parachutist who'd gotten tangled in her lines.

"Now that you're in no danger of freezing to death, why don't you explain what you were doing here?" Cassie asked.

I searched my mind vainly for a believable fib, and finally opted for the truth. "I knew it was winter solstice, and I wanted to observe your ceremony."

"All you had to do was ask, Tori. We welcome any visitor who comes with an open mind."

I was glad for the dim light for I knew I was blushing.

"Did you expect to catch us sky clad? Maybe carrying on a satanic ritual? Killing babies? You see, I know all about the rumors that have gone around town."

I didn't respond. There was no need to.

She glanced at her wristwatch. "It's so late, we might as well call it a night. We've already closed the circle, so you might as well come along and have some refreshments with us, if you like."

The way she said it was more of a command than an invitation. I followed her out into an adjoining room, where the others were waiting. Now I realized they were all wearing sweaters or sweatshirts under their filmy gowns. I wished I was. My wet hair had dripped all over the top of my borrowed gown, and I was chilled to the bone.

After all the ritual and mysticism, I was truly surprised when they served cupcakes and decaffeinated coffee. My teeth chattered as, for the first time in my life, I turned down a piece of cake.

Cassie draped a plaid blanket over my shoulders. "We'd better get you home," she said. "Did you drive?"

"T-t-t-truck. N-n-n-next b-b-b-block."

"I'll take you there." As Cassie put on her coat, the other women hugged me good-bye.

"Come back," they said. It was a funny thing, but I really wanted to.

While we waited for Cassie's car to warm up, I asked Cassie a question that had been on my mind since I observed the ceremony. "Are you Satan worshipers?"

"Absolutely not! That's a common misconception. Sure, there are teenagers who call themselves 'witches,' and go for the satanic rituals, but Wicca is a nature-based religion and we worship the Mother Goddess, from whom all creativity flows."

"And do you believe in magic?"

Cassie fiddled with the heater control. "Not if you think of it as supernatural power. What I and the others of my coven believe is that there is a way to make use of our psychic talents. We conduct ceremonies in order to alter our state of consciousness."

"For what purpose?"

"To increase our perception of the world around us so we may grow in wisdom and understanding. You'll find it all in chapter two of my book."

I must have looked doubtful, for she continued. "Have you ever listened to a meditation tape or gone to a seminar on self-awareness? What we do is similar to that kind of thing. The ritual 'trappings' we use just help us enter another state of consciousness."

"While I was watching your ceremony, I felt a strong sense of belonging," I said. "I'd really like to know more. I'm definitely going to read your book."

"I think you'll see there's nothing to fear," Cassie said, acknowledging she knew what the local gossips said about her group. "Except maybe from some of the local fundamentalists who see us as a threat. Now, Tori, why don't you *really* tell me why you were here tonight?"

I admitted I'd come because of Bernice's involvement with the coven. "I thought I might learn something that could help me identify her murderer."

"And did you?"

I shook my head. "Nothing. It's another dead end. What's got me baffled is that there's no apparent link between the two murder victims other than that they both were in the Christmas pageant. I need to find a connection between them."

I think that's when the newspaperwoman in Cassie took over, because she said, "I hadn't thought about that, but I guess it won't hurt to tell you this since both Oretta and Bernice have passed over. Oretta *was* in our coven. For a very short time—a couple of years ago." She put the car in gear and drove out of the parking lot.

I was so excited I almost forgot I was freezing to death. "She was? What happened?"

"You know how Oretta was. Always wanting to run everything she was involved in. She wasn't willing to wait patiently for her turn to be the priestess. When she decided to rewrite our ritual to make it more poetic, she and Bernice got into quite a row, and that's when Oretta had a hissy fit and stomped out."

"Did anyone in your coven resent her leaving?" I asked.

Cassie smiled. "Can't say any of us missed her very much." And as if she could read my mind, she added, "We don't go around bumping off people who decided the Craft isn't for them, Tori."

"Do you know of anyone in town who might have it in for someone simply because she was a witch?" I was thinking of bigots like Weezie Clopper.

She shook her head. "I'm afraid you're way off base, Tori. There are lots of religious fundamentalists in Lickin Creek, but I can't think of any who'd get so riled up they'd want to kill us." She paused and looked thoughtfully out the window for a moment. "It has happened in other places, but I'm sure it wouldn't happen in Lickin Creek . . ." Her voice trailed away as if she realized for the first time just how unpopular her chosen religion was.

She parked next to my truck. "Better take a hot bath when you get home," she suggested as I opened the car door.

I shivered inside the blanket. "Like I need someone to tell me. Thanks, Cassie. I'm really sorry I disrupted your ceremony."

"It's all right, Tori. In a strange way, it was actually kind of fun. One thing you should know—we believe in the threefold law, and that means that whatever you do returns to you threefold. It's something I think about every day as I go about my business."

With that gentle and somewhat mysterious warning in mind, I drove home. My wet boots squished with every step as I entered my kitchen and flipped on the light switch. Noel, sleeping on top of the refrigerator, flew into a panic when she saw me in my strange garb.

"I know," I said. "It's not the real me."

Praxythea, a vision of loveliness in peach satin, came in from the front hall, wiping sleep from her eyes. "Oh, thank goodness it's you. I heard a noise and . . ." She stopped in the doorway, and her mouth gaped in astonishment at the sight of me. "What in God's name happened to you?"

"Don't ask," I warned. "And that should be 'What in Goddess's name!'"

With all the dignity I could muster, I wrapped my blanket tightly around me and swept out of the kitchen.

CHAPTER 20

Sing we joyous all together

"YOU'RE A VERY LUCKY LADY," PRAXYTHEA said as she poured a cup of coffee for me.

The aroma of vanilla and hazelnuts rose from my steaming cup. Where had she found gourmet coffee in Lickin Creek? I winced and repositioned the ice bag I'd tied on my head. "I don't feel very lucky." Below the knot on my forehead where a would-be rescuer had clobbered me with a pole, a black eye was threatening to erupt. I was also covered with bruises, and my stomach smarted where most of the skin had been scraped off. At least I didn't have to worry about getting a tetanus shot. I'd had one a few months ago thanks to an unfortunate incident at the launderette.

"I meant, think about what would have happened if those women had been less understanding and had called the police. After your very recent brush with the law over the same offense, it's quite likely you'd be drinking your coffee in a jail cell this morning."

I hadn't thought of what I'd done at the cold-storage house as trespassing, but she was right. All my efforts to solve a crime and help Luscious had only succeeded in losing me my cat and nearly ruining my reputation.

Praxythea refilled our cups and placed another of her

freshly baked homemade cinnamon buns on my plate. I decided she was nice to have around.

"Tell me what it was you were wearing when you came home last night," she asked.

"It's called a 'goddess dress.' Cassie said she orders them from the Red Rose catalog."

"Let me get a pencil. I want to write that down."

I was pretty sure I knew what Praxythea would be wearing on her next TV appearance.

The grandfather clock out in the hall struck the hour. Reluctantly, I pushed away from the table. "I've got to get going. Trinity Evangelical is having its Christmas luncheon and greens sale today, and I promised to take some pictures for the paper."

Praxythea jumped up. "That sounds so delightfully old-fashioned! I'd love to pick up some fresh greenery to decorate the house with. Some holly for the mantel and maybe some pine boughs for the staircase. Is it all right if I come along?"

"I'd like the company."

I dressed in a hurry and we drove across town to the church. Judging by the number of vehicles in the parking lot and along the side streets, at least half of Lickin Creek was in Trinity Evangelical today. The sign on the door announcing the Christmas pageant had been canceled was a sad reminder of the tragedy that had happened here a few days earlier.

As we entered the basement auditorium, a woman seated at a folding table said, "That'll be five dollars, please, if you're going to have lunch."

"I only came to take pictures . . ." I began, but Praxythea whipped out her wallet and paid for two lunches.

"Your names, please," the woman asked. "I need to put you on the list."

"Praxythea Evangelista."

"The TV psychic?" When Práxythea smiled her acknowledgment, the woman jumped up from the table and came around to shake her hand. "Take my picture, please," she said to me. "My kids aren't going to believe this without proof."

I obliged, and she returned to her station.

"Name, please?" she asked, looking at me.

"Tori Miracle."

While not expecting the same enthusiastic welcome she'd given Praxythea, I was a little disappointed when she asked, "Any relation to the Merckles over in Big Pond?"

"No. And it's Miracle."

"It's a miracle the Merckles aren't all in jail. Have a nice lunch."

"I'm not hungry," I told Praxythea. "I just finished breakfast."

"You can pretend to eat a little. I'm sure the money's going for a good cause."

We picked up brown plastic trays and got in line. Although it was just now noon, at least a hundred people had already been through the line and were now eating at the long tables that filled the hall.

We carried our heavy trays over to a table and sat on metal folding chairs. "Good grief, there's enough food here for an army," Praxythea said, staring aghast at the heaping plates and bowls in front of her. "And what's worse, I don't even know what most of it is. Except for the fried chicken."

"I tried to warn you," I said. "One thing about living in Pennsylvania is that the natives take food seriously. Since I've been here for several months, I can probably identify most of it for you.

"The slices are scrapple. Don't ask what it's made of if you want to enjoy it. And this is corn pudding. These cute little things are 'pigeons,' or steamed potato dumplings, and if you're afraid we don't have enough starch, we also have a side order of deep-fried potato balls."

Praxythea picked something out of the oyster pie and sniffed it. "Are oysters typically found in Pennsylvania-Dutch cooking?"

I nodded. We were just getting started. I went on with my description of the food. "String beans with ham, sauerkraut with dumplings, corn bread, lettuce salad with hot boiled bacon dressing—"

"Why are the eggs pink?" Praxythea stared at the bright yellow and pink sliced eggs on top of her salad.

"They're soaked in beet juice. And of course we have the usual assortment of sweet-and-sours. Different kinds of chow chow, apple butters, preserved fruits, and homemade pickles."

"They don't eat like this on a daily basis, do they?"

I said, "Look around you. Does anybody here look undernourished? Even the air in Pennsylvania is fattening."

Although I had finished off several cinnamon rolls only a short while ago, the aromas drifting up from my tray were making me hungry. Conversation stopped, and we concentrated on eating. Praxythea ate everything, the first time I'd ever seen her do more than nibble daintily at her food.

We were settling down to Montgomery pie and coffee when Primrose Flack mounted the steps to the stage and took the microphone. "Good afternoon. It is really wonderful to see such a terrific turnout for our Christmas luncheon. The greens and baked goods will be on sale shortly in the next room, but before that we have a real treat in store. Our own choir soloist, Lydia Wrigley, is going to sing Andrew Lloyd Webber for us." She led the applause as a chubby woman in a purple suit and feath-ered hat came out on stage and bowed.

Praxythea leaned over to ask, "Why doesn't she sing Christmas carols?"

I shrugged. "I don't think she knows anything else." I felt like a real old-timer, since I'd heard Lydia sing at least six times, always an Andrew Lloyd Webber medley. She stood smiling directly at me, and I realized she was waiting to have her picture taken. I obliged.

In a clear soprano voice, Lydia Wrigley began her first number, "Wishing You Were Somehow Here Again." It was a song that always brought back melancholy memo-ries of people I'd cared for who'd disappeared from my life. It affected me even more strongly now that it was Christmas and I was feeling so alone. I whispered in Praxythea's ear, "I have to leave. Do you want me to give you a ride home?"

She shook her head. "I'm having a lovely time, and I still want to pick up some pretty things for the house. Don't worry about me."

I popped into the next room and took a few pictures of the greens. By the time I had my coat on, Lydia was singing "Love Changes Everything." Sure does, I thought, thinking of how drastically my life had changed because of Garnet. Last Christmas, instead of attending a concert in a church basement, I went to the Christmas show at Radio City Music Hall. And that was only the least of the changes I'd made in the past year.

Outside, the light snow that had fallen glimmered like diamonds on the pavement. A familiar-looking woman came toward the church from the parking lot, and I real-ized I'd seen her at the coven meeting last night. She appeared not to recognize me as she hurried into the church.

Across the street was a drugstore, and since I still had

time to kill before my appointment with the clown at Raymond's art studio, I went in to talk to the pharmacist on duty.

His horrified reaction was funny, to say the least. "You want to know about what?"

"Cyanide," I repeated. "For Pete's sake, I'm not looking to kill anybody. I only want to find out if it's possible to buy it in a drugstore."

"Absolutely not," he said emphatically.

"How about insecticides? Do any of them contain cyanide?"

"No! Not since *Silent Spring*." He looked suspiciously at me. "Why do you want to know?"

"I'm doing an article for the *Chronicle* about the different poisons we come across in our daily lives—and how we can be more careful with them." I was amazed at how easily the fib rolled off my lips. Actually, it wasn't a bad idea and maybe I *would* write that article someday.

He began to look interested. "Good thinking. There's poisons in lots of things. Even the stuff on a firefly's bottom that lights up would be poisonous if you ate enough of it."

I had no intention of eating even one firefly's bottom, but I thanked him and turned to leave. "Water," he called out. "Drink too much water, and it'll kill you."

On the street, I turned my collar up against the arctic wind and figured it was close enough to two o'clock to drive over to Raymond's art studio.

A big bunch of helium-filled balloons marked the entrance to the studio, reminding me that the clown had carried balloons in the parade. I parked and walked over. The window was full of flowers and signs: WELCOME, GALA GALLERY OPENING, ADMISSION FREE, ART SHOW TODAY, REFRESHMENTS INSIDE, BUY YOUR CHRISTMAS GIFTS HERE. Since there were only a couple of vehicles parked on the street, I had a feeling that Raymond's gala gallery opening wasn't going too well.

My original belief that the clown was simply drumming up business returned to me, and I almost left, but my natural curiosity won out. With pounding heart, I pushed open the door and went inside.

There were two couples in the large front room, holding plastic cups of punch and looking uncomfortable. Raymond entered from a back room, wearing a jaunty beret and an artist's smock, and carrying a plate of cookies. He stopped dead when he saw me and dropped the plate, and although his mouth opened and shut, no words came out.

"Merry Christmas," I said, pretending nothing was out of the ordinary. The four visitors all leaped forward to help pick up the mess.

Raymond stared down at the cookie and plate shards with a horrified expression, but when he looked back to me he seemed to have regained his composure, for he was smiling warmly.

"How delightful to see you," he gushed. "I'll just bet you've come to do an article about my show for the *Chronicle*."

I didn't have a chance to correct him. He practically seized me by the arm and dragged me over to the card table in the corner. "Do have some punch. And some of my delicious homemade cookies."

The liquid in the bowl was red, and the melting sherbet floating on top was lime-green. Christmasy, maybe, but not very appetizing.

"No, thanks," I said. Since my clown hadn't showed up yet, I decided to take a look at the large, brightly colored canvases hanging on the walls.

Raymond was still gushing. "I am so delighted you are here. Thrilled, actually. You are going to just love this.

I'm showcasing my most talented students today. Aren't we all just thrilled, everybody?" The two couples exchanged perplexed glances, then shrugged and nodded that they too were "just thrilled."

The canvas I stood before was bright red splashed with white. Tacked to the wall below it was a piece of cardboard with the title "Cat-astrophe," and next to that was a photo of a gray and white tabby. I looked again, and the little white splotches turned into paw prints.

The next painting was called "Re-pussé." The accompanying cat picture was a calico. More paw prints, this time on a very pretty blue background.

Confused, I turned to see the two couples nudging each other as if sharing a good joke.

"I don't understand," I said. "These don't look like paintings. They look like a cat stepped in some paint and then walked on the . . ." Light dawned. "Your students are *cats*?"

A rude noise burst from one of the two women. It sounded exactly like a snicker that she tried to cover up by finishing her punch.

"These photos—these are your students?"

"I have given a few artists the opportunity of a lifetime the chance to nurture their God-given talents in a loving environment," Raymond said seriously.

"Cats!" I couldn't believe what I was seeing and hearing.

"Certainly you've heard of them. My students have been hung in some of the finest galleries on the East Coast."

"I'm afraid I haven't kept up with who's hanging where."

"I am only a teacher," he said piously. "I take no credit for my students' accomplishments. They have all the talent."

A little bell over the door rang as the two couples made their escape. I was alone with Raymond, teacher of cats.

"How about some more punch? Oh, silly me, you never had any to begin with. Well, so nice of you to come. I don't want to take up any more of your valuable time. Do stop back another day." Raymond was tugging on my arm, gently pulling me toward the door. For a shopkeeper with only one possible customer, he was in an awful hurry to get rid of me.

I pretended not to understand and shook off his arm. "As long as I'm here, I want to see everything."

"Oh, dear!"

Next in line was "Puss in Boots," footprints on a silhouette of Italy, painted by a gray Persian. The one after that was "Puss-café," and the orange and white cat artist in the photo was most definitely my own Fred!

"Where is he?" I asked, in a voice so low it frightened even me. "Where is my cat? What have you done with him?"

"I don't know what you're talking about—"

I grabbed Raymond by the collar of his bright red artist's smock and shook him. "Don't lie to me, or you'll regret it for the rest of your miserable life!"

"In there," he gasped, pointing to a curtained archway in the back of the room.

He staggered when I released him and clutched at his heart. I didn't believe for a minute that he was having a heart attack. And I didn't care if he was. I rushed through the curtains, into a small sitting room/kitchen combination, where half a dozen cat carriers stood along the wall.

Fred's plaintive wail was instantly recognizable.

"Baby," I cooed, pulling him out of the container.

Maa-maa, he meowed.

"Yes, sweetie, Mama's here." There are times when he tries to talk, and this was one of them.

"I thought I'd never see you again." Tears flowed down my cheeks, as I hugged his warm, soft body.

"How could you?" I demanded of Raymond, who had padded into the room. "How dare you steal my cat?"

"I was going to bring him back, really I was. Remember when you told me he had artistic talents? That's when I knew I had to check him out."

"I told you what?"

"At the market, you told me he'd painted a design on your kitchen floor."

"Good grief! I was only trying to make conversation. You sneaked into my house while I was sleeping and stole him, didn't you?"

He nodded, looking so sheepish I would have laughed if I hadn't been furious with him.

"Why didn't you simply ask me if you could borrow him for a few days?"

"Like you'd let me take your cat!" Raymond flung a pudgy hand up to his chest. "My heart . . ." he gasped.

"Stop it, Raymond. You are not getting any sympathy from me."

When he suddenly turned a strange shade of grayish-blue and collapsed on the couch, I realized he wasn't kidding.

"Shall I call an ambulance?"

"Pills. Over there." He waved a hand in the direction of a rolltop desk. By the time I got back to him, Fred was curled up on his lap.

He took a pill and recovered quickly. Rather too quickly, I thought, but then I'm no expert on heart conditions. Fred was content to stay where he was.

This was a good sign, I figured. It meant that Raymond had not mistreated him, for Fred was a good judge of character and would never have anything to do with someone who had hurt him.

"Can I get you a cup of tea or something?" I asked.

"My, yes. That would be lovely. There's a full kettle on the stove and some peppermint tea on the counter. Fix one for yourself, too, dear."

While I waited for the water to boil, I looked around the small room and realized the couch on which he was sitting was a sleep sofa. This was obviously where Raymond lived. There were no paintings in here, only framed photographs, dozens of them covering every inch of wall space and sitting on every flat surface.

"Family and friends," he said. "Mostly all gone now." His voice was mournful.

I picked up a photograph of a beautiful woman to take a closer look at her gorgeous beaded Victorian gown. "She's very lovely. Who was she?"

"Grandma Zook. She was a great beauty. The toast of Lancaster."

I replaced it next to a smaller photo of a group of children that obviously dated from a more recent time, the sixties, I'd guess.

He saw what I was looking at and said, "That's me on the left." The chubby little boy who smiled at the camera long ago bore a close resemblance to the rotund gentleman on the couch.

"I'd have recognized you anywhere. Who are the others?"

"Just some of the kids I used to hang out with." He came over and took the photo from my hands. "That's Oretta Clopper there." He indicated a dainty blonde child with a shy smile.

"Wow. Did she ever change."

"In many ways. She was such a sweet little girl, but

she grew up to be one stubborn bitch—never would admit that the animals at the shelter had talents that needed to be nurtured." He smiled, but it faded quickly. "That little boy kneeling on the ground in front of us was Eddie Douglas."

I took the photo and studied the dead child's face. So this was what Eddie had looked like. Sandy-haired. Freckle-faced. An ordinary kid, who should have had a chance to grow up to be an ordinary man. From the age he appeared to be, I guessed the picture must have been taken only shortly before he disappeared.

"He was younger than you, wasn't he?"

"About five years."

"Kind of odd he hung out with you older kids, wasn't it?"

Raymond shook his head. "All the neighborhood kids played together. It didn't matter how old they were."

"Who's the little girl on the end?" I asked. "She looks to be about Eddie's age."

"Well, of course she does," Raymond said. "That was Eugenia Douglas, Eddie's twin sister."

CHAPTER 21

Sorrowing, sighing, bleeding, dying

"PRAXYTHEA, I'M HOME. AND I'VE FOUND Fred." The echoes in the dark interior of the house signaled that I was alone. In addition, there were none of the usual signs that Praxythea had been there: no cookies baking, no coffeepot on the stove. I wondered what she'd found to occupy her in Lickin Creek on a quiet Sunday afternoon, but I wasn't really concerned. Women like Praxythea seem to have unlimited inner resources.

I put Fred on the floor and placed a bowl of Tasty Tabby Treats in front of him. No telling what he'd been eating during his ordeal. Noel approached him cautiously as he gobbled his food.

"Yes, Noel, it's Fred," I told her.

She sniffed him from head to toe. After deciding it really was Fred, she knocked him on his back with one swipe of her front paw and began to lick his stomach. Fred just lay there with a goofy expression on his face, so I left them alone.

Coffee would be nice. I'd grown accustomed to Praxythea always having a fresh brew going. I filled the pot with water, found the coffee, then gave up when I couldn't find the filters and fixed a cup of instant. Sometimes the old ways are the best ways.

I still couldn't get over being astonished at what I'd discovered at Raymond's. Why hadn't anyone in town mentioned Eddie Douglas's twin sister? A call to Cassie gave me my answer.

"I'd completely forgotten," she said. "It happened a very long time ago. And the Douglases weren't local. The father moved here to work for the defense contractor. They'd only been here a year when the tragedy struck."

"Still, it seems odd," I persisted.

"Think back thirty-five years in your own life, Tori."

"I wasn't even born."

"Exactly. Neither were at least half the people in town. If they were around, they were involved with their own lives, their own families, and their own problems. A family who moved in and out of their world in one year wouldn't make much of an impact."

I understood what she was getting at. "If the sister's still alive, she should be notified. Do you have any idea of how to go about looking for her?"

"I'll try the police in the Texas town where the parents died. If they can tell me something, I'll call you back."

While I talked, Noel had rolled Fred over and begun a major attack on his ears. He didn't seem to mind.

I wondered about the mystery clown. He'd never shown up at Raymond's. Even out of costume, I was sure I'd have recognized him simply by his height. What had been his purpose in luring me there? As I looked down at my cats, I thought it was almost as if Fred had somehow sent him to me. Fred, seeing I was looking at him, narrowed his blank eyes to golden slits and said, *Prrrp*. He was a dear, there was no doubt about it, but not even Fred had the brains to do that. There had to be a more realistic answer.

The cats, having emptied the bowl of Tasty Tabby Treats, disappeared into the interior of the house for a well-deserved afternoon nap. I put some lettuce in Icky's container and changed the water in his bowl. I yearned for someone to talk to—other than a lizard—someone with whom I could share my happiness over finding Fred.

I shook off the gloom before it had a chance to overwhelm me. I'd ignore the things I couldn't change and concentrate on what I could do, which was finding the person or persons who had killed two women in the past week.

After a quick phone call, I went up to my room to see how bad I looked. Really bad, I noted. The bruise on my forehead had moved down during the day, and my eye was now swollen and an ugly purplish-blue. I tried to cover the area with makeup with little success. In the hope it would draw attention away from the disaster area, I put on some bright red lipstick. One last look in the mirror—I shuddered and tried not to think of myself as looking like the female equivalent of the parade clown.

Dr. Cletus Wilson lived about a half mile away, a distance I would normally have walked, but not with the snow coming down as hard as it now was. His house would have been an exact duplicate of mine, except it had been carefully and expensively restored to its original splendor, while mine was in danger of collapsing any second. New cedar shingles covered the exterior, windows with many panes reflected the sunset as though on fire, porches were freshly painted.

Before I could touch the lion's head door knocker, the door swung open and a smiling Dr. Wilson greeted me warmly. I felt like Little Red Riding Hood meeting the wolf and controlled the impulse to say, "My, what big teeth you have." He didn't strike me as the type of person who would find that funny.

While he helped me out of my coat and hung it on a mahogany and marble hall tree, I gazed in awe at the huge display of guns, swords, and banners hanging on the walls of the entry hall.

"What do you think?" he asked, squeezing my shoulder.

I moved sideways, shaking off the offending hand. "It's like being in a museum."

"Come into the living room. I've got lots more to show you."

He wore a red brocade smoking jacket with a black velvet collar and had tied a white silk scarf around his neck like an ascot. Except for old black-and-white movies on *American Movie Classics*, I'd never seen anything quite like it. "Nice outfit," I commented. "Did you pick it up at an antique store?"

Ronald Coleman beamed at me. "How nice of you to notice. I have a fondness for the elegance of days gone by."

The living room was warm, unlike my own barn of a house, and a fire sparkled in the marble fireplace. Dr. Wilson handed me a stemmed martini glass. "With a twist," he said. "So much more elegant than olives."

I hate martinis, but I took the drink and sipped it with a murmur of appreciation for the twist.

He directed me to the Empire sofa. I realized immediately that I'd made a mistake when he sat next to me, way too close.

"So glad you called," he said, blasting me straight in the face with his denture breath. "After we met at bingo the other night, I thought you would."

What a conceited ass! And you'd think a dentist could afford a decent set of choppers.

"I am so anxious to see your treasures, Dr. Wilson." I fluffed up a throw pillow and wedged it between us.

He leered, misinterpreting my remark as a witty double entendre. "I'll be happy to show you what I've got. And please call me Cletus."

"I meant Civil War treasures," I said, with a giggle I hoped sounded girlish and flirty.

"Of course you did." I expected the Monty Python troupe to jump out with a "nudge, nudge, wink, wink."

Cletus led me into an adjoining room, where the walls were lined with glassed-in shelves. "No one, outside of the National Park Service, has a more extensive collection of Civil War artifacts," he said proudly.

"I believe it!" I gasped at the enormous cannon in the center of the room.

"Had to reinforce the floor with steel beams to hold that little number."

We circled the room, while he explained the significance of every item in every case, down to the last bullet. When I thought we were finally done, he announced, "And now, on to the jewels of my collection." He slid open a pocket door to the next room.

My parents and I had once fled a country during a coup d'état, where the revolutionary army hadn't owned as many guns as Cletus had in this room.

"Does all of this date from the Civil War?"

"Sure does." He pointed to a rifle hanging from the wall. "This one here's one of more than thirty-seven thousand muzzle-loaders discarded on the Gettysburg battlefield—nearly half of them jammed during the battle. That one's a Spencer, the first repeater to use metallic cartridges."

As we moved down the line, Cletus described in great detail, and with a good deal of relish, the carnage caused by each type of weapon. "And even though this here

Henry could fire twenty-five rounds a minute, it never got to be as popular as the Spencer."

We'd come full circle. I longed for a drink. Even another martini would be welcome.

"I have a real treat for you," he announced. "Follow me, my dear."

Now what? I wondered. Flame throwers? Hand grenades? Land mines? Mummified soldiers? Against my better judgment, I followed him down a flight of stairs to the basement.

"My very own firing range." He flung open the door and stepped aside to let me in. "And I've just had it soundproofed, so that bitchy Mrs. Kauffman next door won't have any more cause to complain. Here, put these on," he said, handing me a set of earmuffs. "We'll take a shot or two."

The target was a life-size depiction of a soldier in a Confederate uniform. "I don't really want to shoot at a person, even a make-believe one," I protested.

"Have it your way." He pressed a button. The soldier fell back and was replaced by Bambi, with a white circle drawn right over her heart.

"That's *much* nicer." My sarcasm seemed to blow right over his head.

After carefully wiping his hands on a clean towel, he took a gun from a satin-lined box and held it up for me to admire. "This is a Colt 1860, the principal sidearm used during the war."

"Model 1860? Is that the gun you reported stolen? The one found at the manger?"

"Same model. Different gun. Luscious picked up the other yesterday."

"Did he say why?" I wondered if Luscious had told Cletus that we suspected his gun had been the one used to kill Oretta Clopper.

"Uh-uh. Guess he wanted to check it for fingerprints. See if he can catch the punks that broke in." His face turned purple as he began a rant about the Lickin Creek crime wave. According to Cletus Wilson, all evil in the world stemmed from males between the ages of thirteen and eighteen. "It's a damn shame when a man's home is invaded like that. Some nights I can't even sleep for thinking about it. They all need lined up and shot."

It struck me as funny that even an educated dentist dropped *to be* from his sentences, like most Lickin Creekers did.

"How did they get in?" I asked. "With all these guns, you must have pretty tight security."

"Thought I did, but I forgot about the damn door here in the basement. It's so well hidden by shrubbery that only kids from this neighborhood who live in similar houses would know about it being there. They broke out one of the glass panes, then just slid the bolt open. I've taken care of that now. Got a steel door in. Nobody's going to break through that baby." Ronald Coleman had been transformed into Charles Bronson.

The hidden basement door was the same way some-one had invaded my house. I agreed with Cletus that it had to have been done by someone familiar with the way these old houses were built. What I didn't understand, though, was why nothing had been taken from my house. And very little of value was taken from his, and even that was all found in the manger. Maybe he was right about it being teenagers out for thrills. Cletus's Civil War artifacts were obviously valuable, and Ethe-lind's antiques were worth thousands. A professional burglar would have cleaned out both houses.

I still wondered if his story about the robbery was a cover-up. "Were you here when they broke in?" I asked.

"Uh-uh." He smiled slyly. "I was at a friend's house,

if you know what I mean." Again, "nudge, nudge, wink wink."

I smiled like a conspirator. "You naughty boy, you have a friend, and you're flirting with me."

"We have an understanding, her and me."

I restrained the impulse to scream, *She and I*, and asked, "Were you at her house the night of the fire when Oretta Clopper was killed?"

"No. My friend was staying here that night. Why are you asking?"

"You do know that Oretta was shot, don't you?"

He nodded.

"The police and the fire chief think the fire was set to cover up her murder. If you were home, I thought you might have seen or heard something that would help the police find her killer."

"I see," he said. "Sorry I can't help, but I was otherwise occupied, if you know what I mean."

"Would you be willing to give me your friend's name and address? Perhaps she noticed something you didn't."

"I don't suppose she'd mind," he said. "We have nothing to be ashamed of." He wrote something on a scrap of paper and handed it to me. I glanced at it, didn't recognize the name, and stuck it in my pocket. If the woman backed up his story, it was a classic alibi.

He placed the gun in my hand and stood close behind me. "Now, Tori. Let's try a few shots." His breath was hot in my ear, as he said, "I always bring my girlfriends down here for some target practice. You can tell a lot about a gal by the way she handles a weapon."

I placed the gun on the ledge and said firmly, "Dr. Wilson, I am *not* one of your girlfriends. And I am *not* going to shoot at Bambi or any other target you put up. I was a reporter on the police beat in New York for too many years, and I've had the misfortune to see firsthand the kind of havoc guns can cause."

Unabashed, he adjusted his ascot and smiled at me. "Can I offer you another martini, my dear?"

⌒

For some reason, the second martini went down a lot smoother than the first. Before I left, I was feeling quite warm and content. Even Cletus didn't seem as noxious as I'd first found him.

When I entered my house, Praxythea was sitting at the kitchen table with Fred on her lap. In one excited burst, I told her the story of Fred's adventures and amazing rescue. My voice trailed off as I realized she wasn't giving me her total attention.

"Is something wrong?" I asked.

"Not at all."

I could tell by the glint in her emerald-green eyes that something was very wrong. I waited for her to say more.

"I'm sorry, Tori, but I have to leave," she said.

"You mean right after Christmas? I didn't expect you could stay for much longer."

She studiously avoided looking at me. "Now, Tori. I have to go now. My friend sent his plane. It's at the Lickin Creek airport, now. I've been waiting for you to come home so I could say good-bye."

Her suitcases were next to the door.

Stunned, I sat down and stared at her. "What about our old-fashioned Christmas? All our plans? I was really looking forward to it."

"But you have so much, Tori. I didn't think he cared, but it turns out he needs me more than you do. I'm sorry."

I have so much? What could she possibly mean? Wasn't I the loneliest person on earth? I thought of all the people in the world who were so much worse off, and my despair slowly vanished. It was time to climb off my pity-pot. "I understand. Really."

"There's one thing I'd like to ask of you," Praxythea said.

"Ask away."

"I wonder if you'd mind if I took Icky with me? He and I have bonded over the past few days, and I know he'll miss me."

She wanted to take the lizard! Hallelujah. God works in mysterious ways.

"He's really not mine to give away," I reluctantly pointed out.

"But he's homeless. Now that Oretta's gone, who's going to find a home for him?"

"Good point. He's yours." I walked over to the terrarium and chanted, "Adios, sayonara, adieu, dzaijyan, lakon, aloha, auf Wiedersehen, ciao." I could think of no more ways to say good-bye.

"Have you been drinking, Tori?" Praxythea stood at my side with a disapproving look on her face.

"Two martinis," I admitted.

"I'd stay away from them in the future if I were you."

Outside, a car horn tooted. "That must be the taxi," she said. "Can you help me carry Icky's stuff out?"

As we picked up his home, some papers that had been under the terrarium fell to the floor. "Let them lie," I said. "I'll get them later."

"They could be instructions for his care and feeding. We'd better look at them."

I gathered the pages into an inch-high stack. "For Pete's sake," I said as I looked through them. "*Death in the Afternoon* by Oretta Clopper. It's a copy of Oretta's play! I see she continued with the tradition of stealing other people's titles."

"She must have dropped it when she brought Icky in," Praxythea said.

"Accidentally on purpose. When she asked me if I wanted to read it, I made some sort of excuse about being too busy. My guess is she left it here knowing my natural curiosity would get the better of me."

I tossed it on top of the Christmas catalogs stacked on the counter and took hold of one end of Icky's abode. "We'd better get you on your way before the weather turns really bad."

After she left, in a flurry of promises to come back as soon as possible, I sat down at the table and drank the last cup of freshly-brewed coffee I'd probably have this year. *Things could be worse,* I thought. *After all, I've got a nice place to live, a job, some new friends, and a baby brother due any minute. I don't need Praxythea to have a nice Christmas.*

To break the extraordinary silence, I turned on the radio. Public Broadcasting was offering Tchaikovsky's *The Nutcracker.* "The Dance of the Sugar Plum Fairy" painfully reminded me that Oretta's adaptation of the ballet had ended up being "The Death of the Sugar Plum Fairies."

Even the cats looked dejected. Fred probably wished he was back at the art studio where he was a star. We were all startled when the phone rang with a call from Luscious.

"I don't believe this," I shouted, after he was finished talking. "We can't just quit!"

"I don't have any choice, Tori. Marvin Bumbaugh and the mayor just left my office. They said there have been too many complaints about you, and they want it to stop. Now!"

"But what about your job?" I stammered. "We've got to find the killer or you'll be fired."

He sounded as low as a man could possibly be when he said, "You don't get it, do you? They gave me two weeks' notice."

"But they can't do that."

"They can, and they have. It's over, Tori. All over."

CHAPTER 22

Dashing through the snow

ON MONDAY MORNING, I MOPED. NOT BE-
cause I was still feeling sorry for myself—I'd gotten over that; I didn't need to depend on other
people to make me happy—but because I felt terrible about what I'd done to Luscious. Instead of helping
him, my investigative efforts had cost him his job.

I spent the afternoon reading Cassie's book on witchcraft. Although I'd never belonged to a church, I always
felt I was a spiritual person, and her depiction of the
Wiccan religion touched a spot deep inside me where
something had always seemed to be lacking. I was determined to find out more.

On Tuesday morning, Greta called and guessed immediately that something was bothering me. "What's
wrong, Tori? You sound like you've lost your best
friend."

"I made the mistake of weighing myself this morning," I said. "It's ruined my whole day."

Greta laughed. "Christmas is no time to worry about
your diet. And speaking of not dieting, what are you
planning to bring tonight?"

"Tonight?"

"Tori, you haven't forgotten the Gochenauer family Christmas Eve celebration, have you?"

"Of course not!" I hadn't forgotten; it was just that Christmas Eve had snuck up on me. "What would you like me to bring?"

"A couple of pumpkin pies would be nice."

I agreed, knowing the Farmers' Market had extended its hours for the holiday. If I hurried I could get there before it closed at noon.

"And do bring your houseguest," Greta said.

"She's gone."

"I thought you two were going to have an old-fashioned Christmas."

"We are—just not together."

The silence on the other end of the line told me what Greta thought about Praxythea's sudden flight.

I found myself apologizing for Praxythea. "She's a busy woman . . ." I began.

"Aren't we all?" Greta said with a sniff.

She made a good point.

I practically flew to the market, arriving just as the last of the vendors was draping sheets over her display case. Luckily for me, she had a few pies left, and I bought them for half price, relieved I wouldn't have to learn to bake today.

"Bad storm's on the way," the pie woman said. "Better stock up on bread and milk."

I did as she suggested and was halfway home before I realized I never drank milk!

The storm had been pummeling the Carolinas for two days and was now affecting Lickin Creek. An icy wind cut right through my jacket as I left the market, and fine sleet burned my face. The roads would be "slippy" tonight, the term Lickin Creekers used to describe icy driving conditions.

Depending on which news station you listened to, the storm could blow out to sea, or it could overwhelm the valley. But they all described it as the "storm of the century," and urged listeners to prepare for the worst.

I spent the afternoon readying the house for the coming storm. There was little I could do about the flapping shutters, the rotting front porch, or the slate shingles peeling off the roof. I did round up all the candles and flashlights I could find, and placed them and a box of matches on the kitchen table.

I brought in wood for the fireplace, and I filled the bathtubs with water, so I'd have drinking water and be able to flush toilets.

The radio station, now calling itself Storm Watch Central, broadcast a minute-by-minute description of the blizzard as it rushed up the Atlantic seaboard.

Feeling as if I were back on a Pacific island battening down for an oncoming typhoon, I locked all the doors, including the one in the basement, and placed rolled-up towels on the windowsills to cut down on drafts.

With the bread and milk I'd bought at the market, three bags of Tasty Tabby Treats in the pantry, and plenty of kitty litter, we were prepared for anything short of nuclear war.

Although the house creaked and groaned under each blast of wind, I felt fairly safe, reassured by the fact that the old mansion had survived many storms in its lifetime.

". . . . storm of the century," the radio repeated.

Could this really be the worst storm in a hundred years? I wondered. Somehow, I felt that "Storm Watch Central" was exaggerating the seriousness of the situation, but whatever might happen, I was ready for it.

Over the course of the afternoon, the phone rang a few times. One poor soul was trying to sell his quota of credit cards before closing up for the holiday. I wished

him a merry Christmas and told him my credit rating
would never allow me to have a Visa card.

Another caller was Murray Rosenbaum, actor/Italian
waiter and my best friend and neighbor in New York. He
was calling from Dayton where he was spending Hanuk-
kah with his parents. He promised to send me a can of
caramel popcorn from his father's factory and wished me
a happy holiday.

After hanging up, I felt lonelier than ever. I missed
Garnet, even though I was now sure our relationship was
over. And I missed Alice-Ann. We'd always exchanged
gifts and called each other on Christmas, even when we
lived far apart. This year, in hopes of a reconciliation, I'd
bought a small Amish quilt for her. It waited under the
tree, but I'd had no word from her.

". . . winds of up to eighty-five miles per hour," the
radio said.

I kept hoping Greta would call to say dinner was canceled, but the Gochenauers are a hardy clan, and Greta
would hardly let a small thing like the "storm of the
century" stop her from celebrating Christmas in her
traditional way.

With the house battened down to the best of my ability, I settled on a couch, with the cats on my lap, to
reread a favorite Christie mystery. Ethelind's library had
a wonderful collection of mysteries by British authors.
Not surprising, considering she was a flaming Anglo-
phile.

". . . small-craft advisory for the Potomac River and
the Chesapeake Bay." Storm Watch Central was right on
top of the situation.

In the late afternoon, I reluctantly put the book down
and went upstairs to dress, choosing what I hoped would
be an appropriate outfit for Greta's dinner party. A long
green velvet skirt and a white satin blouse, both with

designer labels, and both from my favorite shop, a place in New York that sold "nearly new" or "previously owned" clothes for next to nothing.

I added three gold chains, studied myself in the mirror, then removed two. Greta was a flamboyant dresser, but the rest of Garnet's family was quite conservative, and I didn't want to look too "New Yorkish," as one elderly aunt had suggested when she first met me.

It was too early to go, so I set the kitchen timer to let me know when it was time to leave and sat at the kitchen table to finish my book.

When the bell rang, I thought at first it was the timer. But the cats jumped down, leaving globs of hair on my green velvet skirt, and ran toward the front of the house. Sometimes they were a lot smarter than I—at least they recognized a doorbell when they heard it.

I made a futile attempt to brush off the cat hair as I followed Fred and Noel to the front door. Unlike New York, there was no peephole. Most people in Lickin Creek felt there was little reason to worry about who might be at their door. I thought for a moment about the two dead women, Oretta and Bernice, who probably had gone blithely about their business until the moment they were murdered. Most likely neither of them had a peephole.

The door was ripped out of my hand as I opened it. Along with a blast of snow that covered the carpet in the foyer came Mrs. Poffenberger with her baby in her arms.

"Come in! Quick," I said, although she was already inside. I leaned against the door to shut out the howling gale.

"Can I take your coat?" I asked, wondering what on earth she was doing here.

She shook her head. "Can't stay. The kids is in the back of the truck."

"Good grief." I looked out the window and saw a whole bunch of snow-covered blanket-wrapped lumps in the open truck bed.

"That's not safe," I said.

"I don't got no choice, miss. I thought a lot about what you said to me—about doing what's best for the kids—so I'm moving to West Virginia. My sister'll help out till I can get a job."

I was surprised but tried not to show it. "What does your husband think of this?" I asked. I couldn't imagine him taking it calmly.

"He don't know nothing about it. I been sneaking things out a little at a time—diapers for the baby, the blankets. I ain't taking much—we don't got much. The furniture and TV is rented."

"Aren't you afraid he's coming after you right now?" I glanced nervously at the door, fearing that the outraged Mr. Poffenberger might burst through it any minute.

She allowed herself a glimmer of a smile—the first I'd ever seen. "He ain't going nowhere. He done dressed up in a Santy Claus suit and got stuck in the chimney."

"Chimney? You have a fireplace in a mobile home?"

"He was going to climb down the chimney of the barbecue grill in the backyard. He got stuck tight and fell asleep. Probably have to smash it apart to get him out." This time she smiled broadly. "Funny what a man thinks is clever when he's drunk."

"But the weather. It's snowing. He could freeze to death."

She shook her head. "I throwed some blankets over top of him. He'll be warm enough till he comes to."

The mental picture of a sleeping drunk in a Santa Claus suit stuck in a barbecue grill was funny in a grotesque sort of way, but I still was worried about his safety. What if he didn't "come to" in time? What if he was stuck there all night? The situation was potentially dangerous.

"I'm sorry, Mrs. Poffenberger, but I'll have to call the police to get him out of there."

Her face sagged. "Can you give me an hour's head start? Please, miss. You don't know what he'll do to me if he catches us."

The abused woman and her children deserved a chance for a better life. I wanted to help, but all I could do was give them the gift of an hour's head start. I was sure Mr. Poffenberger could survive for one hour, even in the snow. "You've got it," I said. "I hope everything works out for you."

She shifted the baby onto her left shoulder and extended her hand. "Thanks, miss. You always done spoke nice to me. Like a schoolteacher. And you found Kevin. I couldn't go without saying good-bye."

I took her hand, feeling extremely touched. Yes, I'd found Kevin, but my involvement with Mrs. Poffenberger had been minimal. Apparently, even that was more kindness than she'd experienced in a long time.

"Call me if you need anything," I offered.

She nodded. Her eyes were misty, and I realized mine were, too.

"God bless you," she said and was gone in a flurry of wind and snow.

"Merry Christmas," I whispered into the empty darkness. The only answer was an ominous creaking from the porch roof above me, and I pushed the door shut.

It was nearly time to leave for Greta's. I retrieved the pumpkin pies from the refrigerator, looked around the kitchen for something to carry them in, and spotted my bingo pie basket prize. Perfect! I could put the pies in it and give the basket to Greta as a Christmas gift.

I lifted Fred out of the basket, blew out the cat hair,

and put the pies in. It was cleverly designed with a footed stand inside, so the pies could be stacked without being squished. With the addition of a red bow I took from the Christmas tree, the basket looked quite festive. I hoped Greta would like it.

Before I left, I gave the cats their early Christmas presents: two catnip mice. Fred was ecstatic. Noel pretended indifference, but after I said good-bye, I peeked through the kitchen window and saw her rolling happily on her back with her mouse clutched between two white paws.

The roads were a lot worse than "slippy," they were downright dangerous. I passed several cars abandoned in snowdrifts, but Garnet's truck had both four-wheel drive and snow tires, and I drove safely, if slowly, to the outskirts of town where Greta's Fine Swine Farm was located.

The long driveway was already full of pickups and SUVs, so I had to park at the end near the road and hike through the ankle-deep snow. Halfway to the house, I was glad to spot a familiar car, Ginnie's Subaru. It was typical of Greta to invite someone whom she suspected would be lonely at Christmas. Greta was as genuinely concerned about people as she was about whales, dolphins, baby seals, rain forests, spotted owls, bald eagles, and brown trout.

At long last, I reached the large farmhouse. I paused for a moment in the snow to admire the Currier and Ives scene before me. The two-story farmhouse was like hundreds of others in Caven County: redbrick with tall, narrow windows trimmed with white wood, and second-floor balconies flanking the center section of the home. Each window held an electric candle topped with a small white flame, and the side-by-side front doors were decorated with large wreaths of real greens and pinecones.

When Greta and her late husband, Lucky Carbaugh, had purchased the farm from an Amish family, it hadn't even had electricity or running water. They'd spent years remodeling it into the comfortable home it was now.

I entered without knocking, as was the custom at Greta's house, and began to shed my coat and sloppy boots. The double living room was packed with people, and I didn't have the faintest idea who most of them were.

Nearly six feet tall, Greta towered over her short, stocky Gochenauer relatives. From her vantage point, she saw me and swept across the room to greet me. As she moved I heard bells, which meant she was wearing her favorite silver ankle bracelets from India. Tonight she wore a brilliant yellow caftan decorated with a blue, red, and green Indonesian batik print. Brass earrings from Pakistan dangled nearly to her shoulders. Several strands of multicolored agate beggar's beads from Taiwan hung around her neck. Her gray hair was twisted into a coil on top of her head with several lacquer chopsticks protruding from it. Good thing she's tall, I thought, or those things could put out someone's eye.

Comparing her to the rest of Garnet's solid, conservative Pennsylvania-Dutch family, I often wondered if she'd been adopted. She was probably the only person in Lickin Creek who could get away with dressing like that.

She seized me with an embrace that painfully mashed my face into her beggar's beads. "I'm so glad you're here at last," she said, welcoming me and chastising me for being late in the same sentence. "Come on in. Everybody's dying to meet you."

She suddenly spotted the pie basket and gasped. "For me? You are absolutely amazing, Tori. How did you know I collect Longaberger baskets?"

I smiled knowingly. Good for me—apparently I'd

made the right gift choice, whatever a Longaberger basket was.

Greta propelled me through the room, introducing me right and left, and interrupting conversations that dealt with farm crops from alfalfa to zucchini. If I heard it once, I heard it a zillion times: "What do you hear from Garnet?"

Nothing, I wanted to scream. *He doesn't write, he doesn't call. I have been dumped. You want to make something of it?* But I smiled, murmured my nice-to-meet-yous, and somehow made it around the room without crying.

The walnut grandfather's clock in the corner chimed the hour. "May I borrow a phone?" I asked. "I have to make a call."

Greta led me into the kitchen, where food covered every available inch of space. There was nothing like a Lickin Creek potluck supper to bring out the cooks' best recipes. The good smells made my stomach growl as I dialed Hoop's Garage.

A breathless female voice answered, "Yeah?"

"Is this Hoop's?" I asked.

"Yeah. Look, Tori, I'm just getting ready to close down, so if you'uns need a tow, you'll have to wait."

I silently cursed the New York accent that made my voice so instantly identifiable in Lickin Creek. "I need to talk to Luscious, please."

"Is it an emergency?"

"Of course."

"He's gone home. Wait a sec. I'll get his number."

I heard her rummaging through a desk drawer. In a few moments she was back. I thanked her and dialed the number she'd given me.

Luscious's mother answered and said they were just getting ready to leave for church.

"I really have to speak to him, Mrs. Miller."

She sighed, and soon Luscious was on the line.

I told him about Mr. Poffenberger trying to play Santa Claus in the barbecue grill.

"He's stuck . . . where?"

"You heard me. You'll have to get him out of there soon, Luscious, or he's liable to die from exposure."

"Aw, Tori. My mom'll kill me if I miss church."

I felt like a slimeball, but I said what I knew would get him moving. "Garnet would do it."

"I'm leaving now."

"Thanks, Luscious . . . and Merry Christmas."

"You, too."

I returned to the living room, where tables borrowed from the local fire hall were being brought in from the back porch. This required participation by everybody there. The men to carry them in, the women to wipe them off, and the children to cover them with table-cloths. When they were finished, we all admired the patchwork-quilt effect—every woman there, but me, had brought her favorite tablecloth from home and none of them matched.

Greta organized us into a line, and we filed into the kitchen through one door. There, we filled our Styro-foam plates from the mountains of food that covered the counters, then exited through the other door, where Great-aunt Gladys handed each of us silverware rolled up in a red paper napkin.

I was glad when Ginnie brought her plate over and took the chair next to me. "Thought it would be nice for both of us to sit with someone we know," she whispered.

"Bless you," I said. "I've met so many people I am totally confused. Am I wrong, or is everyone here named Zeke?"

"Only the ones who aren't named Gladys," Ginnie said with a sly smile.

I unwrapped my plastic silverware and tasted the oyster stuffing. It was wonderful. Ginnie nudged me with her elbow, and I noticed that nobody else was eating.

"Grace," Ginnie warned. "They're going to say grace."

"Oops!" I put the fork down and hoped nobody had noticed my faux pas. I was too used to eating alone in front of a TV.

Great-uncle Zeke came by filling our jelly glasses with nonalcoholic sparkling grape juice. "Sorry about this," he whispered to each person confidentially. "It's because of Greta and A.A."

"No need to apologize," I told him when he stopped at my place. I was glad that Greta was taking her involvement in A.A. seriously.

At last everyone was seated, and another Uncle Zeke said grace.

The food was turning cold, and I was aching to eat, but it was not yet time. Buchanan McCleary stood up and tapped on his water glass with a spoon to attract everyone's attention.

Several dozen Gochenauer and Carbaugh heads turned to stare at him.

Buchanan raised his jelly glass. "I propose a toast," he said. "A toast to our hostess, my lovely bride-to-be, Greta Carbaugh."

Greta blushed and looked up at him adoringly with dewy teenage eyes. The family members gasped, coughed, and even managed a few choked words of congratulations.

"It's going to be a June wedding," Greta said, cheerfully ignoring the minor furor Buchanan's announcement had caused. "And you're all invited." She reached for her glass, which wasn't there. "Uncle Zeke, you're drinking my juice," she said with a smile.

"Oh! Sorry," the old man on her left said. "I never remember, is mine the one on the right or the one on the left?"

"It doesn't matter," Greta said, planting a kiss on his wrinkled cheek. "At my wedding dinner, I'll see that you have two glasses of your very own."

"Nothing like young love," Ginnie said with an exaggerated sigh.

"They're young at heart." With that gentle chastisement, I took another bite of my stuffing and found it no longer tasted as good as I first thought. While I didn't resent Greta's happiness, I was ashamed that my first thought had been, *It should have been Garnet and I.*

Ginnie innocently rubbed salt into my wounds by saying, "Maybe you and Garnet can make it a double wedding."

I tried the turkey and found it tasteless. How could she be expected to know? The problem with always keeping your feelings to yourself is that nobody is there to help out when you really need it.

I fooled around with the food on my plate and listened to several of the uncles discuss the pros and cons of round hay bales as opposed to the old-fashioned square ones. "They can be dangerous," one said, referring to the round ones. "Just last year, Farmer Stone got crushed by one. Ruined his tractor, too."

"How much do they weigh?" I asked, thinking of the little square bales associated with hayrides.

"Fifteen hundred pounds, at least," he told me.

"Sure, you gotta handle them with a little care, but they save money," another uncle argued. "I can do it all myself—used to be I needed a crew to make square bales."

"Ain't no big deal," chimed in another. "Just keep the bales close to the ground, and you don't tip over."

Someone tapped me on the shoulder, and I turned to see one of the aunts smiling at me. "I'll bet those men are boring you to death," she said.

"Well . . ." I began.

"You just turn around and join us gals, Tori. We're talking about the Quilt Guild."

The scintillating dinner conversation ended when the pies were brought in. The choices were endless: mincemeat, cheesecake, cherry, apple, and pumpkin. Greta put several small pieces of several different flavors on a plate and passed it down to me. I ate it all. Funny how I can lose my appetite for nutritional foods, but hand me dessert and there's no stopping me.

After several servings of pie, a few of the men began to groan and undo their belts. That seemed to be the signal for some of the children to clear the tables. Within fifteen or twenty minutes, the room was back to its predinner look, with the tables stacked up once more on the back porch.

"Everybody gather round the piano," Greta ordered. "We're going to sing Christmas carols." She passed among us, handing out mimeographed song sheets that looked like they'd been used for at least forty years.

An aunt whose hair bun was covered by a starched white net bonnet sat down at the piano and began to play "God Rest Ye Merry Gentlemen." A few of the women began to sing, and soon the men joined in.

Something had been nagging at me since the start of dinner. I tried to focus on the song sheet before me, but somehow I couldn't concentrate. What was bothering me? I closed my eyes and tried to shut out everything that was causing sensory overload. And I remembered.

CHAPTER 23

That night revealed and told

"TORI, ARE YOU ALL RIGHT?"

I opened my eyes and saw Ginnie staring at me with a concerned frown on her face.

"You looked so odd," she said. "I thought you might be feeling sick—from all that pie."

I hadn't eaten *that* much. "I don't know, Ginnie . . . something just came to me . . . let's go somewhere quiet . . . where I can think."

We went into the small parlor that served Greta as a TV room. Hundreds of Santa Clauses—plastic, ceramic, papier-mâché, and even celluloid—dominated the room, occupying every flat surface. There they would stay, I knew, until spring when they'd be replaced by Greta's collection of Easter bunnies.

"Can I get you a glass of water?" Ginnie asked, still concerned that I might be getting ready to throw up.

"No, thanks. I'm not sick. Really." I sat on the plaid sofa and patted the cushion beside me. "Sit down. Maybe if I can talk this out, it'll make some sense to me."

Ginnie moved aside a needlepointed Santa Claus pillow and joined me on the couch. "What is it? You look terribly serious."

"I think it is something serious. Remember at dinner, when Uncle Zeke drank from Greta's glass by mistake?"

She nodded. "Sure. So?"

"So, it's been nagging at my subconscious ever since. Then, while we were singing, it came to me."

"What came to you? For Pete's sake, Tori. You're not making any sense."

"Give me a minute, Ginnie." My voice sounded curt, even to me. "I'm sorry. What I'm trying to say is it made me think about Bernice drinking poison from the Goblet of Life."

"And . . ."

"And I suddenly thought maybe her death was really a mistake."

"You mean you think the poison got into the cup by accident?"

I shook my head. "No. I mean I think someone put the poison in the cup intentionally, but then the wrong person drank it."

"That hardly seems possible, Tori."

"That's what I thought, too, but when Uncle Zeke and Greta talked about him drinking Greta's juice, it made me recall the first rehearsal I attended. And I remembered it wasn't Bernice who drank from the Goblet of Life—it was Oretta."

Ginnie's eyes widened. "You're right. I remember that now."

"At the break, Bernice went up to Oretta and started to argue with her. I didn't stick around to listen, but I'll bet Bernice was reminding Oretta that according to the script she was the one who was supposed to drink from the goblet."

"But the killer didn't know that," Ginnie said.

"Right. Oretta got carried away by the moment at rehearsal and drank the stuff by mistake. The killer must have decided right then that he could kill Oretta by putting poison in the cup."

"Only at the dress rehearsal, Bernice drank from the cup as she was supposed to and got the poison meant for Oretta."

"Right." My mind was in high gear now. "When the killer realized he'd murdered the wrong woman, he had to revise his plan—he paid a late-night visit to Oretta, shot her, and started the fire to hide the crime."

Ginnie picked up a Santa Claus snow globe from the coffee table, shook it, and watched the miniature snow fall for a minute. "You could be on to something," she said. "But there's something wrong with your scenario. Two things, actually."

"What?"

She put the snow globe down. "The killer must have known that an autopsy would reveal that Oretta had been shot."

"Of course. There had to be another reason he set the fire." I realized Ginnie had said there were two things wrong with my interpretation. "Help me, Ginnie. What else have I come up with that's offtrack?"

"It's just that you keep referring to the killer as *he*. It could be a woman!"

"Excuse me," I said with a hint of sarcasm in my voice, "if I wasn't politically correct. I referred to the killer by the masculine gender out of convenience. Actually, I have given some thought to him—or her—being a woman."

"Really? Who?"

"Weezie Clopper for one. But don't you breathe a word to anyone, or I'll deny I ever said it."

"Weezie? Why?"

"She had a grudge against Bernice and even sent her one of her poison-pen letters. But if I'm right about the intended victim being Oretta, then that rules Weezie out."

"Weezie and her husband had a feud going with Matavious and Oretta about the Clopper land," Ginnie pointed out. "I've always heard that to find a murderer you should look at the money angle."

"True. But Oretta really wasn't involved. The land was inherited by Matavious, and he held the title in his name. Killing Oretta wouldn't stop the sale." I stood up. "I'm going to go home, fix myself a cup of tea, and think about this some more. I'm sure something will come to me."

"Do you want me to come with you? Two heads are usually better than one."

"No, thanks, Ginnie. I need to be alone."

By the front door, I thrust my feet into my boots while Greta tried to keep me from leaving. "It's so early. We still have the scavenger hunt to do, and Santa will be arriving by sleigh in about an hour."

"Something's come up," I told her. "I really have to go."

She hugged me. "Drive carefully," she said, opening the front door.

As if I had a choice. "Thanks for inviting me." The windblown snow hid the fields around the farmhouse from my vision. I stood at the top of the porch steps for a moment and pulled the hood of my quilted jacket over my hair. Behind me, I heard Greta call out, "Okay, kids, it's piñata time!"

The door clicked shut, and I wanted to go back in, to the place where everybody was happy and warm and having fun, but I knew I couldn't. There were pieces of the puzzle to be put together, and I needed to be alone to do it.

In some places, the snow had drifted up to my knees.

It slid inside my ankle-high boots and turned my toes into ice cubes. The wind gusted so strongly I had to cling to the trucks parked along the driveway to keep from blowing over until I finally reached Garnet's truck. Although I was worried about the battery, it started up right away and I moved out onto the main road, saying a little prayer of thanks to the inventor of the four-wheel drive.

The roads were not as bad as I'd expected. Judging from the drifts of snow on the shoulders, the snowplows had been through at least once. But driving was still difficult, and sensible people were sitting out the storm in their homes.

When, at long last, I drove through the gateway of the Moon Lake development, I was struck by the total darkness around me. Black clouds above obscured the moon, and there was no light at all coming from any of the mansions' windows.

Power failure! Thankfully, I'd prepared for the worst.

I lit several candles and greeted the cats, who showed me they were very glad I was home by leaning up against me and meowing pitifully.

"I thought you guys could see in the dark," I said as I stroked them. "A power failure shouldn't bother you at all."

When they'd been soothed by a handful of Tasty Tabby Treats I went upstairs and stripped off my green velvet skirt. It had seen me through many a winter party in New York, but one Pennsylvania farm Christmas had done it in. Oh, well, I thought, dropping the soggy thing in the trash, it was time for a new Christmas outfit. Comfortably dressed in a warm sweatsuit, I joined the cats downstairs.

Although the house was heated by oil, the thermostat

was electrically controlled, so the temperature was dropping rapidly. The cats helped me prepare a fire by batting crumpled newspapers around the front parlor while I tossed match after match into the fireplace. Once it finally caught, I felt as proud as if I were Daniel Boone. My first fire!

The ringing of the telephone startled me. I'd assumed if the power was off, the phone would be out of commission, too. Cassie's voice cut through the static. "Tori, I've been trying to reach you all evening. I finally got through to the sheriff's office in Jasper, Texas."

"What did you find out?"

"Not a whole lot. The sheriff said he remembered the Douglas murder-suicide very well because it was his first case as a deputy. He said the saddest part of it all for him was seeing what happened to Eugenia after her parents died."

"What happened?"

"There were no relatives to take her in. So she was placed with a foster family. The worst happened there. She was physically and sexually abused for at least six months before anybody found out."

"That's awful."

"It was. He said she was so traumatized that she had to be institutionalized."

"Forever?"

"No. After about six months, she was adopted by an out-of-state family. He never heard any more about her."

"Can the family be traced?"

"He says it can't. I guess we'll never be able to let her know about her brother's body being found."

"Might be just as well," I said. "After all the horrible things that happened to her, she's probably better off putting it all out of her mind."

"I agree. Goodnight, Tori, and Merry Christmas."

"Merry Christmas to you—and thanks, for everything."

I went back into the kitchen and put on water for tea. Thank goodness the stove was gas. While I waited for the kettle to whistle, something tickled my memory like a barely remembered tune, then faded away before I could grab hold. Something about adoption. Reverend Flack saying his wife's problems came from her having been adopted after her parents were killed in an accident.

When the kettle came to a boil, I prepared tea in one of Ethelind's Staffordshire teapots and covered it with a flowered tea cozy. I loaded up a silver tray with the teapot, a mug, artificial sweetener, a bowl of potato chips, and an unopened package of chocolate chip cookies. I always think better with food on hand, and I had a lot of thinking to do tonight.

Back in the parlor, wrapped up in a crocheted afghan, with the fire going, several candles lit, a cup of hot tea in one hand, a cookie in the other, and the cats on my lap, I settled down to do some serious brainstorming.

Something had come to me in a flash right after dinner at Greta's, and I was pretty sure I knew who could have committed the murders, but even though I was now sure that the intended victim had been Oretta, the "why" was still beyond my grasp.

I reached for another cookie when suddenly a rumbling noise seemed to come from the very bowels of the earth. The cats sat up, startled, as it built to a crescendo that ended with a crack and a burst of lightning that momentarily turned the room as bright as day. My mug flew into the air, and the cats shot off my lap and sought refuge under a marble-topped table in the corner.

After my heart stopped pounding, and I'd wiped up the tea I'd spilled, I laughed at them. " 'Fraidy cats—scared of a little lightning."

Another clap of thunder shook the house. "Maybe you guys know what you're doing," I said. I'd never heard of thunder and lightning accompanying a snow-storm. I longed for a battery-operated radio to tell me what was going on, but that was the one thing I hadn't thought of earlier in the day.

Covered with another afghan, I tried to recapture my train of thought. During the past week, I'd spent a lot of time in the company of some very strange people: a TV psychic, a goddess-worshiping witch, a cat artist, a re-covering alcoholic–drug addict restaurateur, an amorous arms collector, a bingo buff, a hymn-playing scamstress, a cavorting chiropractor, and a child serial-killer-in-training. But I hadn't come up with any evidence that pointed to any one of them as a murderer.

"Damn," I muttered after a few minutes. "Nothing makes any sense."

Noel, still under the table, consoled me with a com-forting chirp.

How could I find Oretta's killer when I knew so little about the woman? If only I'd had the opportunity to get to know her better. What did she do in her spare time besides write bad plays and save animals?

That thought made me pause. Animals. Someone, pre-sumably the murderer, had rescued all the animals in Oretta's house before setting fire to it. Had Oretta done something at the shelter to incense a fanatical animal lover?

Something else occurred to me. Oretta's passion had been writing. What if she hadn't limited her plagiarism to Shakespeare and the Bible? Perhaps the answer lay in Oretta's own, or stolen, words. What if someone had written a wonderful play and shown it to Oretta, only to discover later that Oretta had incorporated it into one of her own works?

Nothing in the Christmas pageant had struck me as unusual, except for the terrible writing, but there was the copy of the play she'd artfully left behind when she'd brought the lizard in. It was the only thing of Oretta's that had survived her death.

She'd claimed it was her "masterpiece," a play even better than *The Bad Seed*. I'd purposely avoided reading it, dreading the woman's pretentious prose. But . . . everything else had been destroyed in the fire, and now I knew I had to look at the play. Maybe, just maybe, the answer I was looking for was there.

The manuscript was in the kitchen, half-buried under the Christmas catalogs. After refilling the potato chip bowl, I carried chips and script back to the living room.

I glanced at the title page and smiled at the title, Oretta Clopper's last attempt at plagiarism, *Death in the Afternoon*. With a sigh of resignation, I turned to Act I.

It was the worst writing I'd ever had the misfortune to read, but I couldn't put it down. Like the play Oretta had mentioned, it was about children. If I hadn't been directly involved so recently with Peter Poffenberger, the young wannabe serial killer, I would have thrown it down in disgust, but because I now knew without a doubt that children are capable of evil I kept reading, for Oretta's play was a thinly veiled account of Eddie Douglas's death.

In the first act, a little boy follows the older children to the quarry, where they have a secret clubhouse. The kids regard him as a pest, and when he falls in the water, they taunt him and throw rocks at him until he goes under and never comes up again. In the second act, the children, afraid of being punished, swear a blood oath not to tell anybody what happened.

I went back to read the cast of characters. The leader of that charming group of children was described as "a girl of great beauty and creative ability." Not surprisingly, her name was Loretta. Loretta's cohort was Richard Shook, "a chubby but artistic child."

As I read on, I was convinced that I was not reading fiction—Oretta hadn't even changed Eddie's name—that Oretta had written a play about the terrible thing she and Raymond Zook and possibly some other playmates had done. Why had she written it? Had it been an attempt to clear her conscience? In the past, this was the kind of thing I would have talked over with my best friend, Alice-Ann, but that was now out of the question. And I knew Maggie was out of town recreating the Civil War. I thought for a moment, then picked up the phone and called Ginnie Welburn's number. There was no answer, so I assumed she was still at Greta's house.

Before I had a chance to get resettled, a crash, far above, shook the house. What had happened? A tree? The roof? What? When the building stopped shaking, I took a candle and went upstairs to check on the damage. In a third-floor bedroom, a falling tree had smashed through a window. There was nothing I could do to fix it, not now with the storm at the height of its fury, so I moved everything I thought was valuable into the hall and shut the door against the howling wind.

Halfway down the stairs, with the candle flame casting eerie shadows on the wall, I suddenly thought I heard something in the front of the house. I stopped. Listened. Heard nothing but the wind. And yet, there had been a sound—I was sure of it. I wanted to run back to my room, lock the door, pull the covers up over my head. But that wasn't the adult way to face formless fears. Besides, my cats were down there. Near-panic set in. What if the door had blown open? They could be lost in the storm! What if they'd knocked over a candle? What if . . . ? "Stop acting like an idiot, Tori," I scolded myself. "Go downstairs and find out what's happened."

In the front parlor, I found the cats were standing on their hind legs looking out one of the front windows.

I whistled with relief. What I'd heard had probably been them, moving around. "Is it still snowing?" I asked.

My answer was a crack of thunder followed by a bolt of lightning. Both cats screamed and scurried under their table.

I was transfixed by what I thought I'd just seen in the window before the drapes fell back in place. A face. I rushed to the window and looked out, but of course there was nothing there. My imagination, triggered by the storm, had gone into overdrive.

After I threw another log on the fire, I tried to call Greta's house, but apparently the phone lines had finally gone down. I wondered how much longer this storm could go on, and once again, I longed for the comfort of a portable radio.

Noel came out from under the table and gave me one of her looks that called me a "stupid human."

"What's wrong?" I asked her. She answered by strolling out of the room with her twitching tail straight up. I followed her into the front hall, and from there I heard the sound of someone or something pounding on the front door.

I stood close to the door and yelled, "Is someone there?"

"It's me. Ginnie." I could barely hear her voice over the roar of the wind.

I unbolted the door, and it blew open, admitting Ginnie Welburn and a lot of snow. The porch creaked ominously as I shut the door as gently as I could. Noel screeched and ran from the hall.

"I tried to call you a little earlier," I said.

"I came straight from Greta's. I have something I wanted to give you." I noticed she had a plastic-wrapped bundle tucked under one arm.

"You shouldn't have . . . I didn't get you a present," I protested.

"It's not really a present. But don't open it until tomorrow, please." She placed it on the hall table, hung her parka on the hall tree, and went into the living room.

"What a lovely fire." She was rubbing her hands together in front of the fireplace.

"You look frozen. I'll get some tea," I offered. When she didn't say anything, I hurried back to my frozen kitchen. The water in the kettle was still hot, so it took only a minute or two to come to a boil. I refilled the teapot, grabbed another mug, and went back to the living room, where Ginnie was seated on the couch reading *Death in the Afternoon.*

I filled two mugs with tea and put one down beside her. She flipped quickly through the pages and didn't seem to notice me.

Fred crawled out from under the table and curled up on my lap. I sipped my tea, which burned all the way down.

"So she did give you a copy," she said.

"She didn't exactly give it to me. She sort of left it here for me to find."

"I figured that's why she came down here after leaving my house." Ginnie tossed my copy of the play onto the coffee table. "The day after we learned Kevin Poffenberger was lost."

"The reason she gave me for dropping in was she wanted me to lizard-sit an iguana until she could find a home for it. Now I can see that was just an excuse to leave the play here. But I didn't see it until Sunday night when Praxythea packed up to leave and took the iguana with her."

"That explains a lot." Ginnie sipped from her mug of tea. "Have you read it?"

I said quietly, "Yes, Eugenia, I read it tonight."

Ginnie jumped up and started pacing the length of the room. Back and forth, and back again. Fred, startled, jumped from my lap and ran from the room.

When Ginnie spoke, her words sounded almost child-like. "Eddie and I were twins, you know. Like one spirit with two bodies. Always together. If I hadn't had a summer cold, I would have been with him that day. And he wouldn't have gotten lost. Mummy said it was my fault he got lost.

"I tried to put it out of my mind. For years, I hadn't thought about it. Then Eddie's body turned up in the quarry, and I read Oretta's play, and everything flooded back. Eddie's disappearance. Mummy drinking. And crying all the time. The fighting. The shots. Finding Daddy and Mummy in the bedroom. All covered in blood.

"They took me away to live with another family. There was a terrible man there. He did things to me in the barn—it all came back.

"I called Oretta. Told her it was a great play. When I asked her if it was 'autobiographical,' she was stupid enough to tell me it was—that she'd done something as a child she regretted, and writing about it was her way of getting it off her conscience."

"Why didn't you go to the police with it?" I asked.

"I couldn't have proved she'd really killed my brother, and even if they believed me, she'd never have been punished enough. They'd have figured it all happened a long time ago, when she was only a child. At the most, she'd have been given a lecture and maybe a short sentence, suspended of course. She deserved to die."

"Did Bernice deserve to die?"

She began to cry. "I didn't mean to kill her." Her pacing was more rapid now. Up and down, back and forth. "As you guessed, it was meant for Oretta. I felt terrible when Bernice drank it and died."

"Where did you get the cyanide?"

"In the back of a locked closet in the high school lab where I sub. Years ago, cyanide was used for some science experiments involving the synthesis of complex molecules, but schools were supposed to have disposed of it." She half-smiled as if she'd heard a bad joke. "Most likely the science teacher didn't know how to get rid of it, so he locked it up and forgot about it. Nobody knew it was there. After I read her play and decided to kill her, I remembered the cyanide. I went over to the school and helped myself. A few students saw me, but they had no idea what I was doing."

"I'm going to have to call the police, you know," I said.

She stopped pacing and hovered over me, and I became frightened although I tried not to show it.

"You can't call anyone. The phone lines are down."

I knew I had to keep her talking. As long as she was talking, she wasn't hurting me. "With all the painful memories Lickin Creek holds for you, I'm surprised you came back here to live," I said. "Why did you?"

The pacing started again. "What I told you about driving through with my husband on our way to Gettysburg was true. There was something about the town that appealed to me. I instantly felt as if I belonged here. I didn't remember that I'd lived here before. After all, I was only five years old when it happened. It wasn't until I read Oretta's play that I realized that this was the town, and the reason I felt so comfortable here was because this was the last place where I'd actually been happy—before Eddie disappeared and my life ended."

"Why did you threaten me?" I asked, recalling the disemboweled bean-bag kitty that had been left on my doorstep. "What have I ever done to you?"

She stopped abruptly and knelt beside me. "Oh, no! Tori, you're the best friend I have in the whole world." She seized my hand and rubbed her face with it. "I wouldn't really have hurt your cat. It was just that you were asking so many questions, and I knew it was only a matter of time before you remembered me serving cider to Bernice. And once you'd read Oretta's play, I was sure you'd figure the whole thing out. I only wanted to scare you so you'd go back to New York."

Ginnie got to her feet and walked over to the fireplace. With her back to me, she said, "I need to go home for about half an hour. Put some things in order. Then I promise I'll go to the police station and turn myself in. Will you give me that time?"

I no longer feared her. I believed her when she said I was her best friend. But I was grappling with a new worry, Raymond Zook's safety. According to what I read, he had nearly as much to do with Eddie's death as Oretta. If I let Ginnie go off alone and she killed him, it would be my fault.

"I can't let you go," I said.

As if she could read my mind, Ginnie said, "I'm through killing, Tori. I'll never hurt anyone again."

I shook my head. "I'm sorry."

She spun around, and I had only a brief moment to notice the light reflecting off the poker in her hand before she swung it at my head. It connected with my skull with a horrible crack I'll never forget, and I collapsed in a blur of pain. I might have lost consciousness for a minute or two.

A red haze covered my eyes. Blood! I swiped at it. Tried to wipe it away. I was afraid I'd bleed to death before I could get help. I pulled the quilted tea cozy off the teapot and pressed it against my head as hard as I could to try and stop the flow.

The front door slammed. "Ginnie," I called weakly. "You'll never get away." I knew she couldn't hear me. Not through the door. Not over the storm. I struggled to my feet. By the time I staggered to the front hall, what I'd dreaded for weeks came to pass. The front-porch roof caved in with a splintering crash. I pulled the door open, only to find my way completely blocked by the fallen roof.

A car engine roared to life out front. Ginnie drove a four-wheel-drive vehicle, like most of the people I knew in Lickin Creek, so she'd have little trouble getting through the snow. Was she going home? Or was she, after all, going to kill Raymond Zook? Whatever she had planned, I knew I had to follow her.

In the kitchen, I checked my wound in the mirror on the hall tree. It wasn't nearly as bad as I'd feared, and I recalled someone telling me that even small head wounds bleed profusely. The pressure from the tea cozy had stopped the worst of the bleeding. I rinsed some of the blood off my face, put on my heaviest parka, and went out into the stormy night.

The truck engine leaped to life when I turned the key. God bless that battery manufacturer! I drove around to the front of the house, where the tire tracks left by Ginnie's car in the snow were easily visible.

Just as I feared, the tracks didn't lead to Ginnie's driveway, but continued to the highway. She wasn't going home. At the Moon Lake gate, I could tell she'd skidded a little as she pulled out onto the main road. I did, too. Because it had been cleared at least once, the snow wasn't as deep as it had been on the development's roads, but under the several inches of fresh snow there was now a solid sheet of ice.

The windshield wiper strived valiantly to remove the heavy snow, but it fought a losing battle. I was left with only a small hole to peer through, and I worried about losing the trail Ginnie left. Several times, the truck slid sideways. If I went off the road, I'd probably freeze to death before anyone found me. I gripped the wheel tightly and tried to remember what I'd heard about driving in snow. What came into my head was "stay off the roads." Too late for that now, I thought.

After driving for a very long time, I realized we weren't heading toward town, because even at five miles an hour we should have been there already. I had no idea where I was. All I could see through the front window was a small area of snow-white road illuminated by my headlights. The rest of the world was black.

The snow hitting the windshield had a hypnotic effect. It seemed as though the truck were no longer on the road but was flying through space. I was completely alone in the world. Maybe even out of this world, somewhere in another dimension. I plowed on, until I suddenly realized the tire marks I had been following had vanished.

I managed to get the truck turned around, even though I twice backed into a snowdrift that tried to hold me captive.

After a few minutes, I picked up the tracks again, although by now they were nearly obliterated by the driven snow. Ginnie had turned onto a nearly invisible side road.

Gritting my teeth, I said a little prayer—there must be a patron saint for fools—and drove in the ruts Ginnie's car had created. It was barely more than a trail, but the driving wasn't too bad because there was less snow than

I would have expected. I realized the trees that nearly met overhead must have sheltered the road from the worst of the storm.

Ginnie's car was stopped up ahead with the lights still on and the driver's side door open. I pulled up behind it and wondered what I should do next. I'd only followed her to prevent her from killing Raymond Zook. I hadn't thought about being trapped in the woods with her. My painful head wound was evidence that she was dangerous.

I slowly realized her car was empty, that there were footprints leading away from it. Where was she going? Where were we? In the back, I found a long metal tool I suspected was useful when changing a tire. It wasn't much, but it could be some protection if Ginnie tried to attack me again.

I followed the footprints deep into the woods. Just when I thought I was lost forever, the forest disappeared, and I stood on the edge of a vast white field. A lightning strike nearby illuminated the area long enough for me to see a hill on the far side of the field and realize I'd been here before. Beyond that hill was the quarry where Eddie Douglas's body had been found.

Sheet lightning, accompanied by nonstop rumbling, lit the night sky as brightly as if it were high noon. One flash came quickly after another. The eerie light allowed me to see a trail in the snow, leading across the field and up the side of the hill, and I knew Ginnie had gone that way. As the lightning once again illuminated the area, I saw a black figure silhouetted against the sky at the top of the hill.

"Ginnie," I cried. "Come back. It's too dangerous . . ." My words were swept away in the howling wind.

When the lightning flared again, she was gone.

CHAPTER 24

I heard the bells on Christmas Day

THROUGH THE KNEE-HIGH SNOW I PUSHED, following the tracks Ginnie had left in the snow, until I reached the edge of the quarry. There, the trail ended.

I called her name a few times, although I knew it was useless. Ginnie had chosen to die, like her brother, in the dark, cold waters of the quarry.

I struggled back to the truck, got it turned around, and drove as fast as I dared to the highway. As I attempted to pull onto the main road, the truck skidded on the ice. I gripped the wheel helplessly as I slid sideways across the road and down an embankment on the other side. Thanks to the seat belt, I wasn't hurt, but Garnet's truck groaned pitifully once and died.

The damn door was stuck. I couldn't get out. I'd probably freeze to death in an hour. I vented my frustration by pounding on the window with my fist. It hurt me a lot more than it hurt the truck. The door suddenly flew open, and I nearly tumbled out.

"Whoa, miss," a man said. "You okay?"

"I am now," I gasped to the man who had caught me.

"Geez, lady, you're hurt bad." He was gazing at my wounded forehead.

"It's just a flesh wound." I grabbed the tea cozy and applied pressure.

"What in God's name were you doing driving on a night like this?" he asked.

"It's a long story. What are *you* doing on the road?"

"I'm a trucker. Trying to get home to West Virginia for Christmas. Thought I could beat the storm. Can I take you to a hospital?"

I shook my head, a motion that caused so much pain I resolved not to do it again for a long time. "Just drop me off in Lickin Creek, please."

"It's right on my way. Come on." He gave me a boost into the cab of his eighteen-wheeler.

The truck barreled down the highway as if there were neither snow nor ice outside. High up in the cab, protected from the storm, I fully understood the meaning of the song "King of the Road."

He dropped me off at the small brick ranch house Luscious Miller shared with his widowed mother. "Merry Christmas," he called, after making sure someone was there to let me in.

Luscious, in blue flannel pajamas decorated with red fire engines, opened the door. As I passed by him, I sniffed discreetly and was relieved not to smell alcohol on his breath. We sat in his small living room, and he listened carefully as I told him what had happened. "Give me two minutes to get dressed," he said and disappeared down the hall.

In a minute and a half, he was back. Since the phone lines were down, the only way we could round up a search-and-rescue team was to physically go after them. We started at the Lickin Creek volunteer fire department, where we interrupted a poker game. The officer in charge sent one of his men to get the dive team. The EMTs were ready to go immediately. Not one person complained about having to go out in the "storm of the century."

Luscious led the procession to the quarry in his own four-wheel-drive vehicle. Bringing up the rear was Henry Hoopengartner, the coroner. It took the divers only a few minutes to find Ginnie's body.

It was daylight when Luscious drove me home. The storm had passed, leaving massive devastation in its wake. Barns had collapsed, trees were down, and roofs were ripped off. The manger scene in the square had been completely destroyed, but instead of looking upset the people cleaning up the mess looked as cheerful as if they were at a block party. There's nothing like a natural disaster to pull people together!

I was relieved to find my house still standing, minus the front porch, of course. "Come in and have some coffee," I suggested.

"I'd like that," he said.

The house was like an ice box. "My cats! I hope they're all right."

"They've got fur coats on." Luscious laughed.

They came running in to greet us when they heard our voices. Luscious endeared himself to me forever by picking up Fred and saying, "What a nice big boy he is."

I found an old-fashioned coffee pot and managed to get it working. While I was occupied with that task, Luscious disappeared.

"Luscious, where are you?" I called.

"In the living room."

He was on his knees before the fireplace. "Thought I'd take the chill off for you," he said. "Good thing you thought to bring in all this wood."

His knobby spine strained against his shirt. I hadn't realized he was so skinny. "I'll fix us something to eat," I said.

"Thanks. I could use something."

In New York I would have run down to the deli on the corner, but that was impossible in Lickin Creek. With what I'd learned from watching Praxythea in the kitchen, I managed to put together a rather good-looking breakfast of bacon, scrambled eggs, and toast. I even sliced some of the "world's best fruitcake," laid it on a plate, and added some of Praxythea's crescent cookies.

I piled everything on an enormous silver tray commemorating Queen Elizabeth's coronation and carried it out to the living room. We pulled chairs in front of the fire and ate ravenously.

When I came back with fresh coffee, I found Luscious holding the package Ginnie had left for me. "It says 'To My Best Friend, Tori, from Ginnie.'"

"Go ahead and open it."

He stripped off the plastic wrapper and opened the box. "It looks like a manuscript. And there's an envelope on top with your name on it."

"It's a copy of Oretta's play." I took it from Luscious. "Hard to believe this innocuous pile of paper caused three deaths." I opened the envelope and through tears that nearly blinded me read Ginnie's letter out loud.

Dear Tori,
    By the time you read this, I will have joined Eddie. I should never have let him go off by himself that day. At least now he won't be alone anymore. I am glad, glad, glad that Oretta's dead. She deserved whatever she got. But Bernice didn't, and I'm sorry about that. I was afraid to try poison again after that horrible mix-up. That's why I "borrowed" a gun from that old lech Cletus. When it nearly blew her head off, I knew I couldn't go on

with my plan to kill Raymond Zook. He'll never know how lucky he was.

    You have been a good friend, Tori, and I would never hurt you. Please remember me with kindness.

Eugenia (Ginnie) Welburn.

The knot on my head throbbed, evidence that she would have and did hurt me. But I still wanted to believe she struck me in desperation, to give her time to get to the quarry, and not because she meant to harm me.

Luscious handed me his handkerchief, which I used without even checking to see if it was clean.

"It looks like she intended to drown herself in the quarry from the beginning," he said.

I nodded.

"When did you realize she was the killer?" he asked.

"Last night, at Greta's Christmas Eve party when Uncle Zeke drank out of Greta's glass by mistake, it reminded me that at the first rehearsal Oretta had absent-mindedly drunk from the goblet. Bernice complained to Oretta, and they agreed Bernice would drink from the Goblet of Life at the next rehearsal, just as she was supposed to. As I thought about everything that went on, I recalled Ginnie had been passing out cookies and cider at both rehearsals. It would have been easy for her to place a cup of poisoned cider on the pedestal without anyone noticing. But I still didn't suspect her because she didn't seem to have any reason to kill Bernice. She hardly even knew her.

"But as I came to realize that Bernice wasn't the intended victim, I knew the answer had to lie with Oretta. When I read *Death in the Afternoon*, I discovered the motive. The names of the children who had been involved in Eddie's death were changed ever so slightly, but still recognizable. Oretta became Loretta Klinger."

Luscious said, "Her maiden name was Singer."

"And Raymond Zook was Richard Shook. What she didn't bother to change was the name of the victim, Eddie Douglas, or the name of his twin sister, Eugenia, better known to the other kids as Ginnie. I remembered Ginnie commiserating with me when I said I got upset about people calling me Victoria because that isn't my name. She said she hated it when people called her Virginia. That was because Ginnie's nickname wasn't short for Virginia, but Eugenia."

Luscious interrupted. "I thought your name *was* Victoria."

"It's Tori. I was named for the gateway to a Shinto shrine on Okinawa where my mother went to pray for a baby. It should have ended with a double *i*, but Mother was never any good at spelling."

"Interesting. Sorry. Go on."

"After reading the play, I realized Ginnie had a motive—and it was revenge for the death of her twin brother, or retribution, if you want to call it that, on the woman who was responsible. It must have come as a terrible shock when she read that play. She'd been made to feel such guilt by her mother. When she learned the circumstances of his death—that the children could have saved him, or at least told where he was so his body could have been recovered—she snapped."

"I don't understand why she burned Oretta's house down. She must have known it wouldn't cover her crime."

"The fire wasn't meant to cover anything. She wanted to destroy Oretta's computer and all copies of the play.

She realized if anyone else read it, they'd start looking at her as a suspect. Just as I did."

"Were there other reasons you suspected her—before you read the play?"

"There were. Three days ago, I visited Cletus Wilson." I couldn't help laughing at Luscious's expression. "It wasn't a date. I went over to ask him some questions. He took me downstairs to his shooting range and showed me how to use a gun similar to the one used to kill Oretta. Cletus said he took all his 'girlfriends' shooting. Ginnie had mentioned she'd gone over to his house for a drink and had barely escaped with her 'girlish virtue' intact. That, and the fact that she lived in the neighborhood and knew about the location of the hidden door in the basement, started me thinking about her. I guess she must have decided to steal a gun rather than buy one and risk being identified."

"Do you think she broke into your house, too?"

"I'm sure of it. She came in the same way through the basement. She suspected Oretta had brought over a copy of her play the day she brought me the iguana to take care of. But she didn't find it, because Oretta had hidden it under Icky's terrarium, in hopes that when I found it my curiosity would get the better of me and I'd read it."

"And the bean-bag kitty?"

"She wanted to scare me. She feared with all the investigating I was doing that I was getting close." I felt tears on my cheeks. "Damn," I muttered into Luscious's handkerchief. "I wish I'd had a chance to tell her I understood. I wish I could have helped her."

"Remember what she did, Tori. Murder is the most horrible of all crimes."

What I did remember was the disintegration of my own family after my brother's death. And the guilt I'd carried ever since. How would I feel if I suddenly learned someone else had been responsible and had let me take the blame? And if my parents had killed each other over it instead of dissolving their marriage, I knew I'd feel even more remorse. Even worse things had happened to Ginnie as a child as the result of her brother's death. Although I couldn't justify what she did, I could understand it.

"I should have read the play as soon as Oretta described it as being 'like *The Bad Seed*, only better,' " I said. "I might have stopped this from happening."

"What's *The Bad Seed*?"

"It was a play written in the fifties by Maxwell Anderson, about a charming little child murderess. In the play, she got away with her evil deeds, but in the 1956 film version I saw on TV, the kid got hit by lightning at the end. A neat Hollywood way of resolving the problem of how to punish an adorable eight-year-old killer.

"Oretta told Ginnie and me about her 'masterpiece' the night Kevin Poffenberger disappeared. The search for another missing child must have triggered repressed memories that she needed to get off her chest. The final straw for Ginnie must have been when Eddie's body was found and she realized Oretta's version of his death was fact, not fiction."

Noel rushed into the room and mewed frantically at me. "What are you trying to tell me, sweetie?" I asked.

"I think she's telling you someone's pounding on your back door," Luscious said. "I'll get it."

He was back in a minute, followed by a man whom I didn't recognize at first. My mailman. In civilian clothes.

"Morning, Miss Miracle. See your porch finally bit the dust."

"Lucky you weren't under it," I said, rising. Why was he here on Christmas morning? Was he looking for a tip?

"Big package of mail came in last night from Harrisburg for you. Saw the letters and foreign stamps. Look like they might be from Costa Rica. Thought you might like to have them as soon as possible, so I took them with me."

I grabbed the letters from his hand. More than a dozen of them. All from Garnet! Some postmarked more than six weeks ago.

"Some countries don't got such good mail service as we'uns do here in the good old U.S. of A.," he said.

"Thank you," I whispered, holding the letters close to my heart.

"How about some coffee?" Luscious asked.

"Sounds good."

"And fruitcake," I said. "I'll get it." In the kitchen, I placed my precious letters on the table. I'd read them later, when I was alone.

I started a fresh pot perking, and as I sliced more fruitcake, I heard a knock at the door. Marvin Bumbaugh, accompanied by Lickin Creek's Laotian mayor, Prince Somping, glowered at me as I greeted him.

"Where's Luscious?" he demanded. "His mother said he was here."

"And Merry Christmas to you, too," I said sweetly.

"Oh, yeah. Merry Christmas, ya-dee-ya-dee-ya-da."

I led the two men into the living room, where Marvin verbally launched an assault on Luscious. "I got a call from Henry this morning, Miller. He said there was another mysterious death last night. Some woman what lives in this neighborhood. Not really from here. You'uns better tell me what the hell's going on."

The mayor, whose English was probably better than Marvin's, nodded in agreement. "What's going on?" he repeated.

Luscious's answer was to hand Marvin the letter Ginnie had written to me. "This should explain everything."

Marvin carried it over to the window where the light was better and read it slowly. "Dear God," he said when he was finished. "She killed them both." The mayor took the letter and scanned it quickly.

Marvin wiped his brow with his handkerchief. "Looks like this winds up the murder investigation. Miller, the job's still yours if you want it."

Luscious thought about that for two or three seconds before saying, "Thanks, boss. I'll stay."

Through the window, I saw a four-wheel-drive vehicle coming up the driveway. "Now what?" I said, heading toward the back of the house.

"Western Union," said the teenager at the back door. "This just came for you. Usually we call, but the phones are down."

"Come in." I opened the yellow envelope, scanned it, and began to cry for the umpteenth time that morning.

"Bad news?" the teenager asked.

I shook my head. "Good news. Great news." I ran into the living room waving the paper. "I have a baby brother," I yelled. "A Christmas baby."

"That's wonderful," Luscious said. The others added their congratulations.

"They named him Billy—in memory of my brother." My voice choked, and I couldn't continue.

"I'll get the coffee," Luscious said.

I sat down on the sofa and gazed into the fire. God had given me a second chance to be a sister. This time I was going to do it right.

"Look who I found at the back door," Luscious said, as he came in carrying the heavy tray. He stepped aside with a smile on his face.

"Alice-Ann!"

My best friend in the whole world sat down beside me and took my hand. "I've missed you," she said.

"I thought you were never going to speak to me again," I said.

"After the apple festival, when you found out about Meredith, I didn't want to face up to my disastrous taste in men, so I lashed out at you. I was so wrong. Can you ever forgive me?"

First she'd chosen a lousy husband, then a rotten fiancé. Alice-Ann needed me in her life to steer her away from inappropriate men. I hugged her. "There's nothing to forgive. I'm just happy to have you back."

Fred forgave her, too, and proved it by rubbing against her ankles. "I'm so glad you got him back from that crazy artist," Alice-Ann said.

"*You* were the clown," I gasped. "I can't believe I didn't recognize you."

Alice-Ann giggled and pushed her streaky blonde hair out of her eyes. "I saw Fred 'at work' in the studio the morning of the parade and wanted to let you know where he was. I was going to slip the note under your door, but I couldn't resist handing it to you when I saw you at the parade."

"Fruitcake, everybody?" Luscious asked.

"I brought some eggnog," Alice-Ann said.

A few minutes later, we were all happily munching cookies and cake and drinking eggnog and coffee. Except for Luscious, who whispered, "No eggnog for me. Greta's got me going to A.A."

I looked around the cozy living room at my guests: Marvin, the mayor; Luscious; the mailman; the telegram teen; and Alice-Ann. Although this wasn't exactly the group I would have chosen to spend Christmas morning with (with the exception of Alice-Ann, of course), it worked. Maybe that "threefold law" Cassie had mentioned really did work. I felt as if I were getting back much more than I had given. And this was certainly better than the lonely Christmas morning I had expected.

Despite everything that had happened, this really was turning out to be my best Christmas ever. I raised my glass. "To all of you—a very Merry Christmas."

"Merry Christmas, Tori," they responded. Outside, the bells in the steeples of all the Lickin Creek churches rang out in unison: "Joy to the World."

Alice-Ann, drawing on her vast knowledge of English literature, quietly quoted Tennyson. " 'They bring me sorrow touch'd with joy, / The merry merry bells of Yule.' "

Praxythea Evangelista's Crescent Cookies

1 cup soft butter
1/2 cup sugar
1 teaspoon vanilla
1 3/4 cups sifted flour
1/2 cup each finely chopped almonds and pecans
1/4 teaspoon salt
1 cup confectioner's sugar
1 teaspoon vanilla

Cream butter; gradually beat in 1/2 cup sugar. Add 1 teaspoon vanilla, sifted flour, nuts, and salt. Chill well.

Shape into crescents, using 1/2 tablespoon dough for each, and place on greased cookie sheets. Heat oven to 300 degrees and bake for 25 to 28 minutes. Allow cookies to cool about 10 minutes. Roll in 1 cup confectioner's sugar to which 1 teaspoon of vanilla has been added.

Makes about 3 1/2 dozen.

Praxythea Evangelista's Fruitcake

1 lb. candied pineapple
1/2 lb. candied cherries
1 lb. pitted dates
1 lb. chopped figs
1 lb. chopped pecans (in large pieces)
1/2 cup white granulated sugar
1 cup water
2 tablespoons white corn syrup
3 tablespoons lemon juice
1/2 cup port wine or sherry
4 cups sifted flour
1 1/2 teaspoons cinnamon
1 tablespoon each of allspice, cloves, and baking soda
2 teaspoons salt
1 lb. butter
1 1/2 cups brown sugar
1 1/2 cups white sugar
12 eggs
1/2 cup light molasses

Chop fruit and nuts and place in a glass bowl. Make a medium syrup by heating 1/2 cup white sugar and 1 cup water to boiling point and simmer for 5 minutes. To the cooled syrup, add white corn syrup, lemon juice, and sherry (or port wine). Pour over the fruit and nuts. Let sit for several days in refrigerator, stirring often with wooden spoon.

Line three or four loaf pans (4 1/2″ × 8 1/2″) or one angel food cake pan with brown paper. Grease and flour center post of the angel food pan.

Sift flour, measure, and resift with spices, baking soda, and salt. Cream together butter, sugar, eggs, and molasses. Dust fruit and nuts with about ¾ to 1 cup flour mixture to prevent settling to bottom of pan. Add remaining flour mixture to creamed sugar mixture. Combine with nuts and fruit. Put in pan(s). Place pan(s) in a large baking pan containing ¼ inch water. Pat top of cake(s) with milk to make a film. Heat oven to 250 degrees and bake for two to three hours. (You may have to add more water to the large baking pan during baking process.) Test with straw for doneness. If bottom of cake seems too moist, then remove pan from water and place directly on rack for 30 to 45 minutes. Remove from oven, cool, then invert to remove from pan(s). If cake doesn't come out of pan, run a long knife around the sides and the center post and turn upside down for awhile.

Wrap in cheesecloth that has been soaked in brandy or rum. Place slices of a large Delicious apple on top of the cake. Wrap the whole thing in aluminum foil and store it for awhile.

ABOUT THE AUTHOR

VALERIE S. MALMONT grew up on Okinawa, Japan, studied anthropology at the University of New Mexico, and library science at the University of Washington. She now lives in Chambersburg, Pennsylvania.